DARK WATERS

DEBORAH SIDDOWAY

BLOODHOUND BOOKS

First published in 2024 by Bloodhound Books.

www.bloodhoundbooks.com

Print ISBN: 978-1-917214-48-3

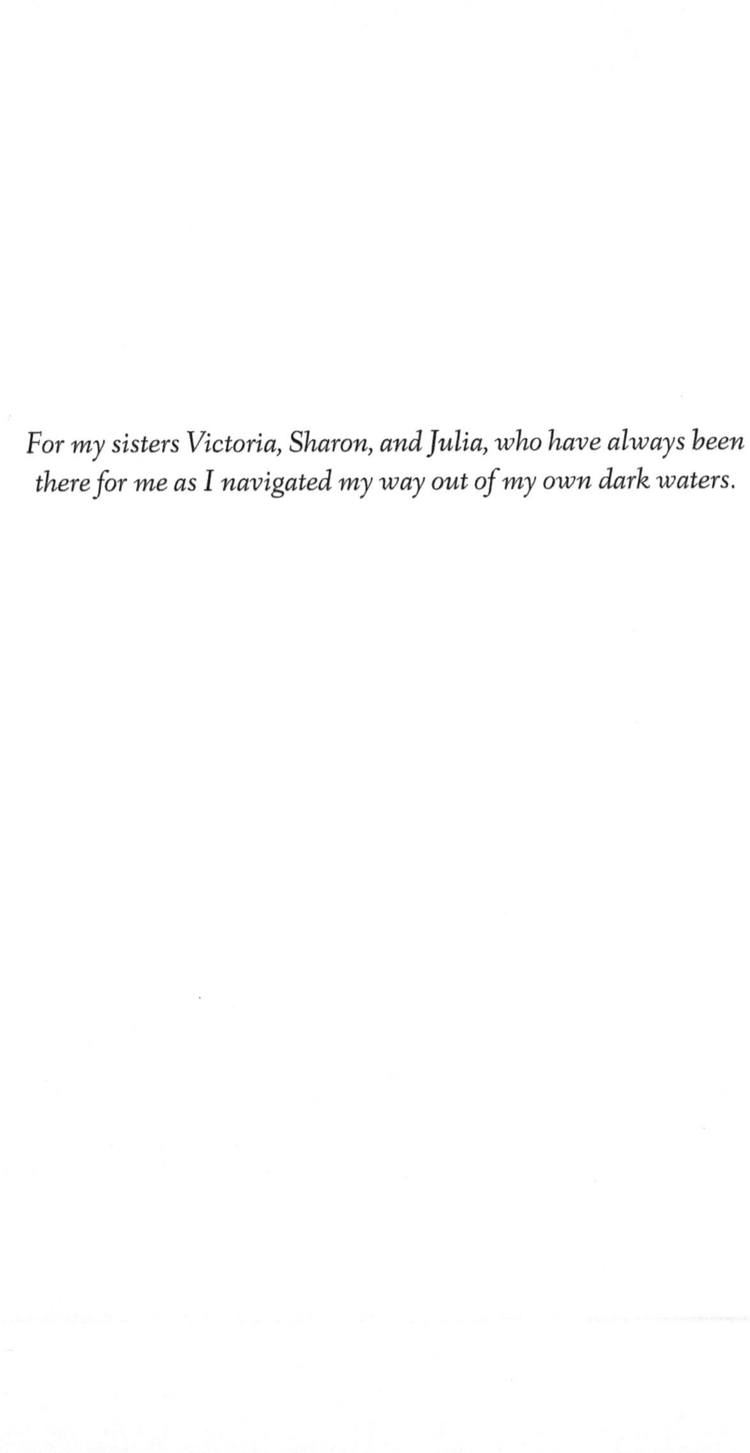

For my sisters Victoria, Sharon, and Julia, who have always been there for me as I navigated my way out of my own dark waters.

'Look before you, lady. Look at that dark water. How many times do you read of such as I who spring into the tide, and leave no living thing, to care for, or bewail them. It may be years hence, or it may be only months, but I shall come to that at last.'
— Charles Dickens, *Oliver Twist*

CHAPTER ONE

S he hadn't seen him. Not at first. Walking back to her flat down the back streets, close to Westminster Cathedral, the cold air settled on her neck, as though icy lips were dropping kisses on her skin. Bloody hell, she'd left her scarf at the office. Again. When would she learn? Michelle pulled the collar of her coat up and pushed her hair behind her ears. The last of the fallen autumnal leaves danced in the air and settled on the damp pavement. As she passed under the light thrown by the Victorian street lamps, she squinted, trying to protect her eyes from the gritty debris that courted the wind.

As the breeze settled once more, dying to a quiet whisper, she widened her eyes. And she saw him. How she wished she could not. He was smiling. There was no malevolence on his face, but she knew what he wanted. Damn it. A flurry of apprehension settled in her stomach, tying it in ever tightening knots. She had not come all the way to London to be found, but she knew in her heart that he was far too aware of who she was, of what she was. She could see from the look on his face. She shook her head, trying to tell him no. Telling him she could not give him what he wanted, what he demanded, from her. But that smile of his, it told her all she needed to know. And he moved closer to her.

As the wall of distance between them was breached, the tight knot of uneasiness in Michelle's stomach transformed into panic. She could not free herself from his gaze, his eyes drawing her towards him with a desperate intensity of need.

'No.' The word was silenced in her throat, unable to sound through the thick mesh of her own fear.

Struggling against the potency of his vivid, demanding eyes, she averted her gaze and picked up her pace, heading with greater urgency towards her flat. Why today? Was it not enough that she had already endured a long and difficult day at work, and this was the last thing she needed? In a city full of millions, it seemed strange to her that it could narrow down to just the two of them, even as she pushed past other Londoners either heading home, or out for a drink or dinner in one of the new trendy eateries that were springing up all around Victoria station.

'Please.' One whispered word, floating through the shadows of the evening, arrested Michelle's flight.

She stopped. It was pointless running from him. He would catch her in the end, no matter what she did. Taking out her phone from her coat pocket, holding it in her hand, as though she was poised to make a call, she turned to look at him. He was about her age, she guessed, but if she was wrong, probably no older than forty. It was always difficult to tell with people like him. His hair must once have been a deep shade of chestnut brown but was shot with a few strands of silver. But those eyes of his, they already haunted her. A muted shade of earthy brown, it seemed to her they were full of infinite sadness and regret. Did he care that he was scaring her? Would her fear make a difference? She suspected whatever it was he cared about; it wasn't her.

Michelle took a deep breath, closed her eyes for a brief moment, trying to find her calm, hoping that when she opened them once more, he would have vanished, sliding soundlessly back into the shadows from which he had first emerged. She opened her eyes. He was still there. Damn. Damn it to hell.

'Okay. I've stopped,' she said. 'Please can you stop following me now.'

When he spoke, his words sounded haggard, forced. As though he had to make an effort after a prolonged silence. 'I've been waiting for you,' he said.

Michelle already knew that. She had known it from the moment she had first seen him, that ethereal presence in the corner of her eye. She nodded, and looked around her, trying to determine how many other people were about, whether they would notice if something was amiss.

'How long? How long have you been waiting?' What a pointless question. It wasn't going to tell her anything of use. But she waited for his answer anyway.

Her words hung in the air between them, like a partly deflated helium balloon still struggling to take flight. His brows furrowed. This did not surprise her. How could he grasp something that no longer had any meaning for him? Time. What did days, hours, minutes matter to him given his purpose with her?

'A long time,' he finally said.

Michelle sighed. It told her nothing, as she expected. She tried again. 'How old are you?' It was the wrong question again, she knew that. But she was deliberately avoiding asking him the right ones because the moment she did, she would be making a commitment to him, and she was not ready to make any promises to anyone. She couldn't. Not now. There was nothing left to give. Not after all she had been through. She had lost everything and was only just holding on.

The same puzzled expression flitted across his face as he considered.

'I can't remember,' he said after his searing silence had not yielded the information she had asked of him. 'I think thirty-four, maybe thirty-five.' His eyes searched out hers again, and she saw the hope peeping out from behind the near impenetrable wall of sorrow.

As she looked at him, his stare binding her to him, she became more aware than ever of the coldness of the evening. She wrapped her coat more tightly around her. The moment was getting closer. The moment where she would have to ask him. And when it came, she would not be able to step away from the answer, even if she wanted to. He would follow her until she gave him what he wanted, as though she had been placed in his path for his deliverance.

She bit her lip, trying to hold back the inevitable, but the words fell from her mouth, carrying her with them.

'How long have you been dead for?'

Dead. It was the finality of it, she supposed. She saw that he struggled to accept it, though if she had to guess, she would bet he had been dead for quite some time, maybe even a century or more. His clothes told her that. The heavy cord of his trousers was so unlike what any London man would wear today; the flat cap perched on his head out of place, even in the cold chill of the evening; the faded rusty brown of his mended coat, which he wore over a grubby white shirt and shabby waistcoat; and the neckerchief tied around his neck all betrayed that he was not of her own time. He was dead. That much was certain. She had confirmed to him nothing more than what he already knew in his heart, but even so, she saw she had shredded his mortality into pieces and scattered it into the cold vagaries of the autumnal wind.

He opened his eyes and looked into hers once more but responded only with continued silence. The confusion evident in his eyes was sparking pity in her heart. Time had no meaning for him, not now. Not ever again.

How many years had passed since she had last spoken with

one like him? It had been so long, she couldn't even remember. She had almost been tempted to believe her gift, as her grandmother had called it, had abandoned her. It was a gift she had not asked for, and never wanted. She had decided a long time ago that her cursed vision was not something to be proud of, not to be courted, and she had pulled down the shutters, blinding herself to that which only she could see. But with her last question to this shadow of a man before her, she had taken the plunge back into the full wilderness of her sight, with the sinking realisation she was tied to him now, like two corpses shackled to an anchor and thrown into the ocean. She would not be free of him now until he was free. And it had been so long since she had done this. She had tried so hard to leave this part of her buried. But he was here, and it was done. Through him, she had resurrected that which she had condemned, and it seemed that even after lying dormant in a grave of her own making for all those years, her sight, undiminished, undecayed, vibrant, was strong enough to make the invisible almost corporeal. She would have to see it through.

'What's your name?'

'Edmund. Ned, if you like. That's what most people call me... I mean, it's what they used to call me.'

'Ned?' Michelle tested the name. She felt the hook of it curving in her mouth, the cold taste of metal confirming she was caught. He nodded, waiting for her to continue. 'Ned, what year did you die? Do you remember?'

'Yes,' he said, 'I remember. Leastways, I think I remember. It was a sickness in the capital. The air had got really bad, full of poison. Lots of people got sick from it. London wasn't like it is now,' he said, looking around him. They were on Emery Hill Street. She had fallen in love with the street from the first moment she had seen pictures of it. It spoke to her of what

London was, the way in which the new was simply layered on over the old, so the streets became like a snake that forged a new skin while forgetting to shed the old, growing thicker and less wieldy over time.

'The air was dirty, black, always full of smoke, the streets strewn with mud and filth. Lots of people died. It was 1848, near the end. Leastways, I think it was. I got sick too. Real sick. I remember lying in misery, my body shaking, and I was cold... so cold. I shut my eyes, fell into darkness, grateful for leaving all the hurt behind. And when I opened my eyes, I didn't hurt anymore. At first, I thought I'd got better, some people did, you know?'

Michelle nodded; people did sometimes recover from illness, at least now they did. But back then? A plague in the city would claim many lives. She sensed a sadness in his spirit as he looked back into the confusion that had followed as he passed through the grey veil between the living and the dead. And then she recoiled from her own intuitive connection to him, appalled at the ease with which her gift had taken hold of her again, without her even thinking about it.

'It took me a while,' Ned continued, 'to realise I hadn't got better. I was just glad not to be in such wretched pain. But then, after a bit, I thought I should be thirsty, as I hadn't been able to keep anything down when I was sick, not even beer. And then I realised that I didn't feel anything. Not hungry. Not thirsty. Not cold. Nothing. And then I started to think I was...' The words seemed to sit rigid in his mouth. 'That I hadn't got better after all. That I was dead.'

Michelle reached out to comfort him. But before she could get close, she shoved her hand back in her pocket. There was nothing for her to hold on to. He was only spirit, sorrow and shadow, drifting in a world he no longer had a place in.

'So I thought I'd better wait. Until someone told me what I was supposed to do next. But no one came. No one,' he said, his eyes penetrating hers, holding her to him as though they were caught up in a current, dragging them together into the wilds of the deepest ocean. 'That is, no one until you.'

CHAPTER THREE

The bottle of Chablis was the first thing Michelle reached for after dumping her bag in the entrance hall to her flat. She had not even stopped to hang up her beloved coat, leaving it in a puddle on the floor as she struggled to collect her whirling thoughts.

She opened up the cupboard and pulled out a wine glass, well, the only wine glass. It was one of the few things she had treated herself to after her move to London. That, and the expensive coat now sitting in a careless heap on the floor. She looked at the glass. It had cost her £40, so it was lucky for her she had need of only one in her life right now. She had others, of course, but they, along with everything else she owned that mattered to her was probably stuck on a ship somewhere in the middle of the ocean; slowly making its way to her. She had left Sydney so abruptly she hadn't really thought through the practicalities of the move.

As Michelle took the first sip of Chablis, it dawned on her that perhaps Ned was the reason she had been drawn to Emery Hill Street, his spirit calling to her unseen from the glossy estate agent pictures. She had allowed her instinct, rather than any logic, to guide her in her choice of accommodation. And this latent instinct had led her straight to Ned. Michelle traced her finger over the swirl etched into the thick crystal of the wine glass, following it from the stem to the rim. Her thoughts continued to dwell on him. She had told him she needed time to think, to make sense of the conflicting torrent of emotions whirling in her head. He was the first spirit she had seen so clearly in quite some time. There were always shadows, flitting about aimlessly in the distance, like black specks swimming across her eyes, but as long as she did not shine the light of her vision towards them, they always disappeared into the darkness, unaware that she could, if she chose, see them. Turning her back on her gift had not been easy. It was like trying to stop hearing the birds singing in the dew-drenched trees of the morning sun, to not feel the warmth of the afternoon sunlight kissing her skin as she walked along the beach, to not smell the drifting scent of lavender and rosemary in a flowering herb garden, or to not taste the oaky melon undertones of a chilled Chardonnay.

It was as though she had to shield herself from what she could see. It required constant effort to keep this self-imposed blindness in place, but her discipline and steely determination, which was so a part of her life, had kept the chains in place. But now those chains had been loosened, the blind discarded, and it was as if she was still blinking as those eyes adjusted to the light once more.

She tried to convince herself she didn't have to care about Ned. She could choose to ignore his wandering spirit, lost in a timeless prison. But as soon as the thought came into her head, Michelle immediately discarded it. She had already made a commitment to him, and they both knew it. She placed her glass on the kitchen counter and went to retrieve the coat she had left puddled on the floor. She picked it up, running her hand over the thick forest-green fabric, smoothing it down, and hooked it on the coat rack by the door. She turned back around to return to the kitchen. Her breath stopped in her throat, and turned to ice. The blood stilled in her veins and she froze, as though a white marble statue on the cold tiled floor of a museum. Ned was in front of her. He had appeared from nowhere, as only a dead man could.

CHAPTER FOUR

'How did you find me?' she asked, her voice emerging from somewhere in the dark hollow of her own fear.

'I don't know,' Ned said. 'I just thought of you, and then I was here.' He looked as though he was waiting for her to say something. But her thoughts had shrivelled like paper thrown on an open fire. 'Is this where you live?' he asked.

Michelle nodded. 'It is. At least it is for now.' She tried to steady herself. To gain the sense of equilibrium that had been tipped off its axis. 'Did you live here? I mean, before...?'

'Oh no. This wasn't here before,' he said, gesturing around him. 'None of this was. Not even that grand cathedral that's here now. Mostly it were a prison. Tothill Fields it were called, a house of correction for the parish of St Margaret's. All these fancy buildings that are here now came after I was sick. But I did live near here. Before. With my wife. We had lodgings nearby. I were working on clearing the Devil's Acre.'

'The Devil's Acre?'

'No better than a swamp it were, but home to thieves and whores. But those that thought themselves better than the rest of us wanted it cleared. Weren't safe, you see. I wouldn't have wanted my wife there.'

At this revelation that he had once been married, something stirred in her, an instinct that this was what she was supposed to do. To try to help him figure out why he was still bound to the heaviness of Earth, when he was a spirit free to soar. Something was holding him back, as though he was a fledgling not yet grown his flying feathers. Her grandmother always said it was something inside them that glued them to our world. Michelle was going to have to find what the solvent was if she was to unstick him.

'Ned, what is it you want me to do? What is it you need from me?'

'I can't really say,' he answered. 'I was hoping you would tell me, you know, what it is I have to do next. You're the first person who can see me. Leastways, the first person still alive.'

Michelle's curiosity, always a danger to her, was starting to overtake her fear of getting involved in this man's life. Or at least, she mentally corrected herself, his afterlife. She wished her grandmother was still around. Michelle had refused to take any of her instruction about the art of her vision while her grandmother had been alive, determined to pretend it had nothing to do with who she was. And now, there was a small part of her sifting through the ash of her regret over that bridge burned. But, in the absence of the wisdom and experience of her grandmother, Michelle decided to revert to the one thing she did know, and that was breaking the simmering mixture of the cauldron of emotions she could sense in Ned down to the salient facts. You could never work on any case without a full appreciation of all of the facts.

She took a mouthful of wine and reached for the notepad and pen on the kitchen counter. She thought about recording their conversation on her phone, but her instinct told her that if she tried it, all she would have is a recording of her talking to herself. Pulling up a stool, she sat, her pen poised. 'Tell me about your wife, Ned. Did you leave her unprovided for when you died?'

Ned's eyes darkened briefly. 'Nelly? No. She died before me. She died about ten years before me, I think.'

'Children, then?' Michelle asked, moving on to the next logical potential hold on Ned.

'Dead before me too,' Ned replied.

He offered no further information, no names, no ages, nothing to give any indication of what they had died of or how many children there had been. Michelle's grasp of the history of the era was pretty poor, especially having gone to school in Sydney where there tended to be a focus on Australia's colonial history, followed by the war years of the twentieth century. But she was pretty certain that the child mortality rates of London at the time must have been high. People of Ned's time would have been hardened to losing their children. Perhaps that was why he was being so matter-of-fact about their deaths. He'd also had a long time to accept the early deaths of his children, as he drifted as though a shadow in the fog between life and death. But there was something in the way he had answered her that arrested Michelle's line of questions. She sensed he was holding something back, as though he had caged something shameful within his heart, like a prisoner condemned to death.

Michelle put her pen down. 'Ned, if I'm going to help you, you need to help me. I need to know as much as I can. Can you tell me about your wife? About your children?'

Ned's silence pervaded the room. It was strange, disconcerting, to have him there yet to only hear her own breath, each of her movements contributing small moments of noise, generating heat and energy that tied her to life, while he stood there, as though in a soundless, cold vacuum. It seemed rude to drink in front of him, but God how she needed that wine. She took another sip of the Chablis, appreciating the cold crispness of it, and waited for him to speak.

'Nelly. She were my wife,' he said. 'I really loved her.' He paused, a slight smile turning up the corners of his lips. 'She were a real pretty girl. She had the brightest, bluest eyes and she had a real good heart. She were a good worker, too. An honest girl. I always thought I didn't really deserve someone as good as her. I was just a navvie on the tramp, you see.' Michelle's confusion must have been evident on her face because he added almost immediately, 'A labourer. Hired by the day. Mostly for work to lay the roads. 'Twas my job to set the granite we used to make them. I moved with the work.

'Nelly were in service when I met her, just as a kitchen maid, like, but when we wed she couldn't work no more. She did a bit of sewing, and we set up our home, such as it was. Nothing so grand as this,' he continued, looking around at Michelle's flat. 'Then, she told me we were going to have a child. And I was glad. Real glad. I suppose I thought that it would make up for... Well, it didn't matter what it was supposed to make up for. The child didn't live more than a moment.'

Ned's eyes were bright with unshed tears. Michelle's heart ached for him, and she was reluctant to cause him further distress by pushing him towards confronting those painful memories, but she sensed they were getting close to something, to the reason underlying the bonds that tethered him to a world that had finished with him. As she closed her eyes, opening her heart to experience his pain, the power of his memories captured her, as though she was caught in the force of a wave pulling her out to face the perils of the sea. His thoughts played in her head as though on a cinema reel. Michelle had never before experienced such a powerful connection with one in spirit form, and her mounting fear went to battle against her curiosity. She wanted to pull back from him, but found that she could not.

'When the time came for the baby...' Ned stopped again, and Michelle sensed his fear for his wife. Dizziness threatened to overwhelm her, as the momentum of the current that had dragged her into the maelstrom of his past took full control, and when she opened her eyes, she was no longer sitting in her flat on Emery Hill Street, a passive listener to Ned's tragic tale. Instead, she had been plunged into the very nightmare of Ned's past, to the wretched room where Nelly had died, as though she, and not Ned, was the spirit haunting her home. The flickering flames from a couple of struggling candles lit the room, but the foetid air hardly provided enough oxygen to allow them to burn bright. Michelle's eyes adjusted to the hazy dimness. She heard the tormented screams coming from the slight figure lying on a dirty straw mattress on the floor, and Michelle was horrified to realise that the woman, Nelly, was little more than a girl. She couldn't have been more than sixteen. And the girl was half mad with pain and terror. She cried out as though she was being torn in two.

Fighting back a rising tide of nausea, Michelle took in the dirt and dust coating the floor, the dank smell of damp and sewage filtering in through the crevices of the wall, the scattered clothing and possessions in the corners. She saw a basin, a pail of murky water. There was nothing to sit on. Just the bed, in a room that was barely the size of her wardrobe. This had been home, then, for Ned. There was something else assaulting her senses: the rusty iron smell of blood.

Her eyes were drawn to the girl on the mattress, the creeping pool of ruby red flowing from her body. There was so much blood. Dirty hands reached between the legs of the agonised child, and Michelle took a step forward to stop her, to try and prevent the grime coating the hands of the woman attending on Nelly contaminating the girl with infection and disease. But Michelle's attempts to seize hold of those terrible hands ended in the futility of empty space. Michelle was the ghost now. She could see, she could feel, she could hear, but she could not touch. And she could not be heard. All she could do was watch as the tragedy unfolded, miserable in her own impotence.

The woman pulled the baby from the womb of the child. There was no cry, nothing to suggest life. Only silence sat against the dying whimpers of the girl on the bed. Michelle saw a small fluttering of the most luminous crystal light diffuse out of the body of the baby and vanish into the brightness of the skies that she could somehow see beyond the dirty ceiling of the desolate room. For the briefest of moments, Michelle was bathed in the beauty of that celestial glow, as though the light of a blazing star illuminated a thousand diamonds.

The absolute serenity of that moment vanished in less than a heartbeat. Once more, Michelle found herself trapped in Ned's memory, back in the claustrophobic confines of the birthing room that had now become a coffin, dripping in death. The woman slapped the lifeless, slimy body of the baby, before sighing and wrapping it in a coarse square of fabric, laying it at the feet of Nelly. The girl's face had taken on an ethereal pallor, and her breath came in short, defeated gasps. Michelle's composure, already weakened, shattered completely as Nelly's spirit parted from her broken body, her empty arms reaching towards the heavens to follow her child. Nelly looked briefly at Michelle, seeing her as only the dead could.

'My baby?' The whispered words stole into Michelle's heart, cutting more finely than any surgeon's scalpel. Michelle nodded towards the light that once more shone through the sorrow and the darkness. She could not speak. Nelly looked into the heart of it, and floated towards it, disappearing as though she had dived into the deepness of the ocean.

Michelle, taking her own shuddering breaths as she fought the urge to sob, found herself back in her flat, Ned standing quietly before her, his wraithlike stillness unnerving after wandering through the dark dungeon of his dismay. It took her a moment to catch her breath, to turn her accusation against Ned.

'Nelly and her child. They're not the reason, are they? The reason that you're stuck here?'

'No.'

Michelle struggled to contain her fury. All the reasons why she had learnt to repress her so-called gift were flooding back to her, drowning her.

'Why the fuck did you tell me all of that? Make me go through all of that?'

Ned stood there, his silence his shield.

Michelle tried to unscramble all she had learnt. It was something he had said. She picked at her memory of the conversation as though it was a festering scab.

'You said something. Something about not being deserving.' Michelle picked a little more off the scab, until it yielded, causing the wound to bleed once more. 'You said when Nelly told you about the baby that you thought it would make up for something. What did you think it would make up for, Ned? What was it you wanted to atone for?' Michelle's anger, heightened by her ghostlike intrusion into the darkness of Ned's past, tore through her like molten lava. She was furious at herself for having let her guard down, for having succumbed to the immersive power of her own gift. Ned looked at her as though he were trapped behind glass, an exhibit in a museum of curiosities. His refusal to answer her only served to fuel her rage.

'Fucking hell, Ned, what the fuck were you trying to make up for?'

Clenching her hands into fists, Michelle closed her eyes, trying to get her temper back under control. She reopened them.

Ned was gone.

CHAPTER FIVE

It was as though she had never seen him at all. It had been nearly a week, and Ned, that blighted apparition she thought had attached itself to her, had not returned since he had vanished from her flat. She was starting to wonder if perhaps the whole encounter with him had been some sort of dream, brought on by the stress and humiliation of what Nick had done, a way to try and deflect her own pain.

Why had she let herself be vulnerable to Ned's thoughts like that? She had allowed her clairvoyance to take over her life, albeit only for an evening. Having replayed it all in her head, Michelle was frightened at the realisation she had lost any sort of control over her ability. She had been taken into the man's past, as though Ned had been a mesmerist trapping her within a trance, and that lack of choice chilled her.

It took her right back to when she was a kid, confused and overwhelmed by the call of the lost spirits clamouring for her attention, their voices echoing loudly against those of the living. It had sometimes been impossible for her to tell what was real when the voices of the dead called to her with just as much authority as the grown-ups who guided her through childhood.

Her poor mum had spent far too many nights with a scared little girl crawling into her bed, seeking refuge from the ghosts that came to her, haunting her dreams with memories of their lives. Alone in her flat, Michelle had no one to turn to. God, how she missed her grandma. And Ned's memories had been too real, too raw. He would be back at some point; Michelle was sure of it.

In the meantime, she tried to live her life, if only to tie her to her new normality as she adjusted to the absence of Nick. She was fast settling into a routine at work, enjoying the comfort of methodically working through files, liaising with barristers, putting court dates into her diary, preparing for hearings, writing letters and instructions, and talking down clients, often hysterical in their desperation to have the residence issue sorted in their favour.

She was still ignoring all of Nick's calls and emails. She couldn't face them. Or him. She supposed at some point she was going to have to talk to him. They were still married. Still had a mortgage together on their beautiful Mosman house. But she wasn't ready to deal with him or any of the stuff that came with him. Not yet.

Michelle picked up the Haynes file, quickly reminding herself of the facts of the case. She had a conference with counsel in Lincoln's Inn Fields later that day and she wasn't going to turn up anything less than prepared. Toby, her trainee, was already making sure all the bundles were in order, and she had also asked him to double-check the school term dates. Michelle was constantly surprised at how few parents were actually on top of when their kids would be off school, especially when they had to share the residence arrangements for the child.

She was acting for the father, a Brit. He had been married, albeit briefly, to an Australian. One child. Marriage fell apart.

Her client had been unfaithful. Of course. Infidelity played a part in the vast majority of the relationship breakdowns Michelle had been involved in sorting out. And the richer the client, the more likely someone was to have cheated. Michelle thought of Nick but cast him out of her mind. She couldn't think about him now. Besides, it was not her job to judge. Just to get the best result that she could for her client.

Still, it was hard not to feel sorry for the ex-wife in this case. She wanted to go home, back to Australia, taking her daughter with her. Of course, Michelle couldn't blame her for that. But she also wanted half of her client's wealth and ongoing spousal and child maintenance, that he could only provide if he stayed in his high-flying job in the UK. The woman was submitting all the usual arguments that were trundled out in these cases: that her family support was back in Perth, that her daughter needed to grow up with her mother who had been the primary caregiver since she was born, blah, blah, blah. None of it mattered. Not really. Michelle had already done a pretty good job of piecing together the huge amount of family support the daughter would have access to if she stayed with her father in London, the happy extended family she was already a part of, and the fact that the nanny, who had been with the family since the child was a newborn, would be continuing in her position if the child arrangement order determined the child should remain in the UK.

Michelle also had the continuity argument running in her client's favour, with the child already having established friendship groups in a lovely, leafy small independent school she was happily settled into. And she had multiple witness statements to that effect; from the headmaster, and the teacher in charge of pastoral care, all of whom had been careful to delineate how detrimental it would be to move the child mid-school year. Michelle was almost disgusted at her own cynicism. The girl was only four and had been at school less than a month.

Reviewing the file, totally on top of all the nuances of the case, Michelle was as prepared as she could be for the conference. Mr Haynes needed to know that he had deployed an effective arsenal in the fight for his child. That was what he was paying for and what the conference was for, to give him that assurance. Michelle had done all she could. It was over to the barrister now.

Michelle sat through the conference with Toby, always ever so eager to please, who furiously took notes in his blue counsel's notepad, as she and the QC guided Mr Haynes through what was likely to happen if the matter progressed to a full hearing, the various possible outcomes, trying to persuade him that if they could possibly negotiate a solution to avoid a trial, it would be preferable, and certainly cost a lot less.

It seemed her client was not going to be moved. Michelle sighed. The intractable ones always made the worst decisions, especially when they could afford upwards of the quarter of a million pounds all of this would ultimately end up costing.

'I know I had an affair and that makes me the bad guy,' he said. 'I hold my hands up to that. But it was a mistake. I shouldn't have to lose my daughter to the other side of the world over a mistake.'

Michelle thought of those words as she returned to the office. A mistake. Is that what all men said when they were caught with their hands in the honey pot?

After wrapping up the conference, Michelle and Toby returned to the office, having despatched Mr Haynes with as much optimism as Michelle had been prepared to offer him. She was confident they were in a good place to get a good result, but family court judges were notoriously unpredictable.

Michelle sat down in her chair, but going over the details of

Mr Haynes's infidelity with the barrister had left her restless, and feeling somehow grotty, as though her own hands were tainted by what her client had done. She was usually able to detach from the moral rights and wrongs of a client's behaviour, because at the end of it all, the only thing that mattered was what was best for the child. But today, the details were bothering her.

'Toby, go and write up your notes of the conference,' she ordered, and as he reached for his Dictaphone and started scrabbling through his notepad, she continued, 'Not in here. Go somewhere else.'

He cast her a reproving look for his banishment as he left the room. But he had the sense not to protest.

'Close the door behind you.'

Michelle watched through the glass door as Toby moved in the direction of the library, stopping to chat to one of the support staff, gesturing back towards Michelle, no doubt complaining about how unreasonable she was. But she didn't care. Not today. Once Toby had vacated their office, a quiet privacy settled over it, as though she was sitting at a dining table in an empty restaurant. Michelle sat back in her chair and picked up her mobile. She tapped voicemails and listened to the first of all the unplayed messages.

'*Michelle. Oh God, Michelle, I'm so sorry, I...*'

Michelle cut off the call. She couldn't listen to it. Not here in the office. Just the sound of his voice caused her throat to constrict, a mutiny of tears threatening to subvert her determination to be strong. She looked down at her hands, could see the tension in her fingers as they curled inwards, trying to contain her emotions. She still wore her engagement and wedding rings, the light in the heart of the diamond reflecting Nick's false promises.

She turned to her PC. She scrolled through all her emails from the last month until she found it. The one from Jen Paxton, with the subject title of Nick Peterson. She had barely noticed it when it first pinged into her inbox. Jen was Nick's secretary and it had not occurred to Michelle that her email would be about anything other than work. Jen often emailed Michelle to keep her up to date with Nick's movements, either because Nick had asked her to, or because Jen had been proactive in keeping Michelle up to speed with what he was up to. Michelle hesitated a moment. She opened the email, reading through it once more, absently twisting the wedding ring on her finger around and around as she read:

Michelle,

I thought you should know that Nick and I have been seeing each other for the last two months. We are in love. He is not happy with you and he wants to leave you, but he feels that he can't. He is only staying with you out of some sense of duty because of what you went through. But I thought you deserved to know. I thought it wasn't fair to let you think that Nick wants to stay with you when I know he wants to be with me. I have not been happy about having to lie to you, and I know Nick has been unhappy about this too. For what it is worth, I am really sorry, but you can't help who you fall in love with.

Jen.

Michelle's heart sank once more as she read it again, a painful echo of that first time, not wanting to believe the words that appeared on her screen. Jen, that young, silly little girl, had been out of school five minutes. It had never even occurred to Michelle that Nick would have been so stupid as to conduct an affair with an employee. He was a partner. And she was his wife, a senior associate at the same firm, on a fast track to make partner herself.

At first, Michelle had tried to persuade herself that it was just a cruel prank. She had trusted Nick with every fibre of her being, and he knew how hard it was for her to trust anyone given the nature of her work, and the battle wounds that still lingered from the breakdown of her own parents' marriage. But when she had picked up the phone, hand shaking, to speak to Nick and told him she had received an email from Jen, the crushing silence on the other end of the line had told her everything that was written in the email was true. Except the part where Jen had said you couldn't help who you fell in love with. She was pretty sure Jen would not be 'in love' with her husband if he hadn't been a partner in the firm, with an expensive, sleek Audi parked in the basement and a house worth millions of dollars in one of Sydney's most exclusive northern suburbs. Jen's only problem, it seemed, was how to manage her lover's wife out of the picture so she could Photoshop herself in.

And when Nick had started to speak, the excuses had poured out of his mouth like acid, the vitriol corroding her heart. 'It was a mistake.' He had said that too. A thousand broken pieces of jigsaw started to piece together in her mind. The long blonde hair she had found on the floor of her bathroom, the way in which she had seemed to be going through her face moisturiser, her hair products, faster than normal. She wondered if Jen had enjoyed playing at being Nick's wife. She thought of the cup in the dishwasher with the lipstick still marking the rim, the way in which her bed had been made, with the pillows with the case openings facing outwards instead of in. Why had she not said something then? She had sensed something was not right, but she had ignored her instinct, brushing aside her unease. Maybe she had become too used to not seeing what she didn't want to see. She had trusted her husband, and she buried her disquiet into that trust, never once suspecting she was digging a pit of her own making.

And with that email, the whole sorry mess came together in her mind like she had exhumed the rancid remnants of her own heart from the filth of the earth, rent open and exposed. Michelle remembered how she had battled the urge to void the contents of her stomach. Her husband had taken that girl to their bed. And it had not been an isolated incident. 'A mistake' was something you did once. Something you tried to learn from. Something you didn't do again because the shame of your mistake, and the hurt it had the potential to cause, taunted you. It didn't become a pattern of behaviour that you tried to keep hidden. Especially from the person you were supposed to love.

And then her dear husband had proven to her once more the importance of making sure you had a firm grasp of all the facts before you tried to deal with a matter.

'How could you?' Michelle had said. 'How could you talk to that girl about our IVF? Aside from Angie, I never talked to anyone about that. It's private. It's our battle that belongs only to us. I didn't even share it with my own secretary, and I was the one that had to have more time away from the office for all the appointments.'

'I'm sorry,' Nick had said. Because really, what else was he going to say?

'And she had the audacity to tell me I deserved to know the truth. Like she was doing me a favour,' Michelle hissed down the phone, 'when all the while she was busy fucking my husband. In my bed. My home. Her truth was only ever going to hurt me.'

'I didn't think she would tell you about the baby.'

Silence. All Michelle could hear was her heart. Beating, erratic, the tempo increasing.

Michelle thought about the years of trying to conceive, the happy nonchalance she had adopted when she and Nick had agreed that the time was right to have a child and she had thrown her pill packet, ceremoniously, into the bin. The two of them laughing before making love on the cold tiles of the floor of the bathroom, wondering how long it would be before they would have the baby they both longed for.

She thought of the months passing, with her period appearing with depressing regularity, the constant repetition of the cycle of hope and despair, as each month came and went and she never once had to even think about taking the pregnancy test they had purchased, like two guilty teenagers buying condoms, when they had first started trying to conceive.

The tests, the needles, the injections into her abdomen, the doctors, the scans, the invasive procedures that dissected her femininity. The bewildering frustration of 'unexplained infertility'.

She thought about the cycles of IVF, the eggs harvested, the cryopreserved embryos transferred during the luteal phase to her womb, each one already a living, breathing child in her heart. Her son. Her daughter. Her hope. She thought about the babies that she and Nick would have each time she underwent this procedure, the little life that she would nurture, feel moving inside her, and bring into this world. She thought about the negative pregnancy tests. The absence of that longed-for line. She thought about her failures. She thought about the emptiness of her womb, the vast desert where life could not take root, and all attempts to seed it were drowned in a tidal wave of her own blood.

And Nick was having a baby.

With Jen.

She had put down the phone, sitting in her office alone. She sat there for some time, struck numb, trapped by thoughts of

Nick in bed with Jen. Jen pregnant. Jen giving Nick what she could not. A tentative knock on her door had called her back to reality. And she remembered she was still at work. It was not the time to surrender control to the turmoil of her emotions. She had turned and waved the paralegal away, and returned to look at her screen, hoping she had conveyed the impression that she was too busy working and could not be interrupted. She had wanted to cry, to scream, to pound the walls with rage, but her pride had refused to allow her to do anything other than sit there. She had sat, staring at the screen, swimming in a cesspit of words, her heart drowning in mud. Already she could hear the whispers. It wouldn't take long. The whole office would know. A partner screwing his secretary behind the back of his wife. Michelle needed no one's pity, and she wanted no one's stares.

Like an automaton, she had requested a meeting with senior management and set in motion the events that would see her seconded to the London office. Each step she had taken, a descent into the realms of her own misery, while retaining the regal air of a woman in control of her own destiny. And she did not allow herself to cry until she reached the hotel room, ignoring all of Nick's frantic phone calls and messages.

Michelle didn't want to think about any of that now, so she turned her mind back to Ned, to the nightmare of his shattered past. He had come to her with hope that she could rebuild the broken pieces and make whole what had been destroyed. But Ned still hadn't returned since that night he had taken her to Nelly's death, and his absence haunted her more effectively than his ghostly presence ever could.

She had not been able to erase the memories of Nelly's death from her mind. Her visit to the depths of the dark recesses of the life Ned had once lived had told her Nelly and the child were an important part of Ned's story. But Michelle had been told countless stories over the years, and sometimes, to tell a good story, you had to abandon truth by the side of the road.

Michelle was convinced Ned had only told her part of his story, leading her to his anguish over the death of Nelly and the baby in the hope it would give her understanding. Like it was some sort of an explanation. But Michelle had already ascertained that the death of Nelly and their child was not what was causing his imprisonment as a timeless shadow. There was something else. There had to be. Something more. Her mind kept taking her to the possibilities. But they were legion. She needed Ned to come back. He knew how to come to her. But she had no idea how to make him reappear in her life, to summon his elusive spirit before her and give her the resolution only he could bring. She would just have to wait.

CHAPTER SIX

Michelle was sipping a light Pinot Noir from her one wine glass on the balcony overlooking Emery Hill Street. There wasn't much to look at, but she liked the feel of the cold air on her face. It somehow made the wine more warming. Her crate of belongings had still not arrived from Sydney, although she realised she had no idea how long it would take for it to get to her. How long did it take to sail halfway around the world? She supposed she might have to try and find out. She had her coat on, a scarf wound around her neck. It was coming up to Bonfire Night, and the peace of the few stars visible was constantly interrupted by the flare of fireworks, the explosions in a symphonic disharmony against the sirens and horns of the impatient London traffic that she could always hear, even tucked away in her little corner of the city.

The branches of the birch trees were bare, exposed to the unpredictability of the approaching winter. Her mind drifted, imagining the birth of the goddess Freya from the flaking bark of the trunk of a birch such as those that peppered Emery Hill Street, Freya's spirit emerging from the confines of the tree, like a human spirit from the body that had once housed it, free to roam the world. Freya, the goddess of love, beauty, sex, fertility. And on that thought, Michelle saw the tree for what it was. Hibernating. Stripped bare for the winter. Devoid of life. Just like her. Barren.

Ned. She saw him looking up at her from the pavement below.

Her intake of breath was sudden as her eyes met his, and she realised she had been waiting for him, silently calling to him as she stood on her balcony. And he had come back. As she had known he would.

She went indoors, closing the door on the crisp, cold air of the evening. She walked towards her kitchen. Ned was there, just as she had expected him to be.

She could only suppose he was ready to tell her the next part of his past. Or maybe, she thought, he had only come back to her because he thought she might have somehow found what he needed to move on. How she wished it was that easy.

'So, it wasn't Nelly and the child,' Michelle said, taking off her coat and unwinding the warm scarf from around her neck. 'There was something else, wasn't there? Somebody else?'

That sadness that she had come to associate with him was there, but there was something more. Guilt.

'Her name was Clara,' Ned said.

'Clara? Can you tell me about her?' Michelle asked, noting the way Ned's eyes closed as she uttered the name out loud, as though just the mention of it was like plunging his hand into a bucket of ice, to test how long he could hold it there before the pain compelled him to snatch it back, to free it from self-induced torment.

'There was a girl,' Ned said, his eyes glazing over as he

walked backwards through the misty memories of his past. 'Long before Nelly. She were a pretty little thing. I wasn't kind to her. I wasn't kind to her at all. But I didn't mean for it to happen. I didn't know.'

The admission was costing him, the guilt etched on his face like a scar. She waited for him to continue. But the words seemed stuck in his throat. They were building up, like something inside of him was dammed.

'Ned,' Michelle said, 'I can only help you if I know what happened. What happened to this girl? What happened to Clara?'

'I were only young myself,' he said, already building up his armoury of excuses.

Michelle recoiled from this abrogation of blame before he had even begun to tell her the story. She had seen it time and time again with clients. Their behaviour was appalling. And yet, they sought refuge in their excuses, all the reasons why what had happened was not their fault, not their responsibility and that blame could settle anywhere but in front of their own fireside. But Michelle couldn't worry about that now. A part of her had been longing for Ned to return to her. The important thing was to try and get a handle on the facts.

Michelle reassured him. 'How old you were really doesn't matter. Not now. I just need to know what happened to Clara. Why she was important to you.'

'I had just come to London. It was growing and there was work, you see. Lots of work for people like me. And I couldn't stay at home no more. My pa, he weren't a good man. When I met Clara, I hadn't been in London for too long. It were a different world, then. You can't see it,' Ned told Michelle, 'because this is what it has always been like for you. But for folk like us, London were a chance to get on, to earn a decent living. Especially for a lad like me, who were young, strong and willing.

It were a place where everything were possible. Even for a lad like me.'

Michelle listened as Ned talked, feeling the pull of the current wanting to take her into his past with him again. She was going to have to be careful. Hold on to her own life to stop from sinking into his.

'Clara were a servant, a kitchen maid, I think, but something had happened with her situation, and she were on the tramp looking for something else. I never knew what had happened that made her have to seek a new place,' Ned said. 'I supposed I never asked.'

Ned's entire being was taut, as though he wanted to take flight, and Michelle was scared he would somehow take her into his darkness with him. As Ned hesitated, Michelle wondered why he was so afraid to tell her about Clara. But she could see from his face that he was fighting a powerful self-loathing. His jaw was set, his fists tightened as he talked, as if he was trying to contain his volatile emotions.

'She had a character,' Ned said. 'But not much else. No family to speak of. I suppose she were ripe to be taken advantage of. Especially in a place like where we were, so close to the Devil's Acre. It weren't no place for a young girl to be walkin' about on her own.'

Michelle was trying to keep a conscious hold on her mind, but his words once more acted on her as though he was a hypnotist, reciting an incantation that would take her into his world without any awareness on her part, and her fear prickled on her skin because she was starting to think he could take her there, to this Devil's Acre, against her own will. She must not allow herself to simply drift along with his words. She had to keep herself anchored to her own life, and to her own time.

'Everyone was looking to the next opportunity,' Ned said.

'Looking to themselves. I suppose I did too. I were right selfish I was. And I were only young.'

Ned's words trailed off into silence again. Michelle sensed the weight of his shame, roped tightly around his body like bindweed around the trunk of a tree, slowly strangling him. As his face twisted and tightened, she could see his struggle. He seemed unable to balance his reluctance to give her the detail of his interaction with this young girl, with his need to unburden himself of the horror of what he had done. God, what had this man done to so torment him?

His voice found him.

'She were searching for a new situation, and I watched her as she made her way along the street, wondering which doors to knock at, her shawl wrapped tightly around her. I thought then that she were a right pretty little thing, with her pale face, her bright eyes, and her sweet little mouth. And all I wanted to do was to... Well, I wanted her like all men want pretty women.'

A sliver of fear snaked into her spine. What had happened to that girl? What had Ned done to her? How could she help him if...

'Ned, what did you do? What did you do to her?'

Ned retreated once more into the safety of silence.

Michelle's grasp on her glass tightened as she tried to keep a hold on her own reality, but she was slipping backwards, hurtling headlong into his past, a prisoner of the torrent of his emotions. Swept away once more into his world, his past, her eyes opened to the sordid streets of a London long since swallowed up by the greed of the passing years. She saw Clara. She felt her, somehow. Her arms itched from the sleeves of the serviceable dress she wore, made of coarse, practical fabric, the long skirt of the dress falling heavily to the ground, over layers of petticoats, adding to the weight of her worries. Her auburn hair was tucked into a cap, and her green eyes were full of fatigue and fear. She could feel the blisters on her ankles inside her worn boots as she made her careful way along the streets, avoiding the worst of the mud and filth that coated the ground. She saw Clara pulling the shawl around her body, taut and secure, in part to guard against the chill of the icy northern winds, but also to try and deflect the avaricious eyes charting her progress. Ned's eyes? Michelle's shoulder ached as she watched Clara shift from one arm to another the bundle in which she carried her meagre possessions.

Michelle was overwhelmed by the frightened despair of the girl. It seeped from her eyes like tears. But more than that, it was as though Michelle could sense what Clara must have been feeling. How, she didn't know. She didn't want to know. But her stomach knotted in hunger, her body shivered with the cold. Clara needed a place to sleep and some food in her belly. She needed a job. She was scared and she was alone. She had nobody in the world to turn to. And God, how this girl Clara needed to be anywhere but where she was. It all seemed wrong. So wrong. The girl looked so alone, so vulnerable, as if she hadn't known what to expect on the streets of London as the darkness and fog of the night closed in around her.

'She were scared when I first went up to talk to her,' Ned said, 'and I really didn't mean her no harm. She were just so pretty I wanted to talk to her. Maybe I wanted to help her too. So I asked her what she were doing in London on her own. She didn't answer at first. Looked at the ground, looked anywhere really, but at me. She were real shy at first. But then she told me she needed a place. That she were a domestic. I told her I could help.'

The years had fallen away from Ned's face, revealing the boyish charm that he had once been blessed with, the deep-brown eyes, the dark hair free of the signs of careworn age, the winning, charming smile that told the girl she could trust him.

All an illusion, but Michelle, lost somewhere in the horror of Ned's past, wasn't sure what was real anymore.

'I told her I would tell her all the houses she could approach for work,' Ned said. 'But I told her it were too late to go knocking on back doors just then. And the night were fierce cold. I told her that I could help her find respectable lodgings for the night.'

Ned's hesitation told Michelle that he was getting to the difficult part of his story. The part he didn't want her to know because maybe he thought she would despise him. He had already suggested his motives were predatory, that she was a pretty young girl, walking the streets in the dark, alone, and even without saying another word, Michelle was certain the hunter had successfully stalked his prey. She needed to get out of his head, but she didn't know how. How could it be so difficult to get out of his memories when it was all too easy to slide into them?

'I took her to an inn where I knew there were rooms, 'cause I didn't want to take her back to the rookery where I bedded down. That were no place for a sweet young thing like her. I told her I knew the innkeeper and that she would be safe enough there for a night. And then I got her a drink. She said no, at first, that she couldn't. But she had no gloves and she were rubbing at her hands like she couldn't warm them up, so I told her a drink would put a fire in her belly, and warm her up from the inside. And then I told her I had already bought it, so she shouldn't waste it. She looked so cold, you see. And she were so pretty, and I were so happy that she wanted to sit and talk to me. And so after she had the first one, I got her another. And then another. And all the while I was talking to her. And after a while, she stopped being so shy, and she were smiling at me, and talking to me too, and I thought that she wanted me like I wanted her.'

Michelle looked at the wine glass in her hand, watched it transform into a clay cup, her focus and her grip on her own reality shifting, leaving her unable to determine which vessel it was that she held, and although she had only had half a glass of wine, her glass, Clara's cup, began to tilt and whirl in her head, and she struggled to place it back on the gleaming kitchen counter of her flat. No, not a wine glass. She was placing the clay cup onto the sticky, rancid wooden bar that she sat before. Michelle could no longer tell where she was, but her mind screamed at her that she was safe in her flat, even as leering eyes skimmed over Clara's body in that inn. She looked up at Ned, struggling to bring his blurred visage into focus, but just as she thought she had succeeded, the kaleidoscope shifted once more, taking clarity out of her reach.

She tasted strong cider in her mouth, not the Pinot Noir she had been drinking, and the voices all around were talking and laughing at her. No, not at her, Michelle tried to tell herself, at Clara. She was being pulled into memories that were not hers once more, and her grasp on her own reality was precarious, as though she was straddling tectonic plates.

Michelle's eyes adjusted to the mists of the past, and with her heart racing, she tried to ground herself, telling herself these were Ned's memories, not her own. But her dizziness, her uncertainty was Clara's. How could it be that the energy of Clara's memories had invaded her consciousness as well? It was as though there was something of Clara buried deep within Michelle. Ned had his arm around her waist and was pulling her to her feet, gesturing to the innkeeper, who led Ned upstairs, and opened a door for him. Ned slipped him some coins, the man pocketing the money in his grimy apron, as Ned guided an unsteady Clara into the room.

As the door closed behind them, Michelle watched as Ned's arms pulled Clara close to him, watched him trace his finger along Clara's jaw, across her cheek, and over her lips. She watched as Ned leaned in closer to the girl and they kissed, Clara responding with an enthusiasm that Michelle suspected was fuelled by the alcohol coursing through her veins. The girl gave a small gasp as Ned's hands drifted towards her breasts, pressing hard against the swell buried beneath the rough fabric of her dress.

Michelle closed her eyes as she remembered Nick, the memories of him invading her thoughts even as she tried to close her mind against them. She remembered him touching her like Ned was touching Clara, and her own body was flooded with a heated desire that cried out for fulfilment. She didn't want to think about Nick in that way, but she also didn't want to see this memory of Ned's, because she could see where it was going. And at least the girl seemed more than willing. The longing inside Michelle was building. Christ, she had become some sort of voyeur. Not this, she shouldn't be seeing this. But she couldn't stop it from playing out in front of her, an unwilling trespasser on what should have been a moment of intimacy between the two. And as Ned's voice played in the background, telling Michelle what had happened, Michelle could see it all. She was a ghostly prisoner of Ned's memories, only spirit, powerless to intervene, voiceless.

She watched as Ned scooped Clara up as though she was the weight of a soul and laid the girl on the bed. It might have been romantic, but the stench in the air told her Clara lay on a mattress that stank of the sweat of a thousand drunken men. Ned lowered himself on top of Clara and kissed her with an increasing urgency, already using one hand to unfasten the buttons of his trousers. The girl responded at first, any doubts she may have had about what she was doing dulled by the alcohol she had consumed. But when Ned started pushing up the swathes of fabric that made up her skirts and layers of winter petticoats, Michelle saw the panic in the girl's eyes, saw her shake her head, try to protest, only to have her words silenced by Ned's mouth crushing down on hers, sucking away her refusal like a vampire draining his victim of blood.

Ned ran his hand along the inside of the girl's thigh, above the strip of fabric holding up her thick stockings, and the girl gasped again. 'It's all right,' she could hear Ned whispering to the girl. 'I'm not going to hurt you. This'll be nice, real nice, I promise, and I'll go nice and slow for you,' and he kissed Clara again. Clara was once more drowning in her longing, sinking back in surrender not only to Ned's needs, but to her own, as Ned's fingers worked ever closer to the top of her thigh, teasing her flesh, feeding the fire of need that was consuming her. Clara's arms wound around Ned's neck, her fingers running through the thick thatch of his dark hair, losing herself once more in the greedy urgency of their lust. The musty smell of damp straw invaded her nostrils and the sounds of raucous singing from the bar below provided the dismal soundtrack as Ned eased apart Clara's legs and sank into her. The girl gave a sharp gasp of pain that hit Michelle as if she had been slapped across the cheek.

'It were her first time.' Ned's voice reached her. 'I didn't know.'

She watched as Ned pushed up from the girl, to look at her face. 'I told her I were sorry and I asked if I were hurting her. She told me no, and so I finished what we had started. I were slow and gentle, kissing her all the time. She were already precious to me and I didn't want to hurt her. I felt real bad afterwards, though, and I stayed with her, I did, holding her tight as she fell asleep. She were real warm, and I felt good next to her, and I fell asleep too. I'd been so lonely since I had come to London, and I liked her. I liked her a real lot.'

Michelle glanced back at the sleeping couple on the straw

mattress, but turned her face away from the tableau Ned had painted for her, of the girl on the filthy bed, Ned's arm flung across her, her skirts still pushed up to her waist, with a thin trail of watery blood creeping down her thigh, as though Ned's touch had created a canal for it to flow down.

'What happened after that, Ned? What happened to Clara?'

Ned's silence was weighted. Michelle watched him swallow before he said, 'I don't know. When I woke up the next morning, she were gone.'

'Gone? Gone where?'

Ned shook his head, mute.

'I don't understand,' Michelle said, looking at Ned. There was something missing still. Something he still wasn't telling her.

'I didn't know it were her first time. I thought she must have been with lads before, because otherwise, what was she doing on the streets at night, with nowhere to go? And she wanted it as much as I did, I could feel it. And when I realised I was the first, I, I... wanted to make sure she was all right. I didn't mean to hurt her,' Ned said. 'Really I didn't. And I didn't mean for what followed to happen either. You have to understand,' he implored.

Michelle was struggling to balance herself, as though she still carried the remnants of Clara's cider in her own body, and she was starting to remember just why she hated the pull that the dead had on her. She wanted to get out. Get out of Ned's head, get out of Ned's thoughts. The creeping arms of claustrophobia were tightening around her. And Michelle then discovered to her horror another unanticipated danger to sliding into Ned's memories. As she turned and tried to run, to get out of that room and back to the safety of her own reality, back to her own time, the ghost of Ned reached out and grabbed her with arms that had transfigured into the brutal corporeal, the raw power of his crushing grip arresting her flight, keeping her trapped within this locked chamber of his past.

'Everything that happened after that, it were a mistake. I didn't know. If I had known, maybe, maybe, things would have turned out differently.'

A mistake. That word again.

'Let go of me, Ned. Let me go.' Michelle tried to free herself from the trap she found herself in, as Ned's face and Nick's face merged together in her mind. The scream that had been building inside of Michelle since she had discovered her husband's infidelity finally found release as the fire of her fury combusted into a piercing cry.

When all that was left was the ringing in her ears, accompanied by the rapid beating of her fractured heart, Michelle found herself back in her flat, to the comforting cleanliness of her own kitchen. The wine glass was shattered into pieces, the remnants of the dark-red wine spilled across the granite top of the kitchen bench as though a pool of congealed blood, with the shards of the crystal scattered through the fluid and on to the floor, as though someone had taken an axe to an icicle.

Ned was gone. Again. She was alone.

CHAPTER SEVEN

It was proving difficult to let go of Ned, Michelle thought, as she sat in her kitchen after work a few days later, her customary wine in front of her, although this time she had poured it into a coffee cup. She hadn't had time to pop back into House of Fraser on Victoria Street and get a new wine glass. It was always closed whenever she passed it on the way home from work. She looked inside the cup as if she were a fortune-teller looking for answers. But they eluded her. Instead, she let the dark red of the liquid calm her, warm her. As she swirled the wine around in the cup, staring into the vortex of the deep burgundy fluid, she did think she was going to have to be careful not to let her drinking escalate. It was just so liberating to be able to drink without the little fingers of guilt prodding her in the back of her neck. She had been abstaining for so long, the potential of a longed-for pregnancy in front of her as though she was the patient donkey trekking after that ever-elusive carrot. It was always within sight. Never within reach.

Donkeys were bloody stupid creatures, she thought. She pushed up the sleeves of her shirt, rubbing the angry mottled skin where Ned's hold had bruised her. She hadn't expected him to become so real like that. She hadn't known she could feel him when she was trapped in his memories. Why hadn't Grandma told her? She frowned into her wine. She didn't want to keep thinking about Ned and his past, but he was troubling her. She was convinced there was something he wasn't telling her. There was more to his relationship with Clara than what he had allowed her to see, of that she was certain. Michelle wallowed in her confusion, wondering what it was she was missing. Ned clearly regretted the night he spent with Clara, and there was no denying it might have been a bit sordid, but who hadn't had an encounter they hadn't come to regret, especially when they were young and flooded with desire? Michelle's mind drifted back to Nick again and she cursed herself for wanting to forgive him. God knows he had done nothing to deserve it.

Michelle's confusion stayed with her. She wanted to forget she had ever seen Ned, wanted to pretend that somehow his spirit would never come back and trouble her again. But at the same time, there was a quiet voice inside telling her he had come to her for a reason. The words came to Michelle as though on the breath of a warm breeze, and Michelle liked to think they were the whispered words of her grandmother, or what she might have said if she had been around to guide Michelle in how to help free those spirits condemned to walk the earth. Michelle thought of her Grandma Ivy, formidable, unafraid of her abilities, and the way in which she had embraced her gift as her calling. When Michelle was little and frightened by what she could see, her grandmother had been the one to give her comfort. She had always said it was only the living that could hurt you, not the dead. Michelle had felt safe with her. She sighed. Perhaps she would try and help Ned after all. And she sensed, on some level, that helping Ned would give her a peace and resolution of her own. That she had, as her Grandma Ivy would have said, seen him for a reason.

Michelle had to give Ned credit. For someone who had been reduced to a wraith, he demonstrated a remarkable restraint, staying away from her, giving her time to consider what she had seen, to wonder why it was that she had to see it, never confronting her with his need for deliverance directly. But she had intruded on a moment of intimacy, and it had somehow made it awkward for her to engage with Ned again, which was ridiculous really, given that what had passed between him and Clara was now nothing more than a fleeting moment lost in the shadows of the past.

Ned. Waiting. Always there, waiting for her, on her walk home from the Underground station, as the cold night sky of November covered her. She saw him every evening, hiding in the shadows of Emery Hill Street, leaning against the black lamp-posts, his arms crossed, watching for her. Waiting for her. In the same blue cap, waistcoat and neckerchief that he had been wearing the first time she had seen him. Michelle could almost see the lights as they must have once been, lit with gaslight, shining like demonic red eyes in the thick fog of the London night, rather than the LED lighting they were equipped with now. But Michelle's appreciation of the old mingled with the new had somehow lost its charm. As had Ned.

However, as the days passed and with her grandmother's serene words playing like a lullaby in her head, allaying her fears and calming her confusion, reminding her there was a reason for Ned coming to her, Michelle was starting to feel ready to confront him once more to see why this relationship with Clara had such a hold on him, over a century after both had long been dead. And being honest with herself, Michelle had to admit she had cultivated a curiosity to see what had happened to Clara after that night with Ned, and to see how

Ned's fate played out so that he was, even now, mired in a guilt so powerful it tethered him to a world that no longer had any place for him.

She was plagued with the need to get to the end of the story, as though she had a half-finished book by her bed that called out to be read, even if she suspected the ending was not going to unfold in the way that she hoped, and was building with all the promise and tension of a crescendo, only to fade to a disappointment.

As she had known from the very beginning, from that first moment she had seen Ned, the ghost that haunted Emery Hill Street, she would have to see this through.

Having decided that she was ready, when she next saw Ned, deliberately keeping his distance from her, leaning against the black pole of one of the street lights opposite her flat, Michelle crossed over the road towards him. He stood as if coming to attention, her presence jolting him from his lethargy. Inserting her earbuds so that it looked to any passer-by that Michelle was on the phone rather than talking to thin air like some sort of crazy person, she approached him.

'I'm ready,' she told him. 'I'm ready for you to tell me what happened next. To Clara.'

'Are you angry at me?' he asked.

'No, why would I be angry at you? You had sex. You had both been drinking. It may not have been wise, but it happened,' she said, wondering why he thought she might be angry at him. Wait. Was there a reason she should be angry? 'Ned, why would I be angry at you? No, wait, can we not do this here? Can you come up to my flat again?'

Ned looked at her, saying nothing, promising nothing, as though he were weighing up her request like he had some other option that could help him.

Michelle turned, crossed back over the road, and walked

towards her building, entering the hall before taking the lift up to her floor. When she unlocked the door, and walked in, Ned was waiting for her. Michelle swallowed her doubts and tried to adopt the frame of mind she always deployed when dealing with the most difficult of her legal clients, the ones who didn't like to tell her what it was that she was really dealing with. And she had collected quite a few of those over the years, from the woman who had falsely accused her ex-husband of sexually abusing their child to prevent him from seeing his daughter, to the man who had hidden all his wealth in offshore trusts in Belize and the Cayman Islands so that his ex-wife was left unable to pay the school fees.

Michelle had seen the very worst of human behaviour, the spite and the greed a spurned ex was capable of. Yet she prided herself in always acting professionally and impeccably. She never let her personal view get in the way of her role as a legal advocate. It was not her job to judge. It was hard at times, especially when you really wanted to leave clients to wallow in their own mud. But your own values had no place when you had a job to do. As she kept trying to impress upon Toby, you didn't have to like your client. You just had to get the best result for them that you could. She had read a saying once, to the effect that if there were no bad men, there would be no good lawyers. It was an adage she held close to her heart. She had always wanted to be a good lawyer. Bad people would make her better at what she did. Perhaps it was best if she did treat Ned on the same basis as she did her clients, not getting emotionally involved, just trying to untangle the knotted thicket of facts that made up the barrier to an acceptable resolution.

She started. 'So after you... After that night in the inn with Clara, what happened? You said she just disappeared, but you must have seen her again, or she wouldn't have such a hold over you now. When did you next see her?'

Ned looked up at Michelle, his reluctance saturating the air between them. But he answered her anyway.

'I didn't see her again after that. Not for months, anyway. And when she did come back, she were in a right state. She told me it had taken her weeks to find me, because she could barely remember what I looked like. She could only remember my name. And I suppose I were hard to find because I moved around a lot. She had been searching the face of every dark-haired man with a blue cloth cap to see if it were me. But she found me in the end.'

Michelle's mind was racing. 'Ned, why did she come back looking for you?' As soon as she asked the question, her heart fell into the cavernous depths of her soul. There was only one reason why Clara would have returned to find the man she had slept with when she was the one who had disappeared. 'She was pregnant, wasn't she?'

Ned nodded, and Michelle saw the guilt shrouding his eyes once more, eating away at his soul the way the worms had consumed his body. 'She told me after that night where we, where we... where we had lain together, she had woken up with a heavy head, and that she were right ashamed of herself for having lain with me when she hardly knew me and there were no promises of marriage between us. She said that the people who had brung her up would have said that she had been evil, that she had sinned, that she had given into temptation, and that she couldn't face me for the shame after I had known her like that. And she were right sorry for that now, because when she knew she were in trouble she didn't know how she could find me. She told me that after that night, she were going to try and put lying with me behind her, and find a new situation. That she wouldn't be accepting any more help from any fellow who offered it. And that she had got a new situation, a good one an' all, where the folk who employed her were kind and treated her well.

'But, after a while, she knew she were in trouble, that she were with child, and that the child had no father because she didn't know where to find me. She tried to hide it for as long as she could, but her belly grew, and told on her, and they dismissed her. Without notice. And without a character. So then she took what little she had and tried to find me to see if I would claim the bairn. And she did find me, but her belly was right big by the time she found me, and it was too late.'

'What do you mean it was too late?' Michelle asked.

Ned retreated into silence.

Damn it, how she was starting to really hate those silences of his. Taking a breath, Michelle considered, and again asked a question she suspected she didn't want to hear the answer to. But she had to know, and she had to hear it from him. 'Did you help her?' she asked him. 'Did you help Clara?'

'No.'

He offered no excuses, no explanations, just stood quietly like a man condemned, as if he was waiting for the torrent of Michelle's anger to rain down upon his head.

'Are you going to tell me why?' she asked.

'I didn't know that Clara were having my bairn. If I had known, I never would have...'

He stopped, looked at Michelle, as if he was waiting for her to piece it together so that he didn't have to say the words himself.

'Nelly,' Michelle said. 'You had already married Nelly by then, hadn't you?'

Ned nodded miserably.

'I already told you I were just a navvie. I had to stand for hiring every day, and there were only just enough money for me and for Nelly, for our food and our lodgings. And Nelly had only just told me she thought that she were with child too. I couldn't take on another woman and her bairn. I were just young, you see, and I were panicked because I had made a right mess of things without knowing. And I didn't mean to be cruel, but I didn't know what else to do. So that's what I told her. I told her that I couldn't take her on because I already had a wife and she had a child in her belly, and I had to take care of them. Clara cried and pleaded, told me if I didn't help her it would be the workhouse for her. But I couldn't help her, you see?'

'So you just turned her away, and left that poor girl to fend for herself?'

'What else could I do?' Ned asked.

'You could have provided some sort of support for her,' Michelle said. 'I mean, you just left that girl with no one to turn to, with nothing, knowing the child she carried was yours.'

Ned nodded again, but he seemed fired up by Michelle's condemnation of his actions. 'I hated myself for having to do it, but I couldn't see any way to help Clara. I had Nelly to think of and we had next to nothing. You don't know what it is to be hungry, to never know if you're going to have work the next day, to have to stand in a line, hoping that the gaffers like the look of you enough to take you on for a job, knowing that it could make all the difference between whether or not you can put a roof over the head of you and your missus. How could I take on Clara and her baby as well?'

'So you chose Nelly over Clara?' Michelle fired back. 'Chose Nelly's child over Clara's?'

'What choice did I have? Nelly and I were wed,' he said. 'And that meant something. I liked Clara, and I might have loved her if she hadn't gone running off after lying with me, but she were gone, and then I met Nelly, and she wouldn't lie with me unless I promised marriage, and so we got the banns read and we wed.'

Silence sat between them as Michelle tried to reconcile what he had told her with what she thought was right and realised that Ned had found himself with a horrible dilemma not entirely of his own making. No wonder he still condemned himself for his failures with Clara. Compassion for Ned was starting to fill Michelle when he added, 'But I suppose I shouldn't have been so cruel to her.'

Her heart sank. Just when she was beginning to think there might be some way to help him.

'You were cruel? How? What did you do to her, Ned?'

'When Clara was standing before me, her hands on her great belly, looking at me with her big sad eyes, I felt bad, real bad. And I didn't want to feel like that. So I tried to tell myself that the baby she had inside her weren't mine. That it could have been anyone's. And besides, it was all her fault anyway, as none of it would have happened if she hadn't gone running off after lying with me, so that I never knew I'd put a child in her before I married Nelly. And I started to get angry at her for making me feel like that, so I told her that it weren't like I knew for certain that the baby were mine. That she gave herself to me easily enough and that I didn't have to work too hard to spread her legs. And I told her that any lad could have taken a walk along Cock Alley with her and that she and her bairn weren't my responsibility. So I told her that I couldn't help her and she should get rid of that what was in her belly.'

Michelle recoiled as Ned's words landed on her as though he wielded a whip. From Ned's description of the state of Clara when she had found Ned, Michelle could only assume that Clara must have been heavily pregnant, and for Ned to suggest that Clara should get rid of the child she carried was unfathomable to her. It was beyond cruel. Grief echoed through the vast hollow of Michelle's own empty womb. Michelle wanted to push Ned as far from her as possible, to force him away from her presence, so she didn't have to listen to his cold rejection of Clara's desperate pleas and his vile suggestion that the girl should subject herself to having a late abortion, her child killed, and her womb scraped empty by some back-street abortionist with a dirty hooked knitting needle. And once more, the pull of the current towards the past was trying to take her. She clung on to her objectivity, as though it was a post fixed into the banks of a rushing river, but his words were weakening her hold. Damn him.

Ned continued, each of his words piercing her heart. 'Clara said she'd wanted to get rid of the baby at first, but she couldn't go through with it mostly because she were scared of the gallows if they caught her at it, but also because she were hoping that she would find me and I would marry her and make it all all right but I told her I would have nowt to do with her or the baby. That I were finished with her. That she should take herself to the workhouse.' Ned hesitated before he said, almost defiantly, 'I told her that were the only place for a whore like her.'

Bastard. Michelle's tenuous grasp on her anger at Ned and her sense of compassion for the girl finally broke her determination to hold on to her emotions, and she found herself caught up in the momentum towards his past as though she had been swept up in the current of a river as it headed towards a waterfall, sending her plunging into the depths of the waters below. She could not turn back to her own time. But on this occasion, she almost didn't want to.

She saw Clara, the young girl, thin, pale, gaunt, her swollen stomach seeming disproportionate to her slight frame. She was starving. Michelle's reality blurred in and out, as she looked down at the sores covering Clara's hands. She could almost feel the burden in her belly moving inside her, the small slight movements of a child only half-formed. For the briefest of moments Michelle's mind looked down to the emptiness of her own womb, wondered how easily some women became pregnant, when her own infertility hounded her like a snarling wolf. But, caught once again in the bonds of a past not of her own, her mind focused on the scene she had landed in.

Clara was holding on to the sleeve of Ned's jacket as she pleaded with him to take pity on her and spare her from the horrors of the workhouse. Her words were laced with fraught desperation. 'Please, please, I'm begging you. If I go to the workhouse, they'll cut off my hair. They'll take my clothes and make me one of them so that everyone will know my shame. They won't let me keep the baby, and it will die. It will die, Ned. Have you seen the workhouse? They all have the graveyards right next door to them so that the journey from the workhouse to the ground is nice and short and they don't have to trouble themselves too much. Our baby will die if I have to go there.'

Ned had fallen silent, and Michelle realised that this retreat into silence was not something that he did solely in his conversations with her to avoid revealing the worst of his crimes. His silence was his refusal to engage with what was unpleasant for him to contemplate, the awful reality of the horrific consequences of his careless actions. Ned shook Clara off, and took a step away from her.

'Perhaps that's for the best,' he said. 'Go to the workhouse.'

Ned turned his back on the girl and walked away, leaving her with her face in her hands, a picture of utter, abject defeat.

'But I didn't mean it,' Ned said. Michelle felt herself sliding back into her own time, into the familiar comfort of her own home. Her heart ached for Clara and the wretched misery she imagined she endured once Ned had abandoned her to her fate.

And she was bloody angry with Ned, but her anger was tempered by the excitement of what she thought she had discovered. She thought she had it. It had come to her with startling clarity as the vision of Clara sobbing into her hands vanished once more into the haze of the past. Clara, heavy with Ned's child. Nelly and her stillborn baby she had taken with her to the grave. Michelle was certain she had found the cornerstone of the building that imprisoned Ned to his ghostly form. Ned had sent Clara away to the workhouse. Had he died without ever knowing what had happened to Clara and the child? And then to lose his baby with Nelly. No wonder his restless spirit was unable to find respite. She was already wondering if the workhouse records had been preserved for Clara's generation, and if so, how difficult it would be to start searching through any archived records to try and find mention of her, and almost immediately she realised she didn't know her last name.

Ned was watching Michelle with caution, covering his face as if he was expecting her anger to ignite and be directed towards him once more. But Michelle was now caught up in the enthusiasm of her plan to help Ned move on. She simply had to find out what had become of Clara and her baby.

She looked at Ned and asked, 'Ned, what was Clara's last name? Do you know?'

Ned seemed disorientated by the question. He thought for a moment. 'Waters. It were Waters.'

'So, all I have to do,' Michelle said, looking at Ned for confirmation, 'to help you make peace with what you did, is find out what happened to Clara Waters and her child?'

Ned looked at her almost as if he pitied her.

'I know what happened to Clara and the child,' Ned said. 'I killed them. I killed them both.'

CHAPTER EIGHT

Michelle was silenced. Her thoughts spinning wildly, she attempted to make sense of his latest confession. But how could she make sense of what was an admission of murder?

'What do you mean, you killed them? And you had better not bloody well disappear on me again.'

Michelle's phone buzzed, interrupting Ned's customary retreat into silence. Without taking her eyes off him, as though she was compelling his spirit to remain in her presence, Michelle picked her phone up off the kitchen counter and swiped to answer.

'Michelle Sikes.'

'Mich, I can't believe you finally answered.'

Fuck. It was Nick.

'Nick, I can't do this with you right now,' Michelle said, as she began pacing the length of the kitchen.

'Michelle, please can we just talk? That's all I'm asking.'

'I will say it again,' Michelle said, 'I can't do this right now. I'm in a meeting...' She turned and glanced to where Ned was standing. He had gone.

'Fuck,' Michelle said, this time out loud. 'Well, Nick, it

appears that my meeting has just been cancelled. So, I suppose I have time to talk. Although I can't possibly imagine that we have much to say to each other at this point.'

'Of course there are things to say. But the first thing I wanted to say, what I have been trying to say since you left, is that I'm sorry. I'm sorry, Mich, more than you could know.'

Sorry for what he had done, or sorry it had caught up with him? She said nothing as she waited for him to continue.

'I know what I have done is unforgiveable and I don't blame you for wanting to get away from all the shit I'm putting you through. But I really miss you, Mich, and I am just so, so sorry for the hurt you must be going through. I didn't mean for any of this to happen. It was—'

'I know, a mistake,' Michelle cut in, as though slicing through ice, the memory of Clara and Ned on that bed still haunting her peace. 'The thing is, Nick, your mistake seemed to happen quite regularly.'

He didn't deny it. Well, now she knew for certain. With his lack of any denial to her statement, he had just confirmed that he had engaged in an ongoing affair with Jen without even realising he had been asked the question. This is why she had always been a much better lawyer than him. Nick was good with the clients, she would give him that, at the networking and socialising, at the reassurance that made them feel as though they were being given the best possible legal representation available. But when it came to actually providing that legal representation, it was always lawyers like Michelle that he relied upon.

'I'm sorry,' Nick said, 'but my head was all over the place with the IVF and everything. I know it was hard on you, but I think you sometimes forget it was hard on me too. I was going through it all, just the same as you. I felt that everything was out of my control, and I hated seeing how upset it made you, yet how brave you were every time we got disappointed. And you were being so stoical, and holding it all together, even though I could see it was breaking your heart.'

'So you thought the best way of dealing with it all was by falling into bed with another woman?' Michelle's words were like ice.

'Mich, I'm sorry, I'm just trying to explain. Because after the IVF and all that, I felt like the only thing we were about was trying to have a baby. That and work were the only things that seemed to matter. And then with Jen, she was being so sympathetic and so kind–'

'I'm sure she was,' Michelle cut in again. How well she could imagine that simpering girl showering her husband with her sympathy.

'Mich, what I'm trying to say is that I suppose everything with her got out of hand. The first time with her really was a mistake–'

'Which suggests that all the other times with her were the result of a deliberate considered action, wouldn't you say?'

'Just let me explain, please, Mich.' Michelle detected desperation in his voice, and ill-disguised impatience. Nick had always hated it when she resorted to legal rhetoric in their arguments.

'Well, it will be interesting to see if you can explain it, so go on, Nick, tell me how you ended up with your dick inside your secretary.' Michelle was holding on to her temper with a strength that came from years of holding all that she was inside of her, never letting go of the control required to keep her gift contained.

Nick sighed, before he continued. 'It should never have happened, but Jen had been staying late at work for some reason, and she said she had to bring some confidential files to me that the client didn't want scanned. It was when you had gone to Canberra for that High Court matter you were working on. Jen and I, we had a couple of glasses of wine, but I swear, Mich, I really didn't mean for it to happen. Even the second and third times I didn't mean for it to happen. But then she got pregnant so quickly, and I didn't know what to do, so I suppose I figured the damage was already done. It wasn't like I could get her pregnant again.'

Michelle wondered if Nick stopped to consider, even for a moment, the words that were coming out of his lying, cheating mouth. No wonder she hadn't been able to get hold of him when she had tried to call him to bring him up to speed about the difficult day she'd had in court, and how much she was looking forward to seeing him. He was too busy shagging his bloody secretary like some godawful cliché.

'When she told me about the baby, I told her she should get an abortion.' She detected the slight tone of self-righteousness in Nick's voice. 'I mean, after all, I am married, and she does know that. She always knew that,' Nick said.

Well, of course she knew that Nick was married. They all worked in the same bloody firm, where everyone knew everyone else's business. Michelle thought of Ned telling Clara that she should get rid of 'that' which was in her belly, like it wasn't a life her body was crying out to nurture, but a regrettable waste product of the pleasure he had taken in her. She thought of the struggles she and Nick had endured together in their efforts to bring a baby into the world, the casual way in which he announced he had 'told' his mistress that she should terminate her pregnancy because it would inconvenience him. Why was it that men thought they had any right to tell a woman what she should do with her body once they had taken their fill of it?

'But she refused,' Nick continued. 'She says she's keeping the baby. She expects me to support it. And I have to do the right thing, Mich. I am going to take responsibility for the baby.'

That self-righteous tone again. Michelle wanted to punch him, and she was pretty sure she might have done so if they were having this conversation in person rather than through the phone. Instead, she steadied her breath, contained her anger.

'As you should. And I'm very happy for you, Nick,' Michelle said through the growing tension in her jaw. 'But I fail to see what any of this has to do with me. You had an affair, which you tried to keep hidden from me. You failed to take precautions to prevent a pregnancy, and the inevitable resulted. As such, you have been caught with your pants down, so to speak. Surely the only thing we have left to discuss would be the terms of our separation?'

'Look, Mich, we had so much trouble trying to get a pregnancy. I guess on some level I thought I didn't need to take any precautions to prevent a pregnancy, because we tried for so long and it never happened. I thought it was really hard to get pregnant. So it really wasn't my fault.' Nick seemed pleased with his logic. 'But don't you see? This could be our chance. We tried and tried to have a baby, and nothing happened. And now I'm having a baby that could be our baby, if you wanted it to be. I don't want a baby with Jen. I want a baby with you.'

Michelle's mind was drifting somewhere in a murky swamp of misery as Nick skirted over the issue of her infertility as though it were an acceptable explanation, a valid excuse for his philandering, not to mention his impending fatherhood thanks to that scheming b– Michelle stopped herself. That woman. His secretary. Wasn't Michelle always reminding her clients that a dignified silence was better than a fraught spat?

'And what about Jen? Where does your secretary fit into this wonderful family portrait you are busy painting?'

'She'll want to see the baby, I suppose. But she's only young, probably too young to be a mother really. It's not like the pregnancy was planned.'

Michelle had no doubt that Nick would have been clueless, but Michelle had come across Jen enough times to know she was not the type to do anything unless there was something in it for her. No doubt she considered having a baby with a well-paid lawyer preferable to working her own way up the corporate ladder.

'But Mich,' Nick continued, oblivious to Michelle's disbelief as he carried on outlining his thinking, 'we are ready to be parents, and we are mature, employed, and could offer the baby a happy, stable family home. We could apply to the Family Court for a child arrangement order in our favour, and Jen could have fortnightly weekend contact visits. Come on, you do this all the time. And you deserve a baby. We deserve a family.'

So, this is what Nick thought Michelle deserved? To be mother to a baby conceived in his lies and betrayal? Yet, for one solitary moment, Michelle considered the possibility of what Nick was suggesting, her primitive desire for a baby obliterating all other thoughts. But she knew in her heart she couldn't take this baby away from Jen, no matter how vile and scheming the woman may have been.

Part of Michelle wanted to take the child, just so she could hurt Jen as much as Jen had hurt her. But she would never be able to live with herself if she did. And even if she did cast aside all her values and take the child away from Jen, it would never really be her baby. It would be his. Nick's. And Jen's. What he was suggesting offered only a lifetime of conflict with every decision made in relation to the child a potential battleground. And every time she saw that child with Nick it would remind her of his betrayal, the way in which he had abandoned his marriage, the years of shared ambition, hopes and dreams, all for an easy fuck. She would think of the way her husband had taken that woman into her bed, in her room, in her home, drinking with her from the wine glasses that Michelle had chosen when she and Nick had married, eating with her from the blue dinnerware that Nick and Michelle had chosen together in David Jones, Jen slipping into the sheets that Michelle had washed and remade the bed with, and where she slept every night, and of Nick making love to Jen with the same passion that he did with her, but unlike her, making the baby that would forever be a part of his future. And now he was asking for it to be a part of hers. She wanted to hit him. It would be like watching his dog shit in her back garden, and instead of clearing it up, taking her to rub her face in the stinking mess every single day of her life.

'I can't believe you would even suggest it. Can you hear what you're saying, Nick? And it's because I do *this*, as you call my job, all the time, that I don't want any part of it. This is your child, not mine. And because it is your child, which you are having with the woman you were fucking behind my back, I don't want any part of you anymore. I want a divorce.'

Michelle had been so busy running away from the hurt Nick had caused her that she had not really thought through what this would mean for her future with him. She supposed a divorce was inevitable, but she had been unaware this was what she wanted until the words came out of her mouth. But once she had said them, she embraced the truth of them, the liberating sense of freeing herself from the weight of her misery. She had been so caught up with trying to resolve Ned's situation that she had given little thought to her own, partly because she had not wanted to imagine her life without Nick in it while knowing this was the only future ahead of her as a result of his affair. But now she had been forced to confront him, the thought of the rest of her future being one where she was chained in marriage to Nick, after what he had done, filled her with a sickening dread.

'I made a mistake, but surely we can find some way to work

this out? I love you. I want to be with you. Not Jen. She was just a distraction.'

'A distraction?' Michelle rubbed at her temple, tying to ward off the oncoming headache. 'You should have thought of that before you fell into bed with her. And you should have thought of that before you forgot to put on a condom,' she said.

Fuck, Michelle thought, as she realised she was going to have to go and get some STI checks. She should have thought of that already. Her husband had been sleeping with both of them without any form of protection. And Jen's actions had shown she was the type that would sleep with anyone if she thought it might get her somewhere. God knows what she had been put at risk of. Her anger rose in proportion to her nausea.

'Put the house on the market,' Michelle fired at him.

Once again, the words had escaped from Michelle's mouth before she even had a chance to consider them. But again, once she had spoken them, she knew she was simply telling him what needed to be done. They would have to sell the marital home. Michelle thought of her beautiful house, with its glimpses of the still waters of the harbour from the top floor, and while she felt the pull of it calling her back home, it was also the very last place she would ever want to be. Everything beautiful about it had been stained and sullied.

A strained silence filtered through the phone. 'That's what I needed to talk to you about,' Nick said. 'Jen is saying that she can't stay in her flat share. That it's not good for the baby.'

'And?'

'I was wondering, since you've moved out and everything, and I know your secondment is for at least six months, if it wouldn't just be better if I moved her in? Into the spare room, I mean. You know, just until the baby is born, and then we can work something out afterwards.'

Michelle laughed. His suggestion was even more

preposterous than the last. If ever there were a case of someone talking out of his arse, this would be it. 'Well, wouldn't that be convenient for her?' Michelle replied. 'Do you honestly think I'm going to agree to that woman moving into my home, Nick, whether I'm there or not? You had an affair with her, and you want to move her in and play happy families with her? Put the house on the market.' And then the lawyer in Michelle kicked in, and because she didn't want Jen to have an easy ride after she had clearly decided to get pregnant to a man she knew to be married, she added, 'And by the way, you are not under any obligation to support her. Your obligation is to the child. The housing issue isn't going to be relevant until the child is born, so that should be more than enough time to put the property through an auction process and for you to take your equity from it and house you and Jen as you see fit.'

Michelle wondered why she was bothering. Jen obviously viewed the child maintenance she would receive from Nick going forward as a more palatable option to paid employment. Did Jen even want to live with Nick, have a relationship with him? She suspected Nick was in the firing line for a lifetime of conflict with Jen, and her experience with women like Jen told her that she, like some sort of demonic Oliver Twist, would always be wanting more.

'So you would represent me if it all goes south?' he asked.

Michelle laughed again. She should have been furious, and a part of her was, but his question was just so ridiculous, she almost couldn't believe that he had asked it. But oh-so typical of him. She was somewhat ashamed that she derived a little sliver of satisfaction from the fact he was already anticipating legal action being commenced by Jen. It suggested to her that the relationship between the two erstwhile lovers was already strained.

'No, are you fucking kidding me, Nick?' Michelle said.

'Even if I wanted to act for you, which I don't, I can't. Nor can anybody in Harpers. Stop looking for everyone else to solve your fucking problems. There is no easy fix here. What the hell is wrong with you? You're a partner in the firm, I'm an associate, and Jen is an employee. There are more conflict issues there than are capable of being resolved and you bloody well know this. In fact, it is nothing but a gigantic bloody mess which I don't want any part of. Besides, the firm is going to have to consider its own position in all of this, because Jen could potentially have an action against it *and you* pursuant to the sex discrimination legislation. She is, after all, pregnant. I shouldn't have to tell you any of this. You know what, Nick? This is your mess. I'm afraid you're going to have to clean it up all by yourself.'

'Mich, maybe we should take some time to consider before we do anything drastic,' he said. 'Besides, it's only very early in the pregnancy. Anything could happen.'

Michelle could hear the unspoken wish behind his words. He wanted Jen to miscarry, so that his problems slipped away with the unformed child in her womb. Did he think it would make any difference to her now whether Jen had his baby or not? She closed her eyes as her disappointment in him completed a full circle.

'Put the house on the market. If you don't, I will. I am perfectly capable of taking care of that from here. And if you decide to make things difficult, I will seek a specific purpose order from the court to allow estate agents access to the property and to effect a sale. I think we both know which way the pendulum would swing in a court hearing between an unfaithful husband and his betrayed wife, especially when that betrayed wife owns most of the equity in the property.'

Michelle had made up her mind. She could never return to that house again, not even to collect any more of her furniture and possessions. It was poison to her now; there was no antidote, and crossing the threshold would only serve to drive the venom deeper into her heart. All that was there for her were images of Nick's trysts with Jen being played out in her mind. She would forever be wondering which rooms they had fucked in, which piece of furniture he had leaned her over, which sofa Jen had reclined her nubile young body on as though she was modelling for Matisse.

'Come on, Mich, be reasonable. If we sell up we would never be able to afford anything so nice. Not on our own. And I do have a baby to think about.'

His sheer audacity! What a complete fucking twat he was being. She could not believe that Nick was deploying his baby to try and guilt her into letting him keep the house. She closed her eyes, wondering what had happened to the man she had fallen in love with all those years ago, when she had first started out with Harpers as a paralegal while she finished her law degree.

She remembered the glint of mischief in his bright blue eyes as he had introduced himself to her at Friday night drinks, pressing a glass of Chardonnay into her hand. The months of flirting that had followed as she focused on passing her law degree, quietly resolved not to get involved in an office romance. He had courted her with admirable persistence and relentless determination, telling her he wasn't prepared to give up, even when she told him that she would be going travelling for six months when she had finished her degree, as she had always planned, and he should find someone else. She remembered falling into bed with him after her farewell drinks before she went off backpacking, thinking that he would have forgotten her by the time she returned. But he hadn't forgotten her. He had waited, just as he said he would, emailing her regularly while she travelled, regaling her with all the gossip from the firm, telling her she was still the only woman he wanted to be with. It was one of the reasons why she had fallen in love with him. He was someone she thought she could trust.

She had been so cautious, not wanting to enter into a relationship that would threaten her career prospects with the firm, conducting the early stages of their courtship with absolute discretion, ensuring she did not go anywhere near Nick's speciality of commercial property litigation so that she never had to work with him directly, before persuading Nick they needed to declare their relationship to the managing partners so the firm was protected from potential breaches of employment and discrimination law. And through all of that, their engagement, marriage, and fight to conceive, Michelle had trusted Nick implicitly. He had never once given her cause to doubt him, at least when it came to the question of other women, something that had become particularly important to Michelle as she chose her speciality and worked with the dysfunctional and fractured relationships of the high-net-worth individuals the firm represented.

But there was one thing Michelle no longer trusted Nick with, and hadn't for some time. And on that thought, the whole conversation she was having with him started to fall into place.

'You haven't told her, have you?' Michelle asked.

'Told her what?'

Well, his relationship with Jen had certainly made him better at feigning innocence. 'That you actually own very little equity in the house. That the vast majority of it belongs to me.'

Michelle had inherited a rather large sum from her grandmother. Her mother was not good at a lot of things, but she was good with money, and had invested Ivy's bequest to her rather wisely on her behalf, leaving Michelle with a significant deposit to put on an apartment when she first started at Sydney University. She had managed to pay off the mortgage on that within a few years. But when she and Nick had come to talk about buying their first home together, she had been somewhat disconcerted to realise he had very little disposable assets to contribute towards a deposit. He was a partner in a top five Sydney law firm, yet had managed to accumulate next to nothing. Nick was a little too fond of spread betting, it seemed, and had lost more money than Michelle cared to think about. So, when they had purchased the house together, Michelle had taken steps to ensure the money she was contributing was protected, drawing up a document that stipulated Nick's share of the equity in the house would be limited to a percentage representing his contribution to the mortgage payments. She had made it pretty watertight. He probably would have benefited from hiring a better lawyer himself.

By her quick calculations, under the terms of that agreement, Nick would now walk away with enough to purchase a small house in the outer suburbs of Sydney. Maybe. If he was lucky. She smiled to herself. Jen really should have taken the time to get a full appreciation of all the facts before she shackled herself financially to someone as she had just done with Nick. Nick earned a shedload more money than most, but he enjoyed spending his cash as well. It slipped through his fingers as easily as he poured vintage Dom Pérignon down his throat. It was Michelle who had been the prudent, sensible one when it came to their matrimonial finances.

'Look, I'll come and see you. I think all of this will be easier if we could just talk in person,' Nick said.

'Don't bother,' Michelle told him. 'It really is a long flight. Besides, I don't want to see you. In fact, I never want to see you again. Do you understand?' She didn't give him time to answer and the lawyer in her then sprang into action, like a jaguar on the hunt. 'As soon as it's possible I will issue an application for a divorce order. Luckily for you I will be filing in Australia because if it was over here, I would have to cite your adultery as grounds. Not that you could dispute that, especially in light of the overwhelming evidence provided by the pregnancy of your mistress.'

'Mich–'

But Michelle was in no mood to be interrupted. Not now. Not by him. 'In terms of the financial settlement that we will need to agree, as the money in the house is already dealt with, we only have to go through furniture and other personal effects. I think we can probably agree not to go after each other's pension funds. Neither one of us needs spousal support as we are both working and earning decent amounts. If anything, I should go after you because as a partner, you earn more than me.'

'What? Come on, Mich...'

'Don't worry, Nick, petty money grabbing just because I can isn't really something I want to do. I just want a clean break. I want to walk away. I will let you know the details of my solicitor once I have engaged one. Once I have, there will be no need for us to talk again.'

Could it be that easy to sever the ties with someone who had been part of her life for so many years? She smiled. It would be just like cutting off her hair.

'Mich, please...'

'Fuck off, Nick.' Michelle cut off the call. She had wasted enough of her time and energy on the waste of space that was her soon-to-be ex-husband.

She had better things to think about. What did Ned mean when he said he had killed Clara and the baby? Could he be a murderer? It just didn't make sense. She believed that he had died of ill health, not at the end of the hangman's noose. He had told her enough detail that, thanks to the wonders of Google, she had been able to figure out what disease had claimed his life and condemned him to his transient state. The cholera epidemic of 1848 had been well documented, and there had been a considerable death toll, with labourers working on the riverbank near Lambeth and Millbank particularly vulnerable.

But maybe he had slain Clara and the child and had not been caught? It would have been possible, she supposed, particularly given the lack of forensic evidence back then, and the fact that the death of an unmarried mother with no family was not going to be a high priority for British justice at the time. The questions in her head were building an impenetrable fortress that blocked out all other calls on her thoughts. She needed Ned to return. She wondered if there was any way to compel a reluctant spirit to communicate with her. Her grandma had never mentioned anything like that being possible. Then again, Michelle had never been all that keen on listening to Grandma Ivy whenever the subject moved on to the mysteries of their gift.

She walked over to her balcony, and pulling back the curtains, glimpsed over the road to the street lamp, hoping to see the spectre of Ned shifting in the shadows. But there was only emptiness under the halo of the light shining through the evening haze.

She opened the door and stepped out on to the balcony, letting the cold wind tease her. Her skin prickled over with goosebumps, but only in response to the freezing temperature outside. She closed her eyes, inhaling slowly, trying to feel any sense of Ned in the street below. But there was nothing, just the quiet whisper of the breeze and the sound of her breath being released, the vapour turning white with the cold, before disappearing into nothingness, lost in the darkness of the night.

CHAPTER NINE

'Cut it off.'

The stylist, Nathan, unravelled her hair from the loose bun she had wound it into, and held it in his hands, dropping it so it fell down the back of the chair in lustrous waves. Looking into her eyes through the mirror, she saw uncertainty reflected in his own.

'It is quite long. Are you sure?'

Michelle glanced at the black geometric-patterned tattoos that crawled up his arm like some poor imitation of an Escher masterpiece, and the piercing through his nose. 'I'm sure. Cut it off. All of it. I want a short bob, to just underneath my ears. Other than that, I don't really care what you do. Just cut it off.' Sensing his continued reservation, she said, not really believing the words, but saying them anyway, 'It's okay. I trust you. Cut it off.'

He hesitated for only a moment, before he started brushing through her hair.

'Do you want to keep the hair?' he asked, looking at it with a kind of quiet reverence. 'It would make a good hairpiece.'

Michelle looked at him, taken aback by the question. She

thought of all the things she had lost recently, of all the hopes and dreams that damned email had stripped from her, the possessions she had left behind when she had got on the plane. Why on earth would she want to hold on to her hair? She wanted to be free of it. She wanted to be free of Nick.

'No, I don't want it. I don't care what you do with it.'

Michelle sat in stillness as Nathan explained that the salon supported a charity that made wigs from real hair for children with cancer, and asked if he could send her hair to them. Michelle nodded, pleased she might bring a little hope and brightness to some poor child, but at the same time wishing Nathan would bloody well just get on with it. He tied an elastic band around the hair, forming a loose ponytail, and picked up his scissors. He waited, poised, looking at Michelle for her approval. Michelle nodded again, and felt a shivering whisper on the nape of her neck, the cool silver of the blade slicing through her hair along the top of the elastic band, like the silence of a falling guillotine.

She was free. She let go of the breath she had been holding, and a little of the hurt that was knotted inside of her went with it.

A couple of hours later, she left the salon with a lightness in her step, imagining she had left a little bit of Nick sealed up in that plastic bag along with her hair. It was time to leave him in the past. How could a simple thing like a haircut lessen the strength of her sadness? She loved her new style. It was sassy and it suited her, even if she did say so herself. Walking back into her flat, she perched herself on the bar-stool in the kitchen, and sat with her head high and her shoulders back. She fired up her laptop.

Clara Waters. Michelle didn't have much to go on, but she typed the name into the Google search engine anyway and pressed enter. Some sort of prison in Oklahoma. Some actress who died in the 1930s. As she suspected, there was not a lot that was going to be of use to her.

She thought for a moment, and typed *London* after Clara's name, hoping it might somehow narrow down the vast quantity of useless results she had just been presented with. It didn't. Damn.

Despite the number of times she had spoken with Ned, she really did not have anywhere near enough factual detail to help her track down any useful information about him and his past. She also realised that while she had asked him Clara's last name, she had failed to find out his own. What the bloody hell was wrong with her that she seemed to become completely incompetent every time Ned turned up in her life?

She took a breath and tried to take inventory. So, what was it that she did know? That a man named Edmund had confessed to the killing of one Clara Waters and her child in an indeterminate year prior to 1848. That was it. As to how he had killed them, or why, she was clueless. It wasn't a lot for her to work with.

She closed her laptop and frowned. Ned had not returned since his startling announcement that he was a murderer. It was coming up to Christmas, November evolving into December before she really even had a chance to mourn the passing days. Coloured lights were starting to adorn the streets of London, the whole city becoming enlivened with festive hope and promise, and a large Christmas tree had been placed in the square in front of the cathedral. It had been decorated with large purple baubles and Michelle was always surprised that the ground underneath the tree was not covered in shattered amethyst shards each time she walked past. There was something rather magical about the shadow of the Christmas tree set before the magnificence of the imposing façade of the front of the cathedral.

Michelle was starting to think she should take herself off to John Lewis and get some decorations for her flat. Part of her also wondered why she should bother given they would just be for her, but maybe getting some new baubles of her own would stop her mind from drifting back to the boxes of decorations sitting in the garage back in Mosman. She and Nick had picked so many of them together, and even though she hadn't been too keen on the koalas in Christmas hats that Nick had picked out, they always made her smile when they unwrapped them and set about decorating their tree together. She tried not to imagine Nick taking the box down and decorating the tree without her. Because when her mind did wander in that direction, she saw Jen with him, her stomach starting to swell as the life inside her grew.

But even though the approach of Christmas kept thoughts of Nick from straying too far from her mind, Michelle was not dreading the holiday as much as she anticipated. When she first noticed the festive decorations going up, Michelle was gripped with a sudden panic as she realised she had no idea how to celebrate the season without Nick. It was almost as if she didn't know what to do. And part of her expected to plunge into melancholy as she faced her first Christmas in years without him. But her decision to come to London was starting to make more sense to her. Being so far away from Nick, from Sydney, from all the memories of Christmas in the sun, was making it easier for her than she expected. For the first time, Michelle was really starting to appreciate what it meant to have a Christmas in the dreary cold of a London winter. The hot, humid and sunny barbecue weather and dips into the pool that came with a Sydney Christmas seemed like a lifetime ago. She thought she would miss it. But most of her Australian memories were tied up with Nick. And her mother. So all things considered, Michelle was almost looking forward to her first Christmas in London, even if she had to celebrate it alone.

Her mum. She was going to have to give that some thought. She had tried not to think about her too much since arriving in London. Would her mum be expecting her to fly back to Sydney to spend Christmas with her? She might as well email her now and try to lay that idea to rest before her mother got the chance to bring it up. She was not ready to go back yet, and she certainly wasn't ready to deal with her mother in person given her demotion, as her mother would see it, from married wife to separated woman. Her mum had really liked Nick, and the thought of talking to her about what he had done filled her with dread. Since arriving in London, she had sent her mum the occasional email, letting her know she was okay, always avoiding the topic of Nick, but their relationship had never been an easy one, especially since her dad had left Australia and returned to the UK after their marriage had failed. On some level, without ever really understanding what had happened between her parents, Michelle blamed her mum for her having to grow up without her dad.

Her dad. Another thorny topic. All she really knew of him she'd derived from her own interpretation of the sentimental birthday and Christmas cards he sent each year, with a cheque enclosed, no doubt to assuage his guilt for his absenteeism. The cards had petered out as Michelle got older, and she just assumed he had got on with his own life, choosing to forget that he had a daughter who longed for him to come back home.

But even without her dad around, it had been so easy to blame her mum for all of the difficulties in their relationship, especially as it was just the two of them. And it had been a difficult relationship, as her mum's relationship with Ivy had been. It wasn't just a generational difference, Michelle could see that, especially now. Since the moment Michelle had been born,

Ivy had turned all her attention from her daughter to her granddaughter, magnifying it tenfold as Michelle got older, if not more. All because Michelle had been born with the one thing that Diane had never possessed. The gift. It became the thing that united grandmother with grandchild, excluding the woman whose blood united the two. And to make it even worse for her mum, Ivy had told Michelle from a young age that the power of Michelle's gift had surpassed her own, even before she had any opportunity to understand, let alone harness, its power. Michelle had never understood how that could be possible until her encounter with Ned. But now that she had communicated with Ned, she could see how easy it was for her to transcend into his time, his life, and immerse herself in the hidden depths of his memories. She suspected that Grandma Ivy had never been dragged unconsciously into the actual past of a ghost in the same way that she had.

On that thought, Michelle turned her attention away from Ned and Clara, and typed into the Google search engine: *psychic medium*. She clicked on the first of the links that looked the most scientific and started scanning through it, looking for something that might help her. The lawyer in her could not disengage from what she was reading, especially when every website she clicked on seemed to contain multiple advertisements to book expensive readings with so-called mediums. Christ, there were people out there who charged more than what her firm did for her legal expertise. And there were obviously a lot of charlatans, frauds willing to take advantage of someone's naïve desperation to reconnect with a loved one they had lost.

But Michelle always trusted in what she could read, having been trained to pick apart the feast of words she was presented with until she was left with nothing but the bare bones of the facts she was searching for. She started reading as much as she could about the terms employed in what was clearly a thriving industry: clairvoyance, clairaudience, clairsentience, and others that she quickly forgot the names of, tallying up eight 'clair' wisdoms, all of them involving the perception of information beyond that which a mere human was physically capable of hearing, seeing or understanding. She wished she had asked Ivy more questions while she'd had the opportunity to do so.

She would have to muddle through on her own. She had seen Ned for a reason. She had to assume it was because she could somehow find a way to help him. But how could she help a murderer? If he would only bloody well reappear in her kitchen again.

'Come on, Ned, where are you?'

And almost as if he had heard her, the phantom that was Ned started to take shape from the shadows, shimmering into her existence once more.

And with that, Michelle truly understood that Ned was tied to her just as much as she was bound to him. There was some sort of connection between them, even if she didn't understand it. It was a lesson that Michelle could have taken from Ivy, but was made all the more potent because she had discovered it for herself.

'Hello, Ned,' Michelle said, with overt purpose in her voice. She was determined to get a full account from him as to what he had done to Clara and the baby, if he had killed them as he had claimed, and to somehow try and figure out, if he really was a murderer, how she was supposed to find a way to liberate his spirit from the guilt it was mired in.

And she wasn't going to dance around the issue. Ned had already drifted for years in the glacial wasteland of his death. It was time for him to look fully into the reflection of the ice.

'You killed them?' Michelle asked. 'You killed Clara and the baby?'

'Yes.'

She waited for him to elaborate. He remained silent.

'How? How did you kill them? You're too much of a coward to have snuck into the workhouse and despatched the poor girl with a knife through the ribs before she was delivered of the child.' Michelle's frustration with Ned was transforming her into the prosecutor from Hades. At the rate she was going, he was going to regret seeking her assistance. 'So how did you kill them? Did you send her food laced with poison? Did you put a pillow over her face as she slept? What did you do?'

Ned looked at her with real loathing in his eyes. But Michelle could see it. It wasn't her that he hated. He hated himself. And for the first time, she understood. Every time he tried to justify himself to Michelle, what he had really been doing was attempting to find some way to reconcile himself with the consequences of his own actions. He despised himself for what he had done and so had become his own gaoler. And despite the passing of all those years since his death, he was still unable to unlock the chains of his own self-hatred and guilt. Michelle needed to understand what it was he had done so she could find some way to free them both. And there was something about Ned's claims that didn't tally up for Michelle. Despite the way he had treated Clara, Michelle still struggled to accept he was a murderer.

'Ned, what did you do?' she asked, more gently this time.

'Nothing,' he said. 'I did nothing.' His sorrow was palpable. She could almost see it. It was as if his sadness and regret sat over him as though a thick grey cloud over the sun, obliterating the warmth and light.

'What do you mean you did nothing? Murder is not a passive act.'

'Clara went to the workhouse,' Ned said, and looked at Michelle as he embraced his confession. 'I suppose I hadn't given her a lot of other choices. And to be honest, once she were gone, I didn't give her another thought. Leastways, not a lot of thought. I tried not to think of her. But it was hard not to wonder if she had been delivered of the bairn, to wonder if she had lived. If the baby had lived. But mostly I tried not to think of her. I had Nelly to think about, you see. And as the months went by it got easier to forget about Clara, especially with Nelly getting closer to her time. So when Clara came back come the summer, I was a little surprised. She had a baby in her arms. It were a boy. My son.'

His son. He said the words. He said them so quietly, a whisper almost, yet the weight of them slammed into Michelle with all the force of an iron-capped boot on the foot of a violent husband. After all his silences, his reluctance to open up to her and to tell her what had happened, she had not been expecting it. Something loosened inside of Michelle. For the first time since she had met him, he had claimed as his own the child that he said he had murdered.

Michelle saw penitence in Ned's eyes, she saw regret in the lost possibility of a future he had decimated through his own actions. And because he called the child his son, Michelle was able to see the possibility of redemption.

'Only, I didn't claim him. I didn't call him mine. When she came back, I tried to turn her away again, but she weren't havin' any of it until she had had her say.'

'What did she say? What did she ask of you, Ned?'

Michelle's frustration once more dissipated into the mists of the evening. No matter how potent it had been, it was nothing against the utter contempt with which Ned held himself. Michelle could only watch as Ned battled against his guilt to tell Michelle his story, the misdemeanours of his past which he was convinced had condemned a woman and her child to death.

'She told me that she had gone to the workhouse, and that

she had spent her confinement there. That they had cut off her hair, and dressed her in the red that they gave to women like her.'

'Women like her?'

'The mothers with no husbands. The whores saddled with bairns with no father to claim on.'

As Ned talked, the hum of his words called to her. This time, though, Michelle did not try to resist the gravity of the downward spiral into the past. She wanted to go. She needed to allow herself to be taken by the flow, so that she could fully understand what had happened all those years ago. When she opened her eyes, she saw Clara, standing before Ned. A supplicant. Clara was all but beaten. That poor, poor girl. Her pride had gone. It seemed to Michelle that she lived only for her baby. Her child was wrapped in a ragged shawl, which she clutched close to her breast. Tufts of Clara's cut hair escaped from the cap they had been tucked into, a mocking testament to her mortification and shame. Her face was pale, her very soul diminished from the trials she had experienced since she had passed through the doors of the workhouse, that archway of tears, subjecting herself to the rules and regulations and the inhumane cruelty that they meted out to those that had done nothing more than have the misfortune to be poor.

And there was something more, something that Michelle could see, but that Ned was blind to, as he tried to avert his gaze from the girl and her child. A pale-blue light surrounded Clara and her baby like a halo, radiating from her skin, seeping from her, dissipating into nothingness. And Michelle understood. Death was close. It was waiting for them.

Michelle once more found herself connected with the girl, as if something of Clara resonated deep within her own heart, absorbing all of Clara's wretched memories since the girl had failed to move Ned to help her, and he had abandoned her to her fate. She saw the long wait she had endured at the gates of the workhouse, sitting in the cold evening air with the other women who had nowhere else to go, before she was seen to plead her case. Michelle saw the looks of distaste and contempt that rained down upon Clara as she explained her seduction, her abandonment and her predicament, and then watched as she fell into silence, as helpless as the child within her womb, as her future was debated. Clara's face was alight with humiliation. She was unable to defend herself, her moral depravity never in question. Michelle saw Clara admitted to the populace of the workhouse, with a complete lack of grace or mercy, walking through the doors with grateful reluctance, her head bowed and her eyes lowered, with nothing but the condemnation of the bureaucracy that had admitted her, and a reminder that she was the most undeserving of the feckless poor.

Her hair had been sheared. They told her it was to prevent the lice, but Clara had seen the lie in their words by the careful way in which they handled her long auburn tresses, the colour of golden oak leaves in autumn. They were far gentler with her hair than they were of her, and the tearing pain she had felt in her scalp as they pulled tightly to ensure they took as much of her hair as possible made her certain that it would be sold. Clara had known she would see neither her hair, nor the proceeds from it, ever again. Michelle thought of the kindness and compassion of Nathan as he had parted her from her own tresses, and her heart wept for Clara. How much more would this girl have to suffer?

Clara was ordered to strip. Michelle could almost feel the coarse brush being raked over Clara's skin, as she bathed in the impossibility of her swollen belly being scrubbed clean of its shame. Michelle was overcome by the strong scent of the soap, a sickly mixture of leather and tar. And she could taste the salt of her own tears.

They had given her a uniform of a rusty crimson dress, the scarlet letter of reproach and shame for all the unmarried mothers who crossed that threshold of despair. And then Clara endured. But she did not live. Time stilled for her inside the grey walls, with nothing but the growing of her belly to mark the dusk of each dreary day disappearing into the dawn of the next.

What was this connection Michelle had to the girl? How could she feel her, see her as if she was her? Michelle wanted to step back from the horror of what she feared was coming. Clara's suffering had not yet come full circle.

Her pains had come, and Michelle saw the shadows of a labour only half-remembered, a disinterested midwife telling her to push as the baby sliced her in two, fighting his way into the world, his fierce determination to live almost enough to wake Clara from her bleak exhaustion.

And as the child was placed on Clara's chest, Michelle observed her awakening. Clara had already been in the workhouse long enough to know that they would give her little enough time with the child before he would be taken from her. Her breasts filled with milk he would not be allowed to drink, the tightness of them choking her more effectively than the rope of the hangman's noose. And Michelle was filled with Clara's absolute conviction that if she did nothing, the child would join the myriad other lost souls in the sodden earth of the workhouse cemetery, a feast for the worms. Michelle's eyes turned outwards, to the mass grave outside of the walls of the workhouse, and she saw the fleeting grey forms of the shadows of those poor souls of the workhouse who had been freed from the misery of life by death.

As soon as Clara was able, she fled, the baby in her arms. Michelle had only one thought thrumming through her mind, an echo of Clara's desperate purpose. Find Ned. She had to find Ned. If he could see his child, his son, he was bound to help him.

It had taken her days. Days of tramping through the Devil's Acre, looking among the throng of dirty labourers for the man who had fathered her child. But while they were long and tiring days, they were even longer nights. Clara had taken refuge in the tide mud with the rats under Westminster Bridge, exchanging the only thing she had left to offer to provide herself enough sustenance so that her milk did not dry out, so that she could continue to feed her son. She would lay him on the damp ground beside her as her face was turned towards the paper bills plastered onto the walls, and some man with a few coppers in his pocket raised up her tattered skirts and petticoats, clawing at her breasts, sensitive and heavy with milk, and sated his need on her. She would focus on the posters that had pictures on them, imagining a story to go with them, ignoring the words she could make out if she made enough of an effort. If she was lucky, the man would pay her enough so that she only had to take one like him each night. She did not need much. But luck had deserted Clara when Ned had walked into her life. She existed as though she was a statue, like that of the Duke of York they had erected at the Mall. Fixed, unmoving, cold. She no longer felt anything other than her desperation to ensure her son survived, closing off her mind each time a man bought her. She would allow him access to her body, but never her soul. The only thing that mattered was her child.

And it was this, the shattered remnants of what was left of Clara, which had found Ned and confronted him with his son, the baby swaddled in what once must have been a beautiful vibrant Indian shawl, a paisley-patterned fabric in shades of red and copper. Now it was tattered and faded, all the colours bleached out of it from exposure to the cruel uncertainties of the outside world, a fitting accessory for Clara whose face, pale and insipid, had been drained of most of the traces of her youthful beauty. Michelle saw Ned's eyes unwillingly drift towards the bundle clutched close to Clara's breast, before the shutters dropped down, and his heart hardened towards her.

'I won't help you,' Michelle heard Ned say, before Clara had even opened her mouth. 'That's no bairn of mine.'

'I don't care about me,' Clara said. 'But he is your son. Look at him. Ned, look at him. He is strong and healthy. He deserves a chance. Please. Pay for our son. Provide for him. I don't care if I have to die. I'm not asking anything for myself. Only for him. Please. Let him live.'

'I already told you,' Ned said, keeping his empty gaze fixed on Clara's face, 'I won't help you. And I won't help him. I can't. I have a wife. And a bairn on the way. How do I even know that your brat is mine?'

And even though Michelle was standing with Clara in the hazy warmth of a London summer afternoon, her whole body started to shiver, as though she had been exposed to the icy winter winds without any hope of a comforting log fire to restore her, or the warmth of a thick duvet to wrap herself in as she lay down to sleep. The cold was enfolding itself around her, drawing her into its indifferent embrace. She saw Clara wilt, her shoulders sag, collapsing in on herself, cocooning the child as though she were his living shroud.

Ned was unmoved. He simply walked away from Clara, as though the child in her arms was nothing to him.

And Clara did not rail against him. She did not scream. She did not become hysterical. She watched the retreating figure of the man who had fathered her child, and simply whispered one word into the gentle winds of the evening, 'Please.'

Ned did not look back. It was as he had said to Michelle. He did nothing. He did not look behind to the figure of the woman he had once delighted in, even if it had only been for one evening. He did nothing.

Clara looked at the baby she held close to her heart, and she scurried after Ned. She clutched at the sleeve of his jacket, slowing him down and frustrating his attempts to free himself of her presence. He stopped and looked at her. But with his arms folded, both Michelle and Clara knew it was pointless to plead with him. 'Ned, please,' she said as she tore at the corner of the shawl her son was wrapped in, ripping a scrap of the fabric from the corner. The shawl was already so threadbare it yielded almost without effort.

In the hand that was supporting her baby, she took the strip of fabric she had liberated and tore the material in half, keeping hold of one portion. 'Take this,' Clara told Ned.

Ned hesitated, as if even taking the fragment that Clara offered him was some sort of acknowledgement he had no wish to give. But Clara was determined and pressed the frayed cloth into his fingers. Only when she knew it was within his grasp did she take a step away from him, so that he could not give it back to her. Ned looked at the fabric in his hand as though he had been handed poison. He opened his mouth, looking like he was about to ask a question.

But Clara would not allow him to speak. Michelle breathed in her quiet determination, the ferocity of the selfless love she had for her son. Ned had already had his say and there were no more words that would help her now. 'I'll take him as a foundling,' Clara told him. 'You won't help me, and it's all I can do for him now. They will feed him. Give him some education, at least, enough so that he can work. With them he has a chance. With me he has nothing. No name. No life. Nothing.'

Clara gestured towards the torn fabric Ned held in his large hand. 'If you want to claim him, take that to the Foundling Hospital. The one in Bloomsbury,' Clara told him. 'They'll match it with this bit of his shawl which I'll leave with him. You'll know he's your son by it. And he is your son, Ned, no matter what you think of me. I shouldn't have gone with you that night. I shouldn't have let you do what you did. But the Lord knows I have been punished for my wrong. You were my first. And the only one until...' Clara's voice faded. Ned's jaw had set and both Michelle and Clara could see that he no longer listened to anything Clara said.

Michelle watched as Ned took the fabric and buried it deep within the pocket of his trousers, as though he were throwing a murdered body into a grave, wanting it hidden from the eyes of the world. She watched as he turned his back on the desperate figure of Clara. And he was right. He did nothing. He let Clara walk away to face an uncertain future in a world that was hostile to women who dared to bring a child into it unwed. Ned did nothing. He did nothing at all.

'His name,' Clara said to the venomous shadow the retreating Ned left behind him, 'his name is Douglas.'

CHAPTER TEN

Michelle's focus shifted and blurred as she came back to her own time, to her own space in her flat on Emery Hill Street. But she wasn't about to let Ned disappear again. She had discovered the next chapter of Ned's story, but it wasn't anywhere near enough. She needed more, so she could truly understand what it was that held Ned tethered to his bleak existence. She had also seen little evidence of murder. So why did he say he had killed them? While his behaviour was reprehensible, abandoning a young girl and her child to take their chances on the streets, it hardly constituted murder. Even in the nineteenth century.

'I didn't hear from Clara again,' Ned said.

'What do you mean you didn't hear from her again?' she asked.

'I mean, that were the last time I heard from her. Ever. The next time I saw her, she were a dead woman walkin'.'

Michelle looked into the shadows of the past, but all she saw was confusion and sadness. Had Ned somehow seen the spirit of Clara after his own death? Perhaps her ghost had waited to confront him on his own passing, to call him into account for the sins he had committed against her and their son in life.

'Dead, like you are dead?' she asked. Ned shook his head.

Michelle continued to think, but whichever way she turned it over in her head, none of it made sense. 'But you did see her again? Ned, what happened to Clara?'

'I were workin' at the time, by the banks of the Thames,' Ned began. 'And everyone had started talkin' about it. They had pulled a woman from the waters of the river close by. And then later that night they pulled out her baby. It were a boy.' Ned almost winced as he said the words. 'The woman were pulled out alive. But the boy were dead. She had drowned him in the Thames.'

'Oh my God,' Michelle said, the significance of his words sinking into her like an axe through her abdomen. 'She tried to kill herself?'

Ned nodded.

'But why did she take the baby? Why did she take Douglas into the water with her? I thought she was going to take the child to the, what did she say it was, some sort of orphanage?'

Michelle could see that he wanted to speak, but the words were struggling to take shape. He shook his head as he battled to give voice to his guilt, and through the hoarse hollow of it, he finally said, 'When she were in the dock for murder, the judge were told the Foundling Hospital wouldn't take the baby.'

'But why not?' Michelle asked. 'Surely that's what they were there for? To take in children, babies like Douglas?'

Ned simply shook his head again.

'For God's sake, Ned, please just tell me what happened. All this bloody silence isn't helping either of us. You may be stuck but you still have a voice. Just bloody use it.'

At that, a sudden thought occurred to Michelle. Maybe she could do this part without having to question Ned directly?

'You said Clara was tried for murder?' she asked.

'Yes,' Ned replied.

'So you didn't actually kill the baby, Clara did?'

Ned looked at her. 'She took that baby into the water because of me. Because I wouldn't help her. I killed him just as much as she did.'

Michelle wasn't about to get sidetracked into discussing Ned's legal or moral responsibility for the death of his child. That could wait. 'Where did Clara's trial take place?'

'The Old Bailey,' he replied.

Yes. At last he had given her something she could work with. 'Okay, I think I need to do some searching on my own. I'll give you a call when I'm ready to talk to you again.' She hesitated as she realised what she had said, like she could contact him as easily as picking up her phone. But she waved him off, while reflecting on how easily the workings of her gift were coming to her. If she simply surrendered to her intuition, she almost did not have to think about how all of her 'clair' gifts worked. It wasn't as if she could actually call him so much, as call *for* him. In any event, Ned seemed to understand her as he turned and vanished once more into the shadows from which he had emerged.

Michelle turned to her PC. She glanced at the time and was taken aback by the lateness of the evening. Part of her wanted to get on with finding out more of Ned's story, but she knew she had a long day at work tomorrow, and she still had obligations to her clients. She needed to get some sleep if she was going to remain on top form. She wasn't going to let anyone down, living or dead.

She switched on the kettle to make herself a cup of herbal tea to take to bed with her. While she waited for it to boil, she scanned her emails. There was one from Angie. Pleased to hear from her best friend, she opened it.

Well, holy fucking shit, Mich. That little slag your husband was shagging is pregnant. I didn't think Nick would be so bloody stupid. Well, I suppose your decision to leave for London makes a lot more sense now. I suppose it really is all over for your marriage. Mich, I'm so sorry.

Trust Angela to get to the heart of the problem, Michelle thought, as she continued reading:

Jen has been walking around the office like some sort of peacock, parading her pregnancy like it's something to be proud of. Seriously, I mean she is nothing but the queen of garbage, spreading scandal in her wake. She hasn't said a word, but somehow the entire office seems to know that Nick's the father. She doesn't seem to care that she's a homewrecker, or that the entire senior management team is pretty pissed off with both her and Nick. Of course, we all know they can't sack her, but I hear that Nick's being pressured to fall on his sword, so to speak.

Well, that was interesting, Michelle thought. No one could make Nick resign from the partnership, but the others could certainly find a way to manage him out the door. Knowing how they worked, it was more than likely Nick would be forced out. And to have his colleagues disapproving of his behaviour was going to be difficult for him to deal with on a day-to-day basis. It was the sort of thing that would eat away at him. He was not the type to put people's backs up. He was more of an affable, get on with everybody type of a bloke. To have the entire office aware of what he had done, especially when Michelle was so well-respected within the firm, well, he was not going to be happy about that. Not happy at all.

Nick turned up at drinks the other night, and the entire room fell silent. He really has managed to turn most of the staff against him. Most of us are pretty disgusted with what he's done, and even the support staff don't seem to want to have anything to do with him. Anyway, with all of this fallout over your going to London and Jen's pregnancy, Nick's just disappeared from the office. Apparently, he's taking some 'personal leave' time. I called in at your house, but he's not there, and it looks like he hasn't been there for a few days. I tried to find out from Jen where he's got to, but she knows we're friends and she is being pretty tight-lipped. Either that, or she doesn't know where he is herself. Or possibly, it might just be because I lost my temper and told her there was a reason they had names for women like her. Dead set that girl is a slap in the face to the sisterhood.

Anyway, I thought you would want to know that I now know all of the reasons why you left. You did the right thing, and I can only guess at how hard all of this must have been for you. My heart is breaking for you, my dear friend. I know how much you wanted a baby, and how hard you worked for it, and it must be a real punch in the guts that Jen is pregnant, on top of the fact that she's having an affair with your husband. She really is the lowest form of scum. What sort of woman has an affair with a married man and gets pregnant? In this day and age, you can't seriously expect people to believe it was an accidental pregnancy? I mean, I know she isn't the most intelligent of her species, but we all got enough sex ed jammed down our throats at school so that no one should have any excuse for getting themselves up the duff unless they actually wanted it.

Mich, I am hoping I can get out to London and come and see you soon. I think you need to have your bestie with you and I want you to know that I'm on your side. All of this will seem so much easier to talk about over a couple of bottles of wine. Then we can go and dance on some tables, just like we did at that beer bar in Brussels. Did we really drink raspberry-flavoured beer? You don't even like beer. I miss you,

Angie xx

Michelle thought of those crazy six months that she and Angie had spent backpacking around Europe and smiled. It had been so much fun. She had first met Angie when the two of them started as paralegals within a week of each other at Harpers. Angie had been the same year as her, but was doing her degree at the University of New South Wales, the greatest rival to the University of Sydney. They had taken their induction at the firm together, and their friendship developed over those first few weeks, bonding over the difficult relationships they each had with their mothers, and then afterwards, they nearly always got together on Friday nights after work, hitting the local trendy wine bars, with Nick always hovering in the background.

When she looked back, Michelle didn't know how she had managed to hold down her job, even though she was only expected to work one or two afternoons a week while she was still at university, finish her degree, and still have time for all the socialising she and Angie did. Their friendship flourished, and in the last year of their studies, they made plans to go backpacking after their final set of exams. They visited as many places as their budget would allow, staying in some interesting youth hostels and cheap hotels. Angie had enjoyed all that Europe had to offer, including the handsome European men, but Michelle had spent those travelling months quietly falling in love with Nick. The night they had spent together before she left for Europe with Angie had spoken to her heart, and with the whirlwind of travel, the packing and unpacking of her backpack every couple of days, Nick's persistence and frequent emails gave her the stability and feeling of home that she missed as the weeks of travel became months. For some reason, she started to believe what Nick had been telling her: that the two of them belonged together.

Nick had been waiting for them at the airport, along with Angie's mum, when they flew back into Sydney. Flying into Kingsford Smith in the early hours of the morning, Michelle had looked out of the window, drinking in the sight of Harbour Bridge, the sunrise sparkling over the water, illuminating the sails of the Sydney Opera House. It was a welcome like no other, and part of her spirit soared as she returned to the city of her birth and childhood. But she didn't really feel like she had come home until she walked out of the arrivals hall, and saw Nick standing there, a bouquet of red roses in his hand, looking gorgeous in his faded denim jeans, a rugby top and a silly grin on his face. She'd flown into his waiting arms.

At least she could always count on Angie to be there for her. Since their European adventures, they had remained close friends, even though Michelle had constantly been part of a couple, while Angie had gone through a succession of unsuitable boyfriends, and they were now working in different areas of the law. Michelle was the only person that knew Angie was getting ready to jump ship and move to a different law firm. Angie was the only person that Michelle had confided in about her infertility and her IVF procedures.

But she had never spoken to Angie, or to anyone else for that matter, about Grandma Ivy and the gift they shared. She wondered what the practical Angie would make of the confession that Michelle could see ghosts. She brushed that thought to one side, figuring there wasn't really a need to tell Angie about her ability, or about Ned or Clara, or their history that she was now trying to make sense of. It seemed strange to her, though, the idea of keeping something so important hidden from her best friend. While she hadn't told her about Jen's pregnancy, it wasn't because she planned on keeping it from her. She had just not been able to give voice to the pain. But now, having read Angie's email, Michelle could almost imagine her in the room beside her, as though the two of them were in the café across the road from the office in Sydney, having a latte and a chat, talking about all the little everyday things that made up their lives. The thought of Angie making a trip over was enough to give her a boost. She typed out a quick reply.

Angie,

That raspberry beer was bloody awful. Never again! At least until the next time. You need to get yourself out here and I will take you for a proper drink. There's a restaurant near Trafalgar Square where they serve the most amazing gin cocktails. You would love it.

Thanks for understanding. I knew you would, but Nick is just too difficult a subject for me to talk about right now. I never thought for a moment he would cheat on me. I never saw it coming, and I feel like such a fool. He's the one who behaves like an irresponsible teenager, and I'm the one having to deal with the humiliation and pain. I guess I expect that everyone at work will be wondering what I did wrong to cause him to stray. I know you'll tell me that actually, what they will be doing is looking at Nick and thinking what a bloody idiot he has been, but I still feel their judgement. I feel like my whole life is now in flux. My future had been mapped out. I was going to be married to Nick, we were going to have children, our family, and bring them up in our home. And now that future's gone, and I can never get it back again. I'm just not sure what the hell I'm supposed to replace it with. I'm hoping that the time in London will give me some perspective.

Michelle stopped for a moment, realising she had actually had very little time to think about what she wanted for her own life since Ned had appeared. Maybe, just maybe, her gift was more of a blessing than the curse she had always thought it to be. She continued:

Nick wants me back. Of course he does. He seems to think we can somehow get past the fact that he's having a baby with another woman. But I don't think I can do it. He even went so far as to suggest that we should apply to the court to get a child arrangement order in our favour, and bring the baby up together. Can you believe that? And I still can't get my head around what he did, how badly he betrayed me. Yet I miss him. Even when I think about what he did, and I hate him, I still miss him. Isn't that odd?

You said you had been to the house. I asked Nick to put it up for auction. Is there a real estate sign up outside? I bet there isn't. I suspect he won't take any action to sell the house while he still thinks there's a chance the two of us will get back together. I've told him that we're finished, but he doesn't believe me yet. He said he wanted to see me. I really hope his disappearing act over there doesn't mean he's on a plane to London.

As soon as Michelle typed the words, she was absolutely certain that this was exactly what Nick was doing. Always one for the grand gesture, she had no doubt he had jumped on a plane to come to see her in London in the hope that his usually devastating charm was going to find a way to persuade her to forgive him, and to try and work past his betrayal. Nick had always used his charm to make life easier for himself. He had such an endearing smile, and a spark in his eyes that made him likeable. You wanted to help him when he turned it on. But Nick's charm was not going to help him win her over anymore. She was no longer willing to be seduced by it like a snake, ready to be soothed by his enchanting music. If she was a snake, she had venom in her fangs and she was ready to strike.

I guess I'll let you know if he turns up. In the meantime, it's getting on to midnight here. I need to get some sleep.
  Miss you too, Angie.
  Mich xx

Michelle pressed *send*, finished making her tea and made her way to bed. She thought she would struggle to sleep, what with worrying over whether Nick would turn up at work and import her humiliation from the Sydney office with him, and also turning over Ned's words in her mind, images of the body of a baby floating on the surface of the waters of the Thames, as though nestled in an infinite dark cradle. She settled under the warmth of the duvet, allowing her hands to settle over her empty womb, wondering to what depths of hopelessness Clara must have descended to so she felt she had no other choice but to end her own life alongside that of her child. Michelle had been inside Clara's heart, only for the most fleeting of moments, and yet she came away overwhelmed by her almost savage love for her son, and her desire to protect him. How could she then wade into the water to die, condemning his life as she tried to take her own?

She switched off her bedside lamp, listening to the hum of traffic outside. As she drifted off to sleep, her last thoughts were of Clara submerged up to her knees in the mud and rising tidal waters of the river, dressed in the coarse crimson of the workhouse like a penitent Magdalene, her pale face clouded in sorrow, her empty arms held straight out before her, with her palms reaching towards the stars, and the tattered shawl that the baby had been wrapped in floating on the surface of the murky river, like a slick of spilled blood, before it sank into the darkness, swallowed up by the waters of the Thames.

CHAPTER ELEVEN

I t would be fair to say that the day was not going well. Michelle already had back-to-back meetings in her diary, only to receive a frantic phone call from one of her clients that totally threw her schedule into chaos, and transformed what was a busy day into something resembling the communications centre for the Home Office while the country was at war. Trying to calm the hysterical woman, Michelle tried to get a handle on what had happened to cause her such distress. It appeared that her client's ex-husband had picked up the children from school the day before for his usual scheduled contact with them. He was supposed to have them overnight and take them to school the next day, but the school had just called her to ask why her children were absent. She had called her ex-husband, who had not taken any of her calls. She was petrified that he was trying to take them out of the country without her consent.

Michelle wrote down the client's surname on a Post-it and held it up to Toby, who had been with Michelle long enough now to know what was expected of him. He jumped to his feet and raced off, before returning with a file thick with court papers and correspondence, a telling testament to what had been an acrimonious marital breakdown and an almost gladiatorial dispute over the children, two boys aged nine and seven. She was not familiar with the case, as she had only been responsible for tying up the loose ends after most of the battle had already been fought in the trenches of the High Court. She checked the nationality of the ex-husband. Russian. A wealthy man who no doubt had his own yacht or jet. Her heart sinking, Michelle realised that if the man's intention had been to take the children out of the country, they would already be gone. He had given himself sufficient time before their absence would be noticed, having already set up a pattern of contact with the boys that would have reassured his ex that he was reliable and would always conform to the court order that was in place.

Trying to explain this as gently as possible to her client was difficult, the woman being adamant that as she had possession of the children's passports it would be impossible for her boys to leave the country. Michelle had to remind her the children had dual nationality, and it was more than likely that her ex-husband had obtained Russian passports for them without her knowledge. It would not have been the first time Michelle had come across this particular ploy, where she had been forced to try to seek the return of children of her clients who had been snatched out of the jurisdiction by utilising the Hague Convention on the Civil Aspects of International Child Abduction, a tedious and expensive business. As far as Michelle could remember, Russia had acceded to the Convention, but she was not sure if it was in force between the UK and Russia. She knew from bitter experience that it was not in force in Australia. She would have to check. And this case was going to have to take priority before everything else she had scheduled for the day. If there was even a small chance the children were still in the UK, she needed to make sure all points of exit from the country were notified and on the lookout, and alert all the ports and private airfields.

Three hours later, and the emergency was over. The ex-husband had called her client, somewhat sheepishly, to say he had taken the children to the cinema, which he had hired exclusively for their use, so that they could see the new *Star Wars* film, which had only been released that day, before the rest of the kids in their classes. He wasn't taking calls because he was watching the film. He was both mortified and indignant at the suggestion that he would take the kids out of the country without his ex's permission. But that was the problem when people had spent months, if not years, locked in a bitter battle over money, possessions, artwork, even the custody of the family dog. There was a tendency for the parties to always assume the worst of each other.

If only all her clients' emergencies ended so happily. She set aside her irritation and started standing down all the people she had drafting urgent court applications should they have been needed, and made a call to the Russian embassy to thank them for their help.

Michelle pretty much played catch-up for the rest of the day, apologising to clients who had been given no other choice but to wait for her while she dealt with the apparent crisis. She had no time to even think about looking into Clara's case. By the end of the day, she looked at the pile of work she still had to get through and sighed. It looked like Ned was going to have to wait. She supposed an extra day would mean little to him, just another grain of sand from the Sahara of his existence through an endless glass tunnel, but it was certainly frustrating for her.

Toby walked into their office, with some draft letters he had prepared for her. She waved at her growing in-tray and sighed again as he set them down in it.

'Is there anything else I can do for you today?' he asked,

unable to disguise the hope in his voice that Michelle would be replying in the negative.

Michelle looked at the time. It was already after 8pm.

'Actually,' Michelle said, thinking quickly, 'yes. I'm sure you know that here at Harpers we like to write articles that might be of interest to our clients, for marketing purposes.'

Toby nodded with a cautious enthusiasm. No doubt he was saying goodbye to any thoughts of heading to the pub.

'Well, I was thinking I should write an article about child maintenance payments for unmarried mothers. I want to go back in time a little to place the current legislative provisions within their historical context. In particular, I think it would be interesting to look at why the provisions are necessary.' Michelle was thinking as she spoke, hoping that what she was asking of Toby made some sort of sense. 'I want you to go through the archived records at the Old Bailey and see if you can find any cases relating to infanticide of infants by their mothers.' Toby scribbled notes in his blue notebook. 'Particularly by drowning,' Michelle added, ignoring the bewildered look that Toby gave her. 'And if you were to come across a case concerning a woman called Clara Waters, I would be particularly interested in that.'

'Clara Waters?' Toby asked, checking he had noted the name down correctly.

'Yes,' Michelle replied. Toby stood with his pencil still in his hand, poised as though waiting for Michelle to continue. But she was not inclined to invent an explanation for her admittedly bizarre research request, so she simply waved him out of the office and picked up the first of the draft letters from the in-tray. Toby looked puzzled, but for once had the sense not to open his mouth. He slipped out of their office without further question. He was a good trainee, Michelle thought, even if he tended to say the first thing that came into his head before thinking it through. She would be sorry to lose him when his seat with her came to an end.

Michelle sucked on her lower lip, as she tried to turn her attention towards the document in front of her. Guilt pricked at her conscience somewhat. Strictly speaking, you were not supposed to use trainees for personal purposes, but Michelle figured the firm would rather she spent her time undertaking chargeable work than waste it chasing after ghosts. And it would be a good learning opportunity for Toby, who had probably never gone over old court records before. Having rationalised her guilt, she turned her full attention to getting the draft letters finalised and ready to be sent.

An hour later, Toby returned with some print-outs in his hand.

'This is all really interesting,' he began. 'Do you know how many women topped themselves by flinging themselves in the Thames?'

Michelle cut him off before he had a chance to launch in. It was too late, and she was too tired to have to engage with his enthusiasm. 'Okay, thanks, Toby, we can go through the detail of your research tomorrow when we've both had a chance to have some breathing space after today.'

He nodded, recognising her dismissal of him, and started gathering his things together.

Michelle looked up at him, almost afraid to ask. 'Before you go, did you happen to find anything on Clara Waters?'

Michelle took a long breath as Toby went back to the papers he had just placed neatly on his desk and shuffled through them, before presenting her with three A4 printed pages.

'The transcript of her trial,' he said, as though he were a sommelier announcing a particularly exquisite bottle of wine, and looked rather pleased with himself as he did so. He certainly looked more awake than he had when she had sent him out on this research task.

Michelle took the pages from him, her heart rate increasing with anticipation as her fingers closed around them. She was getting closer. The papers in her hand sent a shiver of heat through her spine. 'Thanks, Toby,' she said. 'And by the way, it was a tough and frustrating day today, but you did well and handled yourself professionally at all times. Kids being taken out of the jurisdiction means the parent loses months, if not years with them, so we needed to work fast and efficiently. I appreciate that I didn't always explain why I was asking for certain things, and I may not have been as patient as I could have been.' Toby almost raised an eyebrow at her. Almost. 'But if those kids had been taken out of the UK it would have been hell for the mum. And I knew that, so had to work fast. If you do have any questions about what happened or the process that I went through, we can go over those tomorrow as well. But in the meantime, I just wanted you to know that you did incredibly well today.'

Toby puffed up a little as he thanked her, said goodnight, and walked out the office with a jaunt in his step. Her praise was not given lightly. And when she did give it, she meant it. She glanced down at the papers in her hand, focused in on the name Clara Waters, confirming that it was indeed the transcript of Clara's trial, but the moment she started scanning over the words she felt drawn to them. They pulled her towards them like the moon pulled at the waters of the oceans. She wanted what the words had to offer her, the appeal of them almost irresistible. But she closed her eyes, and turned the words face down on the desk, draining them of their power over her. She decided she needed to take the transcript home to read. She did not want to risk slipping into the uncertainty of the past while in her office.

Michelle gathered her things together, slipped the pages Toby had given her into her bag, pulled on her coat and walked to the lift, wrapping her scarf around her neck as she did so. The lift doors opened, and she walked in, pressing the G button. She smiled to herself in the lift mirror, as she pulled on her bobble hat in the same shade of green as her coat. She loved that hat. As she scanned the full length of herself in the mirror, she thought she looked rather like a Londoner now, in her warm coat, scarf and hat, with her new knee-length black suede boots shown to full advantage against the just-above-the-knee length of her amber skirt and the cut of the coat.

Good Lord, she realised she was going to have to write that bloody article about child maintenance payments now to make truth of the lie she had told Toby. Maybe she would get him to write the first draft. It would keep him busy.

As she reached the ground floor, and the lift doors slid open, the smile disappeared from her face. Nick was sitting in the reception area, a medium-sized wheelie suitcase beside him, waiting for her.

He had come to London after all. Fuck.

CHAPTER TWELVE

'Michelle,' he said, as she stepped out of the lift. 'God, it's so good to see you.' He hesitated for a moment as he started to walk towards her. 'You cut your hair.' Was that a note of disapproval in his voice?

He came towards her and went to enfold her in his arms, but she crossed her own arms before he got to her, making an invisible barrier against his desire to embrace her. The thought of him touching her was sickening. She stood awkwardly before him, neither of them knowing how to proceed now that she had refused his welcome. What the bloody hell did he think he was doing just turning up like this? But him being there, in front of her, at that moment, when she was so tired after the fraught day she had just finished, there was a part of her that wanted nothing more than to fall into his arms, go home, get into bed with him and think of nothing else. Because she really didn't want to think about why she shouldn't do that anymore. She didn't want to think about Jen. Or their baby. She thought she had made peace with her decision to end the relationship with him, to murder her marriage and divorce him, but seeing him in person, all her resolve was starting to dissipate as though it were nothing more than a sandcastle set against the full force of the tide.

How was it possible to want someone that you hated? To want to feel their arms snake around your body, and hold you close, even as you could not help but picture those same arms wrapped around the naked body of a younger, prettier woman? How could she feel desire for him flood her body even as her contempt for him filled her very being?

In coming to London, Nick had arrived in a place she had made her own, a home where she could feel safe from the sting of the tail of the scorpion he had brought into their relationship. And his very presence back in her life stirred a cauldron simmering with a vile concoction of her own conflicted thoughts and emotions.

'I really wish you hadn't come,' she said to him, as he looked at her, drinking her in, as though he was a bee seeking nectar for his malnourished hive.

'Michelle,' he said softly, reaching his hand to her cheek, using his thumb to arrest the progress of the tear that Michelle was unaware was making its sorry way down her face. 'I'm so sorry. You don't deserve any of this.'

'Please go home, Nick,' she said, looking down, not even able to meet his eyes. The blueness of them always reminded her of the sky on a bright sunlit day, open and infinite. Michelle was afraid that if she looked into them, she would lose herself in their vastness, respond to the call of them, wanting to soar into the promise they held. But it was all an illusion. It was nothing more than a blue screen on which he could invent his own version of the truth, designed to blind her to the reality that he now offered.

'Let's just go somewhere and talk, Michelle. I've been on a flight for around thirty hours, stopping over in the hell that is

Hong Kong airport, trying to get to you, just so I could tell you sorry in person. The least you can do is hear me out.'

'You have got to be kidding me,' she said.

'Mich, please, just one conversation. That's all I'm asking. I know I don't deserve it. But just one.'

Somewhere inside, one divergent part of her heart shifted, and she made room for his words. That part of her wanted to listen, to hear what it was he had to say. But the other part of her was bristling, as though an angry cat. She had not asked him to come. She had not wanted him to come. She had even told him not to come. But somehow, he had made her obligated to him. Like he had done her some sort of favour when he had left an office hostile to him and flown halfway across the world to make his apologies in person. Bastard. But still, she found herself acceding to his request. It had always been hard to say no to Nick. Some habits were hard to let go of.

'Okay,' she conceded. 'But not here. I've had a long day and I really need to be somewhere closer to home.'

'Then let's go back to your flat,' Nick suggested.

Michelle noticed his reluctance to call her London flat her home. But even though she had only been there for a short time, that little flat on Emery Hill Street *had* become her home, without her really noticing. She thought of the sprawling, spacious house she had left behind in Sydney, with its ultra-sleek open-plan kitchen and dining area, with its high-spec oven and American-style fridge freezer; the vast space of the lounge room with its widescreen TV, a bar propped up in the corner, those areas alone bigger than the whole of Michelle's flat now. But despite the fact Emery Hill Street was just a two-bedroom apartment with nowhere near the space she had shared with Nick in Mosman, it was now more than just a flat she had seen pictures of from an estate agent who was looking to fulfil his brief as quickly as possible. It was a sanctuary from all of the problems she had hoped she had left behind in Sydney. She loved the red-brick building, and she loved the vibrancy of the area. She looked forward to waving to Nathan in the salon as she walked to Sainsbury's, and eating in the little Italian restaurant just a short walk away where even in the autumnal cold you could eat outside because of the gas-fired heaters with the mesmerising comfort of a fiery flame. And the Thai restaurant buzzing with diners always reminded her of the best of Sydney's Oxford Street Asian fusion food and gave her that little taste of home that assuaged the worst of her yearnings. She loved the proximity to all the major iconic London sights, the fact she could take a Tube or a bus to just about anywhere in the city. She had everything she needed practically on her doorstep. Or at least she thought she did. Until Nick showed up and exposed the gaping hole she had opened in her life when she had left him.

'Not my flat,' Michelle said. 'Let's go get a bottle of wine. There's a bar in St James's Park that I really like. It's called the Blue Boar.'

Nick nodded. 'Whatever you want. I'm here for you. I'll do whatever you want.'

'It's expensive,' Michelle added. 'You're paying.'

They left the building and Michelle pointed Nick in the direction of the Tube station. Michelle inhaled the crisp cold air, trying to settle her conflicted thoughts. Nick reached over to take her hand, but she shoved it deep within her pocket. The thought of him touching her, even something so small as holding her hand, was abhorrent to her. She thought if she allowed him to take her hand it would be like allowing him to take control. And he had done nothing to deserve that.

Nick had dressed spectacularly incorrectly for December in London. To give him some credit, he was wearing a thick woollen jumper, which he probably thought would be fine, but having left a Sydney baking in temperatures of over thirty degrees in the shade, the sudden descent into single figures seemed to have left him battling thoughts of freezing to death. He wheeled his suitcase behind him, the noise of it clacking over the pavements like the hooves of horses. Michelle would have staked her life on there being neither hat nor coat inside of it. Vaguely, she wondered if he had even packed clean socks. It was the sort of thing he usually forgot. But, she reminded herself, that was not her problem anymore.

'Once we get on the Tube it'll be a lot warmer,' Michelle told him. 'I've got to the stage where I sometimes wonder whether it's even worth putting on a coat given how hot I get when I'm on the Underground.' In the meantime, glancing sideways in Nick's direction, Michelle could see that he was valiantly striving to avoid shivering with the cold. She slowed her step a little, and then paused, making a play of checking her bag to ensure she had brought those 'urgent' papers with her, knowing full well that the only papers she was interested in, the transcript of Clara's trial, were safely stowed away. The latent promise of the words on those pages sang their harmony to her from the depths of her bag, which sat nestled close to her hip. Having played her little game, she carried on, still walking as though she was in no particular hurry to get anywhere. It was not like she wanted Nick to suffer, she lied to herself, but a little bit of cold never did anyone any harm.

As they approached the barrier to Blackfriars station, Michelle pulled her Oyster card from out of her coat pocket to tap in. Nick looked at her like a little boy lost, seeking help from someone who would usually be all too willing to come to his aid. But not this time.

'Just use a contactless card,' Michelle told him, as she walked through the gates. 'Or you could always go to one of the ticket machines and get a Zone 1 ticket.' She waved in the general direction of the ticketing machines from the safety of the other side of the barrier. She was not going to solve this problem for him. He had been sat for hours on the flight from Sydney, no doubt rehearsing what he was going to say to her. He had almost certainly had the time to assess the basics of public transport in London.

Nick pulled his Mastercard out from his wallet, and held it against the yellow circle of the barrier, until the gate yielded, and he started to walk through, pulling his wheelie suitcase behind him. Michelle tried to swallow her sense of satisfaction as the gates closed before his suitcase had cleared them, leaving Nick cursing them as he pulled at the handle of his case, trying to free it from the indifferent jaws of the gate.

It was hard not to enjoy Nick's frustration, never mind the international transaction fee he had just subjected himself to, as well as the actual cost of the Zone 1 ticket once it was converted from pounds to Aussie dollars. If she had been in a kind mood, she might have suggested a taxi, and picked up the cost of it. But all inclinations of kindness towards him had been killed in her. Affairs tended to be quite psychopathic in their approach to their victims, killing everything good in their wake. There was a part of Michelle that rejoiced in Nick's annoyance, even as she hated herself for her own pettiness.

They caught the next westbound train that arrived at Blackfriars, Michelle saying nothing as the train snaked around the District and Circle line, until they finally got to St James's Park. Every time Nick went to open his mouth, she silenced him with a glare. He should know her well enough to know that she wasn't going to talk about anything before she bloody well had that glass of wine in her hand. It seemed like a much longer journey than normal, even though the lateness of the evening ensured Michelle had the rare luxury of a seat rather than being packed in with a carriage full of resigned commuters, all pressed up against each other, pretending they were somewhere else.

The Victoria Street exit was chained off, so they took the Broadway exit, and Michelle led Nick towards the Blue Boar bar, pointing out the shadows of the spires of the Houses of Parliament and Westminster Abbey, and the lights on the London Eye in the distance. If she was going to be beholden to Nick for his global dash to London to see her, she would rather discharge that obligation by pointing out the tourist sights of London. They walked into the bar and she steered them towards one of the circular tables by the window. She ordered a bottle of wine, not letting Nick even see the wine list. She needed to keep control over the evening, and she didn't want him ordering because she suspected he would try to order something that was familiar to them. The last thing she wanted to be doing was to be sharing a bottle of Chardonnay with the husband who had betrayed her. There were just too many memories she had no desire to revisit.

The waiter brought the bottle of wine, a dry, crisp French Sauvignon, and showed it to Nick, despite it being Michelle who had ordered. Swallowing her irritation at this ingrained sexism that still seemed to abound in a supposedly modern London bar, Michelle confirmed it was the right bottle, the one that she had ordered, and after tasting the wine, Michelle gestured that the waiter should pour for Nick first. When two glasses of it were sitting in front of them, Nick picked up his glass and held it up to Michelle. 'To you, Mich,' he said.

'Sure,' she replied. Taking a sip, she turned her attention towards Nick. What the hell was she doing there with him? She had no more desire to engage in small talk.

'Nick, why are you here?'

'I had to come and see you,' he said. 'I couldn't leave things as they were. You just left. I never got a chance to try and explain.'

Michelle considered his words in quiet reflection. This retreat into silence was not her usual approach to dealing with difficult subjects. It reminded her of Ned. Perhaps she had been spending too much time with him.

'So, go on then. Explain to me why you deceived me. Explain to me why your marriage vows meant nothing to you. Explain to me how you managed to sleep with your secretary in our bed. Explain to me how you managed to get her pregnant. Why don't you try explaining all of that, Nick?' Despite her resolve to stay calm, her voice was rising. She noted the raised eyes on the tables around her. She stilled herself again, retreating into calm, before she continued. 'After all we went through to try and have a baby, to get that woman pregnant... How can I ever look at you in the same way again?'

Nick bristled against her tirade. She could see he had wanted to interrupt her as she railed against him, to defend himself against her accusations, but he waited before he answered her.

'Michelle, I'm not even going to try and deny that I have done something truly awful. None of it was planned. I had an affair. I didn't mean for it to happen, but it did. You didn't deserve it, and I didn't want to hurt you. And after it happened, I really wished it hadn't. You have no idea how much I wish I could go back and undo everything that I did. And I never wanted you to find out. I had hoped the whole thing would just be forgotten, and that Jen would realise we were making a mistake and that she would back off and leave us both alone. But she got pregnant. I honestly didn't think she would get pregnant. I wish I could take it back, all of it, but I can't. It's out of my hands now anyway. Jen wants to keep the baby.'

'I can't be involved in this, Nick, I can't watch you have a child with someone else. It would kill me.' She wondered if he did indeed know how much it would hurt her to see him have a child with another woman, if he could imagine the exquisite depths of pain it would take her to, the crushing void of her own empty womb closing in on her, as though a collapsing cavern, suffocating her.

'You don't have to,' he said. 'I don't want to hurt you, at least, I don't want to hurt you any more than I already have. I could send Jen money and have nothing to do with the baby. I don't want to hurt you,' he repeated, as if trying to persuade her. His hand had reached her leg, lightly caressing the inside of her thigh.

She should push his hand away. Really, she should. But a heat was building inside of Michelle, and she wanted to believe that she was waking up next to Nick in their bedroom back in Mosman, the past couple of months nothing more than a nightmare that she could leave behind as the sun rose in the cloudless Sydney sky, shining its light over the turquoise blue of the harbour.

'Could you really stay out of your child's life?' Michelle asked him. She wanted him to say yes. But at the same time, she knew she could never respect any man who chose to absent himself from his own child's life. A shadowy remembrance of her father swinging her through the air, making the world spin dizzyingly around her surfaced briefly in her mind, before she closed the door on that memory. She could only focus on one hurt at a time.

He nodded, and reached for her hand, stroking her palm with his thumb. Without thinking, Michelle's body leaned towards him, closing the space she had created between them.

'I would do anything for you, Mich. I love you. I have loved you since the moment I first saw you.'

Once more, for the briefest of moments, Michelle indulged

herself with thoughts of going back to Nick, of a life untainted by the devastating legacy of his affair. But it was impossible. They could never be who they were before Jen. That woman had taken something from them both and corrupted it. Even if Michelle never had to see her again, Jen would be there, like a shadow emerging from the darkness, ready to appear in her life without warning at any time, almost as if she were already a spirit intent on haunting her. But it wasn't the dead who could hurt you, as Grandma Ivy so often said. It was the living. And searching her own heart, Michelle knew she could never value any man who turned his back on his own child, who put his own needs above that of the new life he had fathered, however unintentionally. Nick. Ned. Nick. Ned. Both men fathers to babies they hadn't wanted. What the hell was wrong with them?

'I can't. I can't come back to you. I might have been able to get past your affair. And even then, thinking of you with that woman is enough to make me feel ill.' It was worse than that, Michelle thought. It was more like falling off a precipice, knowing you were going to hit the unyielding stone of the ground at some point, but not knowing how long you had to endure plummeting through the air until oblivion rescued you from the dread of the anticipation of the impact. 'But,' she continued, 'you are having a child with another woman, and I can't get past that.'

'I don't want to lose you.'

'You already have.'

Michelle felt herself sinking into the blueness of his eyes, drowning in her own sorrow, the waves of her loss crashing over her, sucking her into the pull of the current below.

'Go back to Sydney. Try to make peace with Jen, and see if you can find some way to be a good dad to your child. But you need to let me go. I think you owe me that.' If he could deploy the language of obligation to compel her to talk to him, perhaps she could harness it to shame him into taking a bow, and closing the curtain on their marriage. 'My life is here now.'

'Do you think you'll come back?' he asked. 'To Sydney?'

'Yes,' she replied. 'But when I do, I won't be coming back to you. All that is gone now.'

Michelle watched Nick deflate with defeat. Or it may have been exhaustion. Those sapphire-blue eyes of his became even more alluring as his glassy unshed tears refracted the light.

What was she supposed to do next? The sensible part of her wanted to get away from him, to leave, to go back to her flat, but a small part of her heart still ached for Nick. Especially as he sat in the chair beside her, the heat of his body calling out a promise of familiar comfort to her, a comfort she so desperately wanted as she battled her grief and loneliness. She wished there was some way she could make their separation hurt them both less, even if a part of her wanted him to suffer for throwing away their marriage so carelessly and so cheaply.

'I suppose we should drink to what we had,' Nick said, reaching for the bottle sitting in the wine bucket beside them, and pulling it from the ice. It was empty.

Michelle wondered how they had managed to finish the wine so quickly. To hell with it, she thought, as she ordered another, even though she suspected she would regret it come the morning. With the day being so manic she had not had time for lunch, and it was already close to 10.30pm and she had not managed any dinner either. She really shouldn't drink any more. But she didn't care. She was sitting in a bar in London, with her husband, about to end her marriage, and the whole tableau was tainted with sadness and jarred inside of her. It felt inexpressibly wrong.

She refilled their glasses and lifted hers up to Nick. 'Cheers, Nick,' she said. 'I suppose it was good while it lasted. We were lucky, at least for a while. But I guess this is goodbye. Go back to Sydney. Go back to your life, and learn how to live it without me in it. As for the house, and the finances, and undoing our marriage, I think it would be better if we left that to emails and lawyers. We don't need to be enemies. I get enough of that with clients.'

Nick had fallen into a defeated silence but tilted his glass to Michelle. Michelle stared out of the window, watching as people made their way along the street. The silence between them was unsettling her, and to cover her unease, she drank her glass of wine more quickly than she had intended. Nick poured Michelle another glass of wine, and they continued working their way through the second bottle, sitting in quiet misery. It was as if neither of them knew how to extricate themselves from the evening, how to walk away from the other. Not so long ago they could sit without talking, and there was a familiar comfort in the silence. Now it felt strained, charged, as they both occasionally glanced at each other, Michelle averting her gaze if she happened to catch his eyes. How the hell had things become so awkward with this man she had only recently been so close to?

She was aware of a vague dizziness. The lights of the bar were coming in and out of focus. Without warning, Nick pulled her towards him, his lips meeting hers. This time, Michelle allowed herself to be taken by him. She wanted to hold on to that which she knew was slipping away from her grasp, to allow him to possess the whole of her one last time. She found an answer to the questions that had been troubling her. How could you want someone you hated? How could your whole body be aching for someone who caused you nothing but pain? As Michelle opened herself to him, she let her hate mix with her desire as though it was some sort of chemical infusion, caring little if the reaction it created was toxic. Just as long as it was sated.

'One more night, Mich, please?' Nick whispered.

Michelle nodded, pushing her certainty that she was about to make a huge mistake to the very back of her mind, as Nick got to his feet to go and arrange a room for the night, taking his wheelie suitcase with him. She continued to drink what little was left of the wine, letting the liquid sink into her with a bewildering disorientation, as the lights of the bar spun around her like a meteor shower. She was aware of the papers she carried in her bag, teased by the potential of the promise they held, but tonight, she needed to put herself first. Ned could bloody well wait. The heat of her desire for Nick was burning everything in its path. Reason, logic, even her hate for his affair were all reduced to phoenix ash in the wake of her need for him.

Nick returned a short while later, without his wheelie case, and holding a hotel key card in his hand. Plucking the wine bottle from the ice bucket to confirm it was empty, Michelle watched as the water ran in channels down the side of the bottle and fell to the floor like tears. Nick took her hand, helped her up and as she struggled to find her sense of balance, he gripped her hand tightly and led her towards the lifts. Michelle pushed all thoughts of Jen and her baby out of her mind. She wanted the man she had loved to fill the aching void inside her, even if she knew it was never going to fix everything that he had broken. Just one last time, she told herself. Tonight, she needed to be with Nick. She needed to say goodbye.

CHAPTER THIRTEEN

It was still dark when Michelle opened her eyes, already feeling the persistent thud of her hangover pressing against her temples. With her heart racing, she tried to orientate herself. Where the hell was she? Everything was unfamiliar. Her tongue sat dry and swollen against the roof of her mouth, like it was a piece of carpet. Trying to slow her breath and even out her heart rate, she took stock of her surroundings, lifting her head to look around her. Sprawled on her front, the heavy weight of her own regret was the only thing covering her nakedness. Nick's arm was flung over her back, as if he was binding her to him, keeping her close. In the few moments it took for her eyes to accustom themselves to the dim room, to focus on where she was, she remembered she was in a hotel room in London, in fact the same hotel she had stayed in when she had first arrived, plagued with jet lag, her heart full of bewildered grief for the life she had left behind.

Fuck, what had she done? She tried to shimmy out from underneath Nick's arm, desperate not to disturb his sleep, although given the state of him, it would probably take a rubbish truck crashing through the window to rouse him. Why had she persuaded herself that it was a good idea to end up back in bed with her cheating husband, the man she was trying to leave? Her mind flashed over last night, and panic flooded her as she tried to remember if she had brought her bag with her from the bar. But she saw it sitting on the chair in the corner of the room, and as relief swept over her body and her heart rate slowed, she tiptoed towards it and then reached inside, finding her phone.

4.03am.

Glancing at the floor, making an inventory of her discarded clothing, and collecting her scattered underwear, she tiptoed to the bathroom, shutting the door as gently as she could. Nick was still snoring. She had only one thought in her mind. She had to get out of there. She had to get away from Nick.

Looking at her reflection in the mirror, she could only shake her head at herself, disappointed that her resolve to keep him at a distance had vanished so completely. It was so much easier to be strong when she didn't have his sad eyes looking into hers, and the promise of a night enjoying his body. Because even though he was a lousy cheat, she had missed him. God, how she had missed him. But that was stupid, and unfair to both of them. Talk about giving the guy mixed messages.

Filling a glass with water, she gulped it, hoping she would manage to keep it down. It would be fair to say that this was not one of her finest moments, and she did not feel great. Actually, she felt as though she wanted to spew up what little there was in her stomach. Holding on to the rim of the sink with grim determination to keep control over the sensation of seasickness that settled on her, she took a few deep breaths, trying to steady herself, placing her cheek against the comforting cold marble surface next to the sink, hoping that her stomach would stop protesting. When the worst of the wave of nausea had passed, she looked at herself in the mirror again. Her face pale, she wished the woman she saw reflected back at her had more strength and conviction. But she could berate herself later. Right now, she needed to get out of that hotel room, and put some distance between her and Nick once more.

Splashing water on her face, and smoothing back her unruly bed hair as best she could, she threw on her clothes, preparing herself to face the walk of shame out of the hotel room, hoping she could slip away before Nick woke up. She scooped up her bag, boots and coat. When she reached the door, she paused, only for a moment, to look at the still sleeping Nick.

Nick.

How could he have done this to her? He was lying on his side, his tanned, muscular body not covered by the duvet. Without thought, she quietly placed her things on the floor by the door, and walked towards the bed. The last time she had slept beside him, she hadn't known the huge tsunami that was approaching, that would engulf them both and tear them apart. This time though, she was making a choice and she was tearing down the fragile bridge that last night had built between them. Slowly pulling the covers over him, as though she was a mother covering her child, she reached down and twisted one of his blond curls around her finger. He was gorgeous, he was her bronzed Aussie beach boy. He always did look better on a surfboard than in the boardroom. Tracing her finger along the line of his jaw, feeling the dip in his chin, tears welled in her eyes. This was the last time she would wake up beside him. It was a thought that left her feeling bereft. She really had loved him. She loved him still really, but she had to let him go. How could she ever be with him again after what he had done?

She walked to the door, collecting her things, and quietly pulled it open and slipped out. She did not look back at the sleeping form of her husband on the bed. Only when she reached the lift and had taken it down to the ground floor did she realise she was shaking, although whether this was because she was still under the influence of the vast amount of alcohol she had drunk or because of the shock of having to part from Nick, she couldn't say. Still unsteady on her feet, she leaned against the doors of the lift as it descended, and almost fell out as they opened. Struggling to keep control over her warring emotions, she sat down in one of the chairs in the lobby, pulled on her boots and zipped them up, trying to ignore the concierge tactfully not seeing her as she did so. He was the same one who had given her directions to St James's Park on her first morning in London. Idly, Michelle wondered if he remembered her.

As soon as her coat was on, and her bag safely over her shoulder, she walked out of the revolving doors, trying not to feel sick with dizziness as she did so. Being with Nick had been wonderful. But it had been maddening and she was furious at him, but more furious at herself. It was as though her entire world was spinning on its axis, losing control, trapped in a remorseless black hole of despair.

Drizzle was falling as she walked onto the virtually deserted street. It was still dark, the streets illuminated only by the electric street lamps that threw their light onto the damp pavement in equidistant intervals. She walked in and out of the shadows. Home, she had to get home. The moon and the stars were hidden by cloud and mist. She looked up to the murky sky, taking in deep gulps of the cold air, trying to let it sober her up, hoping it would unearth the ache of regret that had taken root inside of her.

She should never have agreed to go to bed with him again. Nick would only take it as encouragement. He would now think he had a chance to smooth things over, in spite of Jen and the baby. Seriously, what had she been thinking? Oh, she knew what she had been thinking, but she should have known better. She was a grown, mature woman who prided herself on her intelligence and common sense, and here she was acting like some sort of horny teenager straight from the pages of *Puberty Blues*.

She crossed over Victoria Street, not waiting for the lights to change, and walked in the direction of Emery Hill Street, wanting to get back to the sanctuary of her flat as soon as possible. She was cold, she had a headache, and she needed a shower. She wanted to wash all traces of Nick from her body and feel like herself again.

As she turned on to the familiar pavement of her street, Michelle glanced across to the other side of the road, and came to an abrupt halt. She steadied herself as she saw him, and her sense of shame intensified. Ned, waiting patiently, propped up against the street light, his arms crossed, the drizzle having no discernible impact on him. He was looking at her, unmoving and stern, and made no effort to come towards her. Hesitating, Michelle brought up her hand to wave at him, but as he continued looking at her, Michelle could see that sorrow was prominent on his face. He faded and then disappeared into the shadowy darkness of the early morning light.

Michelle tried to repress the sense of unworthiness and guilt that was overwhelming her soul. She was letting Ned down. But worse than that, she was letting herself down. She shook her head and continued her morose way down the path to the entrance to her building. Her phone buzzed in her pocket as though an angry wasp had taken residence there. She didn't even have to look at it to know it was Nick. He must have woken up. She ignored it and let herself in.

Only when she got inside her flat and closed the door did she allow herself to give in to her grief. Sinking to her knees, her face dropped into her hands, and she poured all the tears of her sorrow into them. She had been doing okay. She really thought she was keeping the fragmented pieces of her soul together as best she could, holding them tightly within her controlled grip.

But now, with the memory of the night they had spent together still playing through her head, his body entwined with hers, his lips caressing her skin, her hands tracing over the contours of his back as she welcomed him sinking inside her, it was almost as if she had to suffer the loss of him afresh. Damn him.

Remorse was beginning to eat away at her, as though he had seeded her with parasites that gnawed at her very soul. She was being consumed from the inside out. She should never have slept with him again. What a silly fool she had been.

She wept until the ferocity of her grief was exhausted, collapsed in a curled heap on the floor, her arms wrapped around her knees as if somehow that could protect her from the hurt Nick had inflicted on her. She stayed on the floor until she was aware of the lure of sleep calling to her with the temptation of a brief sojourn into oblivion, where she didn't have to think about Nick, about Jen, or about the baby they were having. But Michelle was not going to allow herself to give in to her fatigue. She had to keep going and she had to make her life without Nick. Last night had not been wise, but she had made a choice to sleep with him and it was pointless to berate herself for doing so. She was not going to call it a mistake. That would be a cop-out. She had made a conscious decision to spend the night with Nick, knowing that she was putting herself at risk of her emotions spiralling out of control again. You couldn't call it a mistake simply because the completely predictable consequences of your own actions were not to your liking. She was not going to be a hypocrite.

She pulled herself to her feet. It was done, and what she now had to do was get past it and make sure it never happened again. After taking two Nurofen, forcing herself to drink a whole glass of water to counter the onslaught of dehydration, she took a shower, lying curled up on the floor of the shower tray, letting the water fall on top of her, staying in long enough to restore some semblance of humanity back to herself. When she emerged, she no longer felt as though she was dying. Still ill and not quite as sharp as she normally would be, but better than how she had felt when she had first walked through the door.

She threw on some clean work clothes, but chose the black-and-white-patterned skirt, a black roll-neck top, and the black jacket, clothes she would normally only wear on days when she was going into court. But she could not face anything brighter than the simplicity of black and white tones today. She pulled a plain oat cereal bar out from one of the cupboards, and worked her way through it, swallowing each dry mouthful with effort. Perhaps the alcohol would have had less of an effect on her if she had actually eaten last night. But it had been one of those days where eating had really not been a priority. In fact, as she pieced together the events of the day before in her fogged-over mind, Michelle remembered she had not had lunch either. No wonder her judgement had been so very quickly compromised under the influence of all that wine. But it was pointless dwelling on the reasons why she had made the poor decision to sleep with her husband.

The only way to tackle her remorse was to confront it directly. She pulled out her phone, noting the three missed calls from him, and tapped in a message to Nick:

> Nick, I'm sorry last night happened. I'll meet you for breakfast but then I need you to go back to Sydney. The only good thing to come from last night is my certainty that we have no future together. 7:30am. Le Pain Quotidien. It is on Wilton Road.

Pressing send, she then checked her diary to make sure she had nothing urgent to take care of that morning. She made a quick phone call to Toby at the office, knowing that even with all of his enthusiasm, he would not be in yet, but left a voicemail giving him some drafting to get on with, telling him she would be in by 10am. She then dropped a quick email to her secretary to tell her the same, but that she would, of course, be available on her mobile should any clients need to contact her urgently.

Her decisive actions were contributing to an improvement in her mindset. Either that, or the Nurofen were doing a stellar job at killing her headache, and the cereal bar at settling her stomach, so she could function as normal. She glanced at her phone. 6.26am. She had about forty-five minutes before she had to go and meet Nick.

She refused to let her mind think about what she would have to say to him. Instead, she thought of the papers that were still unread in her bag.

Clara's trial. It was only three pages. She had time.

CHAPTER FOURTEEN

Making herself a strong cup of tea, Michelle sat on the bar-stool at her kitchen counter, with the papers spread out in front of her. She took one sip of her drink, the hot, comforting liquid acting like some sort of miracle tonic, and began reading the transcript of the trial of Clara Waters. She was not used to reading historical legal court reports. There had been no real need to since she had finished her law degree. Yet she only had to skim a few lines before it became apparent to her that what she was reading was not a detailed word by word account of the trial such as that which modern lawyers had the benefit of in this day and age, but a sort of summary of what had happened, as well as a précis of the evidence given by all of the witnesses. She began reading:

First session 1838

Before Mr Justice Pendegrast

1121. CLARA WATERS, was indicted for the wilful murder of Douglas Waters, an infant aged about six weeks.

> *Edward David Rudd. I am a policeman in the*
> *Westminster division. On the 19th of August, I was at the*
> *station, when, at about nine o'clock in the evening, a group*
> *of people brought a woman in. She said she had murdered*
> *her child – I asked her in what way and she said, 'By taking*
> *him into the river' – she said the child was around six weeks*
> *old. I went with the woman to the river and she pointed to a*
> *place opposite Millbank Prison, and said, 'It is near here*
> *that I went into the river with my child. The people who*
> *brought me to you pulled me out of the water. But my child*
> *was taken by the tide.' She said she had no money to feed*
> *herself and that she had little milk to feed the baby. She said*
> *the baby was starving. She said that she had taken the child*
> *to the Foundling Hospital, but they told her they could not*
> *relieve her of the child so she brought him to the river. I*
> *made a search for the body of the child. I found it after two*
> *hours, floating on the surface of the water – it was a male*
> *child. The child was not dressed. She told me he had been*
> *wrapped in a shawl. I did not find the shawl. I took the body*
> *of the child to the station. He was examined there by Dr*
> *Elliot – at the time she came in the prisoner was carrying*
> *nothing but a scrap of old fabric. I tried to take it from her,*
> *but she would not surrender the fabric.*

Michelle paused to consider the evidence given by the policeman. She was not familiar with the procedure for modern criminal proceedings, let alone trials for murder that took place in the nineteenth century, but she was wondering if Clara had been given a warning when she had first been taken into the police station that anything she said could be used as evidence against her. There was nothing in the transcript to suggest that she had. But then again, there was nothing to suggest that she hadn't. Michelle did not even know what the rights of an accused were back then. She suspected that whatever they were, they were largely irrelevant when it came to someone like Clara. It was hard enough in the twenty-first century for people to access justice because of the huge expense involved. But for a barely literate woman with no money and no family in the nineteenth century, well, she could only imagine that it would be verging on the impossible for her to have any hope of a fair trial. As it was, Michelle had already established in her own mind that with an alleged confession from the accused, the prospects of an acquittal were already looking pretty remote. She continued reading:

> *Cross-examined by Mr Sendall.*
>
> *Q. That was everything she had about her of any kind – just the fabric?*
>
> *A. Everything – she had not a bite of bread or a farthing of money – she had every appearance of being in the state of poverty that she had described to me – I offered her some food, some bread – she appeared to swallow it without chewing – and she had some coffee. I went to the workhouse where she said she had delivered the child and confirmed that she had delivered a child there. The child had been born living. She spent the night in a cell. I asked if she needed anything. She said her head hurt but that she needed nothing.*

Michelle paused again, looking at the cross-examination in disbelief. That was it? Why had the defence barrister not asked more questions to challenge whether Clara had in fact confessed to the murder? Sloppy or just lazy? He should have focused more on what Clara had actually said, tried to unpick whether it was Clara who had confessed to the murder, or whether she simply let the people who brought her into the station speak for her, condemning herself with her silence. Why did he focus on what Clara had on her person when she was taken in? And why did what she ate have any relevance to the question of whether she was guilty of the crime she had been indicted for, that of wilfully murdering her son? *Christ, I could have done a better job than that, and I am not even a criminal lawyer.* She could only hope that this Mr Sendall did a better job of cross-examination as the trial progressed:

> *George Taylor. I was at the Foundling Hospital on the morning of the 19th of August, on duty. The prisoner came there with a baby in her arms. To the best of my knowledge, she was seen in the afternoon. The baby looked healthy. The prisoner was not relieved of the baby.*

Michelle tried to swallow her frustration as she realised she would be offered no explanation as to why the Foundling Hospital had declined to take the baby from a woman who was clearly both destitute and desperate. She carried on:

> *Cross-examined by Mr Sendall.*
> *Q. I believe the prisoner herself is an illegitimate child?*
> *A. Yes. Her mother had been unable to provide for her and left her with the Foundling Hospital when the prisoner was a baby. The prisoner remained there and was educated and provided for until she was old enough to go into service.*

Now this was getting interesting, Michelle thought, while at the same time she was accosted by a wave of pity for this poor girl who had never been given a real chance at life. Ned had said he knew nothing about Clara, but Michelle did remember him saying that she had no family to speak of. Now she knew why.

Now she knew just how vulnerable and alone Clara had been in the world when Ned had walked into her life. Michelle wondered how old Clara was when she was discharged from the care of the Foundling Hospital and sent out to work. There was a desperate sadness at the thought of her having to take the baby back to the place where she herself had been abandoned and had grown up; the cycle of deprivation and poverty that she was unable to escape from.

And what was Mr Sendall getting at with his cross-examination on the issue of Clara's own status as an illegitimate child? Was he somehow implying that Clara was destined to repeat the sins of her parents by giving birth to another bastard baby that she did not have the means to care for? Again, Michelle found herself perplexed as she struggled to see the relevance of Mr Sendall's line of questioning, while being highly critical of his failure to deal with why the hospital had refused to take the child. Perhaps he considered this to be irrelevant to the question of his client's guilt. Ned had blamed himself for the death of the child because of his failure to act to provide for him, but in her mind, Michelle thought that the bureaucracy of the hospital was at greater fault, because they had been in a position to save his life by simply taking him in.

But, as ever, it was not her job to judge, particularly in this case, where there was already a judge presiding. Trying to keep her mind focused on the conduct of the trial, she read on, quickly ascertaining that the next witnesses were there to give the medical evidence relating to the death of the child. She stopped herself. Douglas. His name had been Douglas. The way in which people kept referring to him as 'the child' or 'the baby' dehumanised him, rendering him nothing more than the subject of criminal proceedings, rather than a living, breathing child, who had somehow survived the lottery of life and death that giving birth centuries ago entailed. How she despised the court for seeming to lose sight of the fact they were dealing with the death of an individual. He was a child. He was just a baby. But he was also Douglas, a little boy, and his life had been lost before he had even had a chance to live:

> *Mr James Elliot. I am a surgeon. I examined the body of the child at about half past eleven at night on the 19th of August. The child had no clothing. I observed that the surface of its body was unusually pale except the skin of the head and face – its eyelids were partially open – I did not open the body – from my external examination, the cause of death appeared to be suffocation by drowning, from immersion in water.*

So, the doctor who had examined the body shortly after it had been extracted from the Thames immediately determined that the cause of death was by drowning. But as she read on, she was starting to be persuaded that Mr Sendall might actually have some purpose to his line of questioning:

> *Cross-examined by Mr Sendall.*
> *Q. Did you hear, before you examined it, that the body had been found on the surface of the water?*
> *A. Yes. I did not make any post-mortem examination – I think there was sufficient appearance on the external body to enable me to say that it had drowned – the mouth of the body was quite closed – it is not usual to find the mouth of a drowned person open – I have seen many drowned persons.*

Two things struck her as she read this final sentence. The first was that it clearly had been a regular occurrence to pull bodies out of the Thames. She thought of the river that ran through the heart of London as though an artery bringing life to the city, the way in which the sun reflected off the surface of the water, the ships going up and down, the banks of the river bustling with tourists and Londoners going about their daily lives. She walked or jogged past it herself most days, and yet it never once occurred to her to consider the dark history submerged in its swollen waters.

Yet on reading the evidence, she could almost hear the weary resignation in the surgeon's voice as he confirmed that he had seen an abundance of drowned souls. Michelle's mind darkened, filling with images of rows of corpses, their shadowy spirits shuffling in a forlorn, funereal procession on the banks of the Thames, waiting for her to see them. She quickly brushed that thought to one side. Even thinking about it scared her. Especially now that she knew from Ned that it was all too possible.

But the second thought that came to Michelle, and the one she chose to focus on, was the way in which the barrister was manipulating the cross-examination of the examining doctor. Michelle was starting to have some respect for this Mr Sendall. She could see he was trying to suggest there was some room for doubt that the child had died by drowning in the Thames, by implying that Mr Elliot had simply assumed Douglas had drowned because he had heard that a child's body had been found floating on the surface of the river. As yet, she couldn't see the point in this, unless he was going to try and establish that Douglas was already dead before Clara had taken him into the water to commit suicide.

And as soon as she had thought this, she could see the wisdom in such a strategy. Very clever. Given the number of witnesses who saw Clara take the child into the Thames, it was not going to be possible to physically distance her from placing him in the water. However, it might be possible to establish that she had not taken a living child into the water, but one that was dead in her arms, and that in her grief for her lost child, she was seeking to end her own life. At the very minimum, if Mr Sendall's strategy were successful, he would at least be able to establish an element of the requisite doubt to justify an acquittal. One thing Michelle did understand about criminal proceedings from her one term of studying criminal law at university was that guilt needed to be proved beyond reasonable doubt. And surely, the forensic evidence at the time was not sufficiently advanced so that the prosecution could indeed prove that Douglas had drowned?

With renewed hope, she continued reading the evidence:

Mr Richard Snow. I am a surgeon. I examined the body of the child on the 22nd of August – there were no external marks of violence – in dividing the skin there was a small amount of fat between the skin and the muscle – the stomach was healthy and contained fluid resembling milk – the lungs filled the cavity of the chest, and were filled with a frothy mucus – the vessels of the brain appeared more congested than usual – the diaphragm descended towards the abdomen – on turning over the body, a little fluid escaped from the nose – in my opinion, the child came to its death from suffocation – from drowning.

Once more she stopped reading to consider the evidence that had just been presented. Someone had decided an autopsy was appropriate. Whether it was the prosecutor hoping to establish beyond any question that the cause of death was by drowning, or the defence hoping to prove that Douglas was dead before he was taken into the water was impossible to determine. All Michelle had to go on were the words in front of her, which she read, bristling each time Douglas was referred to as 'it':

Cross-examined by Mr Sendall.

Q. What was there to indicate that it died from drowning, and not before it was immersed?

A. The frothy mucus, and the blood not coagulating – I infer from that, that the child was alive when taken into the water.

Q. Supposing it to be in a dying state for the want of food, either substantial or fluid, would its appearance immediately before death, or for some minutes before death, be such as to lead a person to suppose it was dead?

A. It might present symptoms of great exhaustion, but not that of death.

And with that, Michelle could see all hope for Clara drowned, fatally submerged in the overwhelming forensic evidence against her. The autopsy had in fact proved that Douglas was living when his mother, the one person who was supposed to protect him, had taken him into the water. And Michelle suspected the prosecutor must also have been hoping to establish that the child had been healthy at the time of his death, with the layer of fat between the muscle and the skin negating Clara's claims that the child had been starving. And as a lawyer, Michelle knew that even if Douglas had been close to death when Clara had waded into the dark waters of the river, it would not change the fact she had killed him, or she suspected, that Clara had indeed intended to kill her son. Michelle desperately searched her memory to try and recall the elements that constituted the crime of murder. There had to be both the *mens rea* and the *actus reus* to make up the crime. Was that right?

She wished she had paid more attention in her criminal law classes. It had been a compulsory subject in her first year of law school, but it was not one that Michelle had been particularly interested in. The only thing she remembered with any real clarity was her mortification of mistaking her criminal law professor for a fellow student on the first day of classes. The man was wearing a pair of Stubbies shorts and thong sandals, of all things. But yes, somewhere in the dusty recesses of her memory, she seemed to recall her youthful professor saying something about both the intention to commit the crime, the *mens rea*, and the physical act of committing the crime, the *actus reus*. In this case, the *actus reus* was not really something she could have argued against. Clara had without doubt taken the child into the waters of the river with the inevitable and foreseeable consequence that the child would drown if she were to let him go.

But, if Michelle had been representing Clara, she thought she would have been able to argue that the *mens rea* component of the crime was lacking on account of the fact Clara was either suffering from post-natal depression or some other incapacity of the mind that meant the *mens rea* was absent. Michelle was willing to take an educated guess that post-natal depression was not an established medical condition at the time, but she could see that Mr Sendall's line of questioning was designed to negate the *mens rea* by trying to show that Clara believed her child to be already dead, or dying when she walked into the waters of the river.

Michelle turned the page, hoping that the next witness was going to be of assistance to Clara's defence. But from what she had just read regarding the results of the autopsy, Clara had knowingly taken her living son into the waters to die. How could anyone defend that? Once more Michelle reminded herself that it was not her job to judge. Lawyers did not have to like their clients, or even condone their conduct. Their job was merely to represent the side of the equation that luck or some ill wind of fate had assigned them.

Jane Rudd. I am the wife of one of the policemen at the station. I was sent...

The sudden loud buzzing of the ringing of her flat's telephone communication system stopped her reading. Michelle looked around her in bewilderment. It took her a moment to identify that the noise was meant for her. She established that it was definitely coming from her flat somewhere, but in the entire time she had been there, she had never heard it before. She followed the noise, and ascertained it was coming from the telephone beside the door to her flat. She went and picked up the handset.

'Hello,' she said tentatively.

'Michelle?'

Nick. Of course.

Michelle wished she was the type of person who could simply hang the phone up and ignore any further attempt to contact her. And it wasn't as if she had not already arranged to see him. She did not appreciate the interruption or the unwelcome intrusion into her home and her life.

'Why are you here?' Michelle asked, not even bothering to attempt to disguise the irritation in her voice. And then as she realised that he had come to her flat, she continued, 'How did you know where to come, Nick? Who told you where I live?'

There was nothing but static on the other end of the phone, yet somehow, she could hear his expectation. She wavered, before she pressed the button with a symbol of a key, assuming it would let Nick in. She heard a click as the door opened and then closed. He was on his way up. She put the phone down and sighed. Reading the case had distracted her.

Michelle went and filled up the kettle and switched it on. She was going to need coffee.

CHAPTER FIFTEEN

Michelle was waiting at the open door of her flat as the lift opened and spat out its contents towards her.

Nick looked bloody awful. Michelle guessed he had woken up, jet-lagged and hung-over, realised she was gone, and just threw on some clothes and came in search of her. Christ, he had not even taken a shower.

'This is stalking, you know,' Michelle said to him as she stepped to one side to allow him entry.

He walked in, and immediately followed the smell of the coffee, heading towards the kitchen. It seemed that he was not inclined to wait for an invitation.

'You just disappeared. You can't run away from me every time something happens that you don't like. We still have things to talk about. This is our marriage, after all.'

'And it was our marriage, *after all*, that you threw away when you went to bed with Jen. Nick, there's nothing more to be said. There is no going back. We need to end this as quickly and as painlessly as we can for both our sakes.'

'C'mon, Mich,' Nick said, 'I have come all this way.'

'I don't care. As far as I am concerned, you can go all of the way back.'

'Take the day off work,' Nick said. 'Please. I'm sure they'll understand. Take the day off and we can just talk everything over.'

Despite the medicinal wonders of the tea, cereal bar, and Nurofen, Michelle could feel the bubbling remnants of her headache threatening to reanimate, like some sort of ghastly Frankenstein's monster. She wished she could make Nick disappear from her life as suddenly as he had reappeared in it.

'What will it take for you to understand? I don't want to take the day off work. I have got far too much to do to spend time talking to you. Moreover, I have no desire to talk everything over. Talking is not going to change the facts. You had an affair. You are having a baby with another woman. We are done. All in all, I think it's a pretty brief conversation.'

'But think about how great we are together. Think about last night. How right it felt.' He moved closer towards her, closing the space between them. The proximity of his body would once have generated a heated longing in her, enough to melt the block of ice she had made of her heart, but all her fevered passion had expired. There was nothing between them now.

And there it was. All the reasons why spending the previous evening in bed with him had been nothing but a bad judgement call on her part. And now she would have to undo the consequences of that because it was not like Nick was going to. He never did. She took a step back from him, seeking refuge in the barrier of space.

Trying not to let the weight of her sadness overwhelm her, she tried to make him understand. 'It doesn't matter how good it was. None of that matters anymore,' she said. 'You're having a baby with someone else, Nick. A baby. Think about what that means.'

'The thing is, it doesn't feel real,' Nick said. 'I look at Jen, and she wants so much from me. She wants me to sort out her flat, sort out medical insurance so she can have the baby in a private hospital. She wants a proper family car so she can drive the baby around safely. She wants me to come to the scan with her and pretend that we are a happy couple. And I'm beginning to realise that I don't actually like her very much. How sad is that? How can I be having a baby with someone I don't even like? And when I think about that, I start to realise I'm going to be stuck with her for the rest of my life. And then when I think about everything she wants, all of which she expects me to pay for, all I keep trying to tell myself is that none of this can actually be happening to me. Not when I'm supposed to be with you.'

Michelle was almost starting to feel sorry for him. And as his blue eyes met hers, she thought of the history they had shared, how her story had entwined with his and been bound together as though a beautiful gold-lettered hardback. Something that she could place on her life's bookshelf and be proud of. She could see her love for him reflected in his eyes. But it wasn't enough. What he had done had all but torn that book in two, ripping the pages into shreds, so that it could never be made whole again. And hopefully he could see that now.

'You need to go back to Sydney,' Michelle said. 'You need to let me go.'

He nodded.

'I need to go to work,' Michelle said.

He nodded again but made no move to leave her flat. She suspected that if she simply walked out and left him there to go to work, he would still be sitting in the same place when she returned at the end of the day.

'When are you going back?' she asked him, hoping to prod him from the lethargy that seemed to have claimed him. He looked up at her, defeated, and made no attempt to answer her question. 'Nick, when is your flight back to Sydney?'

He blinked. She stood with her arms crossed, waiting for his answer.

'I booked a flight back the day after next,' Nick told her. 'I figured I could always move it if I needed to. Will you have dinner with me tonight?'

She thought of all the reasons why she should tell him no. She thought of all the ways in which having dinner with him could hurt her. She thought of the dangers of sharing a bottle of wine with him, and the temptation to allow herself to fall back into his willing arms again. Her mind was screaming at her to tell him no. She found herself nodding at him.

'I'll meet you at a restaurant called Uno,' she told him. 'It's pretty close to here, on the corner of Warwick Way and Wilton Road. But you have to promise me that at the end of the evening you'll go back to the hotel. Alone.'

Nick nodded his agreement.

'Seven thirty?'

Nick nodded again.

'Then I will see you there,' she said as she gestured towards the door. He finally stood up and made to leave, looking like he wanted to say something more. But she refused to meet his eyes, and moving ahead of him, opened the door, stepping back to ensure his exit was clear. Letting him out, she closed the door behind her, wondering why she kept setting herself up to come into contact with him, given the capacity he had to hurt her. She closed her eyes, and leaned her back against the door, listening to the lift doors open and close, hopefully taking Nick away inside of them. Silence. Finally, she was alone with only her thoughts to keep her company.

When she opened her eyes, the relief she was hoping to feel in being left alone was denied her. Ned was in her flat.

CHAPTER SIXTEEN

'Who is he?' Ned asked.

It was not even eight in the morning. She had not had anywhere near enough sleep. She was fighting the hangover from hell. She had got rid of one troublesome male only to be confronted by another. What the hell had she done to deserve this?

'My husband,' she replied.

'You're married?' Ned asked, and then, without waiting for Michelle's confirmation, added, 'He wants something from you.' It was not so much a question as a statement.

'Everybody wants something from me,' she replied. 'Even you.'

His lack of a denial was not missed by either of them. 'But he's your husband. So, you're going to have to go with him,' Ned said. Again, it was not a question.

'It doesn't work like that anymore, Ned,' Michelle told him.

'I don't like him,' Ned said.

'I don't like him much myself at the moment,' said Michelle. And then, as she wanted to move the focus away from herself and her problems, she asked, 'Ned, why are you here? I mean, right now. I told you I would call for you when I was ready, and while I am making progress, I'm not ready for you yet.' She was dismissing him as though he was a client that called too frequently for updates when there was nothing happening. It was a waste of her time, and a waste of their money. But Ned was not a client and her time was nothing to him. Time had lost its currency on his death. But it didn't change the fact that she didn't have anything to tell him yet. Why could he not just wait?

He looked towards the papers that were still sitting on the kitchen counter. 'I've been waiting for you to call for me,' he said. 'I keep listening, but you don't call for me. And I keep waitin'.'

There was accusation in his voice, and Michelle found herself fighting her resentment. 'I'm sorry. I know it must be difficult for you, but I still have a life to lead. I can't give over all of myself to helping you.' A brief twinge of bitterness fluttered to the surface. She had spent many years repressing her gift and there had been a multitude of reasons for her taking that path. She had always thought it had asked too much of her, and this expectation of Ned's that he now loaded on her as though she was his pliable beast of burden was edging her close to overload. 'I didn't ask for this, you know.'

'What are those?' Ned asked, gesturing towards the papers on the kitchen counter.

'It's the transcript of Clara's trial,' she replied, and as Ned looked unsure, she elaborated, 'It's a report of how the trial was run, and who spoke against Clara, and who stood up to defend her.'

He drifted over to the papers, hovering close to them with his brow furrowed. She watched as he attempted to decipher them. She saw his fists clench with the effort, and anger darken his eyes before the papers skirted across the shiny top of the kitchen bench like a gust of wind had caught them, although the air inside of her flat was calm, warm and still. Michelle took a step back, a degree of shock coursing through her spine. She had not known he could connect with the physical. There was still so much she had to learn.

'I don't have much in the way of letters,' Ned said, frustration coating his words, 'but tell me, do those papers tell you what happened,' he asked, 'when Clara were in the dock?'

'It tells me what was said,' Michelle replied. 'But I wasn't there. I don't know what happened. There is a difference.'

His silence was telling. She was learning to read him. Or she was learning to feel him. She didn't know what it was, but she was coming to trust the quiet voices that whispered to her, a latent instinct coming alive inside her heart. Somewhere at the back of her mind, she could see Ivy smiling at her. And all of a sudden, Michelle knew.

'Oh my God, Ned, you were there, weren't you? At Clara's trial?'

Ned looked at her, shifting his weightless weight from one foot to the other, and she knew she was right. Ned had been at Clara's trial.

'I weren't going to go,' he said. 'But there were something about it. After all, it were my boy she killed. My son.'

Michelle quietly noted to herself that once more he claimed the boy as his own. But this time, with more vehemence. She also clocked the change in his attitude; that he now blamed Clara for the death of the child, rather than himself. She could see by the darkness in his eyes that he was holding on to some anger at Clara for taking the child to die in the water.

'I had to go,' Ned continued. 'I wanted to hear what she had to say for herself. I were angry at her for killing my boy.'

'Wait,' Michelle said. A small pocket of fury escaped from her carefully controlled emotional reservoir and bubbled to the surface. 'What did you just say? Did you hear the words that just came out of your mouth? I've seen everything that happened when Clara was pregnant, and then when she brought the baby to you and begged you for your help. You know that. You have taken me to it, little by little, always holding back. You wanted me to be too involved in trying to find out what had happened to Clara, too seduced by the promise of helping you find your redemption so that I would not back away from you in disgust. So, I know. I know, Ned. You told Clara it would be better if the child died. Those were your words. You told her that the child had nothing to do with you. And yet,' Michelle's fury was getting the better of her, 'you have the audacity to stand there and tell me that she was responsible for the death of your son. That she was to blame for the death of Douglas? With no money, and nowhere to go, just what the fuck did you expect her to do?'

'She said that she were going to take him to the Foundling. And even if they didn't take him, she could have taken him back to the workhouse,' he said. 'They always took in the mothers with the small babies. Well,' he paused, 'nearly always. At least he would have had a chance there. But she didn't even give him that chance. She killed him instead.'

'And what sort of chance did you give your son?' Michelle asked.

'I would have gone for him,' Ned said. 'I know it looked like I didn't care, but I would have gone back for him. Especially after my Nelly were gone. But by then it were too late. They were all dead. All of them. Nelly and her bairn. Dead. Douglas, drowned. Dead... And Clara.'

Once more, Ned descended into silence. It settled in the room like a cold mist, freezing all that it touched. Death was everywhere.

Michelle saw the way in which his spirit sagged, deflating under the pressure of her line of questioning.

'Okay, Ned,' Michelle said, quickly checking the time. Now that she was no longer meeting Nick for breakfast, she had some time before she would have to start heading to the office. 'So, you were there. At Clara's trial. I want to hear what happened. Not from the papers in front of me. I can read them for myself. I want to hear it from you.' She pushed the papers to one side. His eyes closed as he weighed up what she was asking of him. And Michelle had already realised exactly what she was asking of herself, anticipating the pull of the currents of the past wanting to drag her into the very heart of his darkness.

Ned opened his eyes.

'I were there,' he confirmed. 'At the Old Bailey. I weren't going to go, but all the folk were talking about what had happened. They all knew. Folk always did. But all the talk were about how Clara had brought the baby to me to ask me for help. How I turned my face against her and sent her away. How Clara had taken the child into the water to die. And they were all looking at me. They all blamed me. Their eyes were on my back all the time.'

She could only imagine the looks of hatred and condemnation that would have been directed at Ned, like knives being shivved in the supple and yielding flesh between each and every rib bone of his back.

'So, I had to go. I suppose I wanted to show them that I cared. Leastways, that I cared about the baby. About my lad. But I got it wrong. I got it all wrong.' Ned shook his head at the memory, as if he didn't want to look further back. But Michelle had travelled too far along this path with him to let him abandon her on it alone. She needed him to take her with him, back into his memories he would prefer to keep buried, back into the past that had long ago been consigned to the dusty pages of court reports and archived records. She wanted to go back and see that time for herself.

She reached out towards him as though she wanted to pull him towards her, remembering only too late that it was impossible to take hold of a shadow. Yet his hand reached towards hers, and as her fingers slid through the cold breath of nothingness, her heart contracted with the disappointment of thwarted expectation.

She withdrew her hand but saw how both her and Ned's eyes lingered on the empty space where their hands should have joined, if only he had been flesh and bone, and not this drifting ghost his guilt had condemned him to be. 'What happened? What happened at Clara's trial?'

'They brought her up, and put her in the dock,' Ned began, his face contorting with his obvious grief at the memory. 'She looked so tiny inside it. Like she were really just a little girl, not a grown woman in the dock for murder. Her face were nearly white. And her eyes...' Ned paused. 'It looked like there were nothing of her left. Like she had died with the baby in the water. She were like a ghost.'

He paused as though he was taking a breath, but the only sounds were Michelle's breathing and the distant traffic floating up from the streets of London below. It unnerved her.

'The policeman came first. They swore him in, and he told of how some folk had brought Clara into the station.'

Michelle pulled out her notepad and pen and started taking notes. While she had already read over the policeman's evidence from the transcript, given the staccato manner in which it had been reported, she figured she may as well get a full account of what Ned had seen and heard. It would give her a fuller picture. She always preferred to be thorough. Ned's account of what the policeman had said in court broadly correlated with what Michelle had already read.

'Then?' Michelle prompted. 'Who gave evidence next?'

Her approach was having its usual desired effect. She was

taking Ned through the trial in exactly the same way as she would a client. She was being matter-of-fact and sidestepping any emotional trap that lay between her and a full appreciation of the factual context of what it was she was dealing with. And this approach had two advantages. Firstly, she was able to get confirmation of the conduct of the trial, and secondly, the unemotional way in which she was handling Ned was also keeping her firmly grounded in her own reality. She was almost starting to feel that she could control her gift, rather than letting it control her.

'It were someone from the Foundling Hospital,' Ned continued. 'He didn't say much, just that they wouldn't take the baby.'

'Did he give a reason?' Michelle asked.

'No,' Ned replied. Michelle noted that Ned did not offer the information that Clara herself had been a Foundling child. But she wasn't going to press him on that point now.

'Who was next?' Michelle asked.

'Doctors,' Ned replied.

Michelle noted the rising red flush in his face as he spat the word out. She ignored the emotion brewing in his voice. She moved on to her next question.

'How many?'

'Two. The first one, he looked at the baby after he had been pulled out of the water. He said that he died in the water. That he had drowned.'

Again, Michelle did not want to press Ned on the finer points of the evidence as she had understood it. She certainly felt it would not be helpful to ask him about his thoughts about the strategy underpinning the cross-examination by the defence counsel. She already sensed that Ned was starting to back away into a cage of his own making, seeking refuge in the prison of his own guilt and remorse. If he chose to go inside it, Michelle would have a hard time dragging him back out to face his past again.

'And the second?'

'He weren't nothing but a Burker,' Ned replied. And there it was. Ned's anger. Michelle could sense it burning inside him. She could feel the searing heat of it. But she sensed something more than that, and it was helping her to understand him better. It was easier for him to feed the fire of his anger than it was to confront his sorrow and remorse. She was starting to identify what it was that was tying Ned to this world.

'A Burker?' Michelle asked.

'A butcher. He cut him open. He cut my boy open so he could poke around inside him.'

The autopsy. It was something that happened in virtually every murder case these days, Michelle would not even have thought to question the necessity of the procedure.

As gently as she could, she tried to explain to Ned why an autopsy had been necessary, and that it was probably because the defence was trying to prove that Douglas was already dead or dying when Clara took him into the water. She also tried to explain, as best she could, why she thought that this had been important and that it could have made a significant difference as to whether or not Clara was found guilty of the murder of Douglas. When she had finished outlining her thoughts, she looked at him to see if he had followed what she had said. His furrowed brow told her that he didn't care whether the doctor had been trying to help Clara or not. The thought of someone cutting into his child's body was still anathema to him.

'They were trying to help her, Ned. They were trying to help Clara,' she concluded, but deciding that it was pointless to press the issue, she moved on. 'But the second doctor said the same thing as the first, didn't he?'

'Yes. He said the baby had drowned. But he shouldn't have

cut my boy up. Everyone already knew he had drowned.'

Skimming over his anger about the autopsy, she tried to take him to his recollection of the evidence of the next witnesses. As she had not yet read their testimony, she was even more interested in what Ned had to say about them. 'Who came next, Ned?'

'Some women,' Ned replied. 'But it were getting harder to keep track of what were happening.'

'Why?' Michelle asked, wondering if it was because the evidence became more complex as the trial had progressed. They had already dealt with the forensic evidence, which was arguably the most difficult for a layperson to follow. It was only because in this case forensic evidence was in its infant stages that Michelle was able to follow it herself. Although she had not yet finished reading the transcript, she anticipated that the rest would be nothing more than circumstantial witness evidence submitted by the prosecutor to confirm the guilt of the accused.

'It were the people. The people that were there. At court that day. They were all whisperin' and lookin' at me. I could feel it. I could feel them staring at me. So I didn't pay much mind to what the women said. I don't think it mattered much anyway,' Ned said. 'It were already plain that she had killed him. The judge were getting ready to take out the black cap.'

While she had not managed to finish reading the transcript, as it stood she was probably inclined to agree with Ned's assessment that the women's testimony added little to the outcome.

'And then the judge asked Clara to speak.'

'Wait,' Michelle said, fumbling for the papers of the trial and scanning through what little was left. She looked for the witness names at the start of the paragraphs. Jane Rudd. George Taylor. Kate Harris. That was it. That was all she had left to read. There was no paragraph starting with Clara Waters.

There was no record of Clara having spoken during the trial. Or if she had, it was not reported. She wondered if Toby had missed a page when he had printed out the transcript or muddled a page with the rest of his research. She would have to ask Toby about that when she went into work, if she ever actually managed to make it in. It had already been a very long day and it had not even really started for her yet.

'Ned, what did Clara say?'

Ned opened his mouth, but the words did not come. He rubbed his tongue along the top of his lip and closed his eyes, shaking his head. His sadness was swallowing her, like Jonah into the belly of the whale, taking her into the cavernous depths of his grief. His guilt. This time, she did not try and fight it. It was what she had been waiting for. She embraced it, fell into it as though a diver off a springboard. She closed her own eyes and let herself be taken and floated into the depths of the misery of his memory.

When she opened her eyes, she was in the courtroom of the Old Bailey. It was strangely familiar to her, although she had never once stepped foot inside there. She supposed all courtrooms had pretty much the same layout with the raised bench with the judge sitting behind it presiding over the proceedings, the tables for the barristers, and the dock with the accused framed inside it. But Michelle's first reaction was not from what she could see, but what she could feel, closing in around her like a swarm of angry bees. The gallery was full, Clara's trial a spectacle for public entertainment. And Michelle could sense it. It was as though she had been transported into a coliseum, with the crowd baying for blood. But their hostility was not for Clara. It was not for the woman who had been accused of murder. It was all for Ned.

Michelle scanned the gallery, searching among the taut and angry faces of the men, and found him sitting with the others, his shoulders hunched over, as though he was trying to make himself appear smaller, his eyes lowered as if he was searching for dust on the floor.

Her gaze was then drawn to the girl standing in the dock. Clara Waters, the accused, indicted for murder, looked small, pale and pathetic, and seemed to be vanishing in the vastness of the courtroom pen, as if all of her soul had been surrendered to it. Her face was gaunt, drawn, the skin under her bloodshot eyes smudged with grey. And those haunted pale-green eyes of hers nothing but hollow orbs from which all the light had fled. She looked as though she had not slept for a week. And Michelle could still see it. Clara was surrounded by the eerie glow of that same blue aura that showed death had set its mark upon her and was calling for her to join her son. Her hands were clasped together, as if in supplication for a mercy she had no expectation of. Her eyes were fixed on the floor and the courtroom was heavy with anticipation. The silence was pregnant. They were all waiting.

Michelle's breathing quickened and her eyes turned in the direction of the bench, towards the red-robed figure of the judge, sitting as though a devil presiding over the gates of Hades. His eyes were dark and guarded as he considered the girl in the dock before him, briefly running his hand along the rich ermine lining adorning the collar of his robes of office, the creamy white complementing the dusty paleness of his curled wig.

Michelle's heart sputtered and went into freefall as her eyes fell on the object set in front of the honourable Mr Justice Pendegrast. It was a square of thick, heavy black fabric, in ominous anticipation of the sentence to come, draped over the edge of the bench as though the darkest of ink spilled from an inkpot, spreading over the floor of the courtroom, blotting out the life of Clara Waters.

CHAPTER SEVENTEEN

The judge asked Clara if she had anything to say before he passed sentence. She looked towards the table where counsel for the defence usually sat. Michelle assumed the barrister sitting behind it was Mr Sendall. He was wearing his wig, and struck an imposing figure being draped in black robes, but he was looking towards Clara with nothing but kindness and compassion in his grey-blue eyes. At that moment, Michelle realised that the man was desperately trying to do his best for Clara, his client, despite the mountain of evidence against her that he had been working so tirelessly to surmount.

This Mr Sendall, who it was so easy to judge as she picked apart what he had done in cross-examination in Clara's trial, was one of 'her people', as Angie would have said, just looking to do the best he could for the client he had been asked to represent. Mr Sendall nodded at Clara, trying to give her some reassurance, and Michelle realised he had almost certainly spent time coaching her in what she should say. Time, no doubt, for which he would not have been paid. Humbled, Michelle looked at Mr Sendall with new respect. It was exactly as she had explained to Ned. She could read from the transcript what had been said, and she could make judgements and assumptions about what she had read, but as to what had actually happened, you could only fully understand from the experience of being in the moment.

Clara looked up at the judge and nodded. A strained silence filled the courtroom. It was tense, impatient, hungry for her words, waiting to devour them the moment she released them. Clara started speaking. Her voice sounded as if it came from the back of a cave in which she had been abandoned and had forever lost her way. The entire population of the gallery leaned towards the sound of her voice, eager to catch its softness.

'I was in service with Mr Roberts and his family, but he had a son who was becoming a man, and I became anxious to find a new situation. I left the service of Mr Roberts and walked within the parish of St Margaret's in Westminster to seek a new situation. It was then that I met a man called Edmund. He told me that he could help me find a new position. He asked me to have a drink with him. I refused. But he persuaded me that I should have a drink with him. I was in his company for several hours.'

Clara paused, and a single tear tracked down her pale cheek, tracing a path through the grime that dusted her face. Clara's words wound themselves around Michelle as though a snake, the cloying closeness of the night that Clara and Ned had spent together still vivid in her mind.

'I spent the night in his company.'

Michelle leaned forward, willing Clara to continue. But there was nothing she could do to help the girl. Once more, she was nothing more than a ghost haunting the lonely corridors of Ned's mind. All Michelle could do was stand there and listen helplessly as Clara confronted her fate. Michelle wondered if the poor girl even realised that she was fighting for her life.

Clara paused again, clearly gathering her thoughts, before

she continued. 'When I knew I was in trouble I tried to hide it for as long as I could. But I lost my place, and I had to leave without a character. I had nowhere to go. And no hope of finding a new situation. I went in search of Edmund and when I found him, I asked him to pay for the child. But he would not help me. He turned me away. And then I knew for certain that he did not care anything for me, only for his own ends. I went to the workhouse. There was nowhere else for such as me.'

Clara stopped her narrative once more, editing out the indignities she had suffered as she submitted herself to the callous care of the parish. A hushed silence sat in stillness over the courtroom as she continued.

'I had my confinement in the workhouse, and I gave birth to a healthy son. He was beautiful. He was perfect.' Clara paused and Michelle could see her struggle to keep herself composed. Mr Sendall sat at the defence counsel's table, silently encouraging her to go on. Clara took a few deep breaths and continued. 'I called him Douglas. But I knew that he would be taken from me if I stayed. So when I was finished my laying in, I took my son and we left. I went back to Ned, I mean to Edmund, to ask him to provide for my son. Our son. But he turned me away again. He did not care what I was to do. He told me that he would have nothing to do with the baby. I told him that our child would die if I had to return to the workhouse. He told me he thought that would be for the best.'

Michelle's eyes drifted towards the cowering figure of Ned in the gallery. He had shrunk inside of himself, as if that was enough to ensure he was invisible to the people who had come to see how Clara's fate played out. But he could not hide from Michelle, either in his life or in his death. She could see him. Her eyes bored into him as though a dental drill intent on piercing the nerve of the tooth, exposing it to the cold air of existence so that he could feel the pain that he had been the cause of.

'I gave him a scrap of fabric from the shawl that my baby was wrapped in. I intended to take my son to the Foundling Hospital so that he could grow up with them and have an education, so that he could get a situation when he came of age. Like I had done. I already knew that I deserved nothing. I chose the path of sin. I did not deserve to live. But my child was innocent of any wrongdoing. I thought he deserved a chance to live.'

Clara staggered backwards as the weight of her own words settled on her conscience. Michelle could see her gasping for breath, trying to rebuild the shattered pieces of her soul back together again, before she was able to continue.

'I left Ned with a piece of the shawl that I had wrapped Douglas in. I tore a matching piece to give to the Foundling Hospital. I walked with my baby in my arms to the hospital, and I waited to be seen. It was a long walk, and I was so very tired. There was a long line of mothers waiting to be seen with me, some with young children, some with babies. We were all hungry. And we waited. When it was my turn, I told them how I had come to have my baby. That I had been foolish, and that I had been seduced, and that the man who seduced me would not pay for his son. But they wouldn't take him.'

Why the fuck did the hospital not take the child? Why would nobody talk about this?

'There was nothing else to be done. I had no food. I hadn't eaten for two days. And the only means I had to get food was to keep myself on the path of sin. But I didn't care about me. It was all for Douglas. But I could not provide for him. My milk was drying up. He suckled but I had too little to give him. My son was starving. His cries got weaker as his hunger took him over. My Douglas was dying and there was nothing I could do to help him.' Clara's tears were silent as though she had reached the very edge of her exhaustion. 'But then I knew what I should do. I was his mother. I was the only one who he had to help him. And I so loved my poor baby boy. I couldn't stand by and watch him starve. It would be a slow and painful death. I wanted to help him. And I wanted to be with him. The river called to us.'

The entire courtroom had plummeted into a deep silence. Ned had shrivelled into as small a being as he could make himself, devoid of spine. The subdued hush of Clara's words held the entire gallery spellbound.

'I walked down to the river when the tide was low. I waded through the tide mud and I walked to where I knew the waters of the river would come to meet us. I weighted my skirts with rocks and I sat with Douglas in my arms and I sang to him as the tide came towards us. The tide started to swell the river. The water came up to my waist. The evening sun was low in the sky and it was a warm day. Douglas had stopped crying for the milk I could not give him and was sleeping. He looked so peaceful. I gave him a kiss on his forehead and then on the tip of his nose. He was warm and soft. I unwrapped the shawl from Douglas and let him roll into the water. The tide took my baby. The tide took Douglas. And then I waited for the tide to take me.'

Clara's tears had turned into a stream, flowing down her face as though they wished to join the tidal waters of the Thames that had taken her son. The entire courtroom was silent.

Clara found the words to continue.

'I sat and I waited to be with my son. But some people came into the water and pulled me from it. They freed me from the stones I had put into my skirts and they pulled me back onto the bank of the river. I fought against them. I didn't want to come out of the water. I wanted to be with my son. But I couldn't see him anymore. I couldn't see where he had gone. I had lost my baby. The people shouted at me and called me a lunatic because I kept trying to go back into the water. But I couldn't find my baby. He was gone. My baby had disappeared into the waters. I told them that I had killed my baby. I told them that I had murdered my son. They took me to the police station.'

Michelle was aware of the indignant murmurings coming from the gallery. She could see the people directing their angry gazes in the direction of Ned. He sat with his head bowed, clearly clinging to the child's hope that if he could not see them, then they would not see him. But the wrath of the crowd swelled like a hive protecting their queen. One man rose from his seat and pointed his finger of righteous accusation towards the cowering shadow that Ned had become. One by one, the gallery rose, until all the men were on their feet.

Someone had taken a handful of Ned's hair, and was dragging him outside. Michelle could hear the judge calling for order, but it was swallowed up by the angry imperative of the crowd. It was as nothing in their need for justice, which they had already decided would not be dispensed within the walls of the courtroom.

Michelle wanted to stay to find out what had happened with Clara, but she found herself carried with the mob outside the courtroom, as though she was nothing more than a cell flowing through a vein in the liquescent blood force of life. She had forgotten that she was seeing only what Ned had seen, that her view was restricted by the boundaries of Ned's memory. The trial in the courtroom was now closed for her as Ned was seized by an abundance of hands and taken out to face the justice of the throng. Michelle noticed that the officers of the court scurried after the crowd but kept their distance. They seemed loath to intervene.

The swarm of angry men bundled Ned outside of the Old Bailey, on to the streets baked in a sunshine that seemed shocking after the claustrophobic darkness of the courtroom. Some men had hold of his arms, another two men held his legs. They were strong men, with broad shoulders and thickly muscled arms, just like Ned's. They were Ned's people. They were probably labourers just like him. Ned bucked and writhed in his captivity, but he was like a fly cocooned in a sticky silken web. He could not break free. A man, his face fired red with fury, was pointing towards something, and Michelle followed the masses. They were taking Ned towards a trough filled with dirty water, a film of brown-green algae coating the surface. Scum always floated to the top.

The man who had hold of Ned's hair forced him towards it, and multitudes of hands pushed against his head and compelled it towards the direction of the dirty water. Ned resisted. He was a strong man, and although his entire body was taut with resistance, he was no match for the will of the horde that sought only to exact their own vengeance for Clara. For her boy.

Ned was bent over the trough of water and his head was plunged into its shallow depths. Hands were pressed against the back of his skull, forcing him downwards, holding his face under the murky water, and drowning him. She could see the violent movements of his body as he struggled to break free. And in the next moment, unrelenting panic took hold of her as she was plunged under the water with him. She wanted to scream but she was afraid that if she opened her mouth, she would be starved of oxygen and the putrid water would flood her lungs. She tried to tell herself that this was not really happening to her, but to Ned. It wasn't real. It was just a memory. But it was as though she had been shut inside her own coffin and lowered six feet into the earth with the muddy clods being rained down on top of the box that imprisoned her. She could find no way out. Her gift was consuming her, as worms would a corpse. As desperation took her by the throat, she tried to take control over what she was experiencing, but Ned's memory was too powerful, and it had too tight a grip on her. Clearing her mind, she started to pick a path to separate herself from him, drifting in and out of Ned's mind, as she fought against the rip tide that had her within its power. A passive observer one moment, and thrashing under water the next. She saw the bubbles floating around her ears, the last vestiges of the precious oxygen that lingered in her lungs dissipating into nothingness, as she tried to free herself from the talons of terror that clawed at Ned's mind. She was choking on her own helplessness.

Finding her strength, she grounded herself back in her own body. Taking a deep breath in, she dragged herself away from Ned's primitive fear. She must take control of how she experienced Ned's memory, and gasping for air that had never been denied her, she stepped back to bear witness. Warm water that stank like pigswill was dripping in rivulets down her neck, and she was still swallowing oxygen as though it was diamonds, but Michelle was almost jubilant. She had controlled her gift, rather than letting it control her. She only wanted to see what had happened to Ned, not experience every moment of his descent into his own personal hell.

Michelle watched as Ned's reckoning continued. There was nothing she could do to help him. But even with the knowledge that she was powerless to intervene, she took a step back, as though she was condoning the punishment the crowd had deigned appropriate to be carried out. A part of her could see the justice of what they did, for Ned to know the dark depths of the water, what it was like to have air denied you, to sink into the murky bleakness of a watery grave, to come close to dying the same death that his son had suffered.

She watched, strangely passive, as the violent movements of Ned's body subsided into nothing more than involuntary shudders as he succumbed to the oblivion of unconsciousness.

His mouth was closing. Michelle wondered if he welcomed death. She saw his body take on that bluish hue, readying his spirit for the moment when it would no longer find respite in the body that had housed it. But at that moment when the shutters of darkness were closing in on him, he was pulled from the water, and the hands that had held him down dumped his sodden form in the horseshit baked onto the ground beside the trough, pushing his face into the swampy mess. The man who seemed to be the leader of the ravenous pack dealt Ned a violent kick in the stomach. It was this that probably saved his life. He started coughing and spluttering, and the blue of the aura that surrounded him dissipated into the brightness of the almost cloudless summer sky.

Ned coiled himself up into a ball, anticipating further blows, wrapping his hands around his legs, tucking his chin close to his chest. The man who had kicked Ned leaned down towards him, and grasping a handful of Ned's hair, pulled his face back with brutal force so that Ned could do nothing else but look into the eyes of his torturer. He offered no resistance. He was spent from the effort of trying to live.

The man curled his fingers into a fist, holding it close to Ned's face, and Ned closed his eyes. Michelle averted her gaze, waiting to hear the sickening sound of bone crashing against bone, flesh tearing into flesh. But it did not come. 'Get up, and get out of here,' the man snarled. 'Leave. We don't want your sort around here. Get up and go.'

Michelle watched as the bruised and battered figure of Ned picked himself up and staggered into the distance. As his figure retreated, Michelle stared as the streets outside the Old Bailey started to fade, morphing into a dizzying blankness until replaced by the familiar, safe contours of her flat. She was back in Emery Hill Street. She reached up to touch her hair. It was dry, carrying the faint blueberry scent of her conditioner. She took a few breaths in, trying to ground herself back in her own reality. The ghost of Ned materialised beside her as she struggled to regain a sense of calm after having absorbed the frantic energy of the enraged mob.

Michelle had heard Clara speak, and it hurt her to remember her words. But she was still ignorant as to Clara's fate. As her breath started to slow, she reached for the transcript that was sitting on her kitchen counter. She had to find out what sentence had been passed. But Ned's words stopped her, and ice coursed down her spine.

'You don't need to look at them papers. I can tell you what happened,' Ned said. 'She were found guilty. The judge sentenced her to death.'

CHAPTER EIGHTEEN

Michelle began pacing the floor of the kitchen as his words settled under her skin like a burrowing tick. She supposed in light of the evidence she had read and heard, that a guilty verdict and the death sentence that followed was the inevitable conclusion. Especially as the judge had already taken out the black cap of condemnation in readiness for his sentencing. But Ned hadn't actually been in the courtroom when the judge passed sentence. So maybe he had just presumed that Clara had received the death penalty and had been consumed by his guilt ever since.

'How do you know?' Michelle asked. 'You weren't there. I saw you being dragged out of the courtroom before the verdict was given.'

'I heard talk,' Ned replied. 'Even after I left and went further west along the river, it were hard not to hear talk of what had happened to Clara. Everyone were talking about it.'

Something stirred in the back of Michelle's mind. 'Her death sentence. After you took me to Clara coming to you with the baby, you said the next time you saw Clara she was a dead woman walking. It wasn't that she had died, but that she was under sentence of death?'

'Yes,' Ned said, nodding. 'After that day in court I never did speak to her again. Not that I spoke to her then. I never got the chance. I were right sorry about that too. I suppose...' Ned paused, looking at the floor before looking up at Michelle again. 'I suppose I would have liked to have told her that I were sorry. I never meant for any of it to happen. I felt right bad about Clara. About the boy.'

Michelle breathed in Ned's regret, and savoured the sensation of it, the soothing calmness settling on her as though balm on her heart. But at the same time, she wondered what it was that he was actually sorry for. Sorry that he didn't help Clara when she first came to him to reveal her pregnancy? Sorry for not offering to provide support for his child? Or, stripping the whole saga back to where their lives had first entwined, sorry for that night he had spent with her when he first encountered her on the street searching for a new position, that moment when his world had collided with hers, and left nothing but a trail of shattered debris in his wake?

Ned seemed oblivious to Michelle's meandering thoughts. 'And that time in the Old Bailey, before the crowd turned on me and dragged me outside, that were the last time I saw Clara. Ever. I didn't go to Newgate for the hanging.' Ned seemed to take a deep breath in, the soundless emptiness of it sitting like a hollow in her kitchen. 'I don't think I could have borne to see her drop.'

Michelle took hold of her kitchen counter, as she tried to steady herself. She had not yet taken the sentence of death to its logical conclusion in her mind, processed the awful reality it would mean for Clara. 'They would have hanged her?' she asked. It was unspeakable. Michelle was horrified at the thought. It was one thing to know that, in theory, as a historical fact, women were executed in such a barbaric manner, but it was another thing altogether to contemplate Clara, the girl that Michelle had experienced such a powerful connection with, suffering such a public and shameful death. Not that she thought Clara had done anything to be ashamed of. It was the world in which she had lived that ought to hang its head in shame. There had been no one to help her, no one to support her. She had given birth to a child that was stigmatised from the moment he came into the world, and there was not a soul that had tried to offer her even a little bit of kindness. It wounded Michelle to think of Clara, that fragile, defeated girl, having a noose roped around her neck and the ground pulled out from underneath her feet, her neck snapped if luck was with her, or stretched beyond endurance as her life was violently choked from her.

Ned looked at Michelle with no emotion on his face. 'Of course,' he said, 'what else would they do?'

'But what about an appeal?' Michelle asked. She was a lawyer. And she had been educated to believe that there was always an avenue of appeal. Some way in which justice could be stripped apart to get the right result. She had seen Mr Sendall, Clara's defence counsel. A weary, middle-aged man worn down by the arduous task he had been called upon to undertake, that of saving the scum of society, the fallen, from their bleak fate. It seemed as if Mr Sendall had genuinely cared about what happened to Clara. Surely he would have done everything he could to avoid losing his client in such a grotesque manner? Where was the justice in hanging a girl who had wanted to die?

Ned looked at Michelle as though he did not understand what it was she was suggesting.

'She made her appeal to the judge. You heard her,' Ned said. 'It wouldn't have made no difference, like. She were guilty.

And once you were found guilty of a murder there were only one place to go. They would have taken her down to Newgate. And they normally hung them within a couple of days after a judge says that they should swing. If she were lucky, she might have had three days before she had to face the rope.'

Michelle closed her eyes. Could it be possible that she had taken this long journey into Ned's past only to have to conclude that the deaths of Clara and Douglas sat fairly on Ned's conscience? That there was a justice to his continued existence in that uncaring window between the life that he once had and death? Was she supposed to help Ned accept that this was the consequence of his actions in life? But even as her mind was turning these unpalatable options over, one thought intruded.

She and Ned were now deciding that Clara had indeed been found guilty, and that the judge had consequently sentenced her to death, purely on the basis of speculation and gossip. If Toby had made that assessment, boy would she have taken him to task, and rightly so. It was so unlike her to jump to conclusions without fully understanding all the facts, and it was even more inexcusable given that the facts were sitting before her in black and white.

Michelle reached for the transcript and started to read through it, picking up where she had left off before Nick had interrupted her what felt like hours ago, even though, Michelle confirmed as she quickly glanced at the time on her phone, it had not yet been an hour since she had managed Nick out of her front door. Ned stood there unmoving as she read the words out loud to him:

'Jane Rudd. I am the wife of one of the policemen at the station. I was sent for when the prisoner came there. Her clothes were dripping wet – I undressed her and examined her – I asked her how she came to take her child into the water – she said poverty made her do it. She said she only had a little milk and that her child was starving – but I thought she had some milk.

'Nice,' Michelle said. 'Just perfect.' Ned raised his eyebrow as if in question, but Michelle was too angry to explain. If she had been hoping for any sympathy to be extended towards Clara from this first witness of her own sex, a woman who should have had some feeling for Clara's desperate struggles, she was sorely disappointed. And to add to her frustration, there was no cross-examination of her. Perhaps Mr Sendall thought there was nothing to be gained by doing so. As for herself, Michelle would have loved to have been able to pick apart this woman's testimony, to have asked this Jane Rudd what exactly it was that qualified her to pass comment on whether or not Clara had sufficient milk to feed her baby. A small thought drifted into Michelle's mind. She wondered if perhaps Jane Rudd was childless, whether, like her, she had not been able to conceive, or had given birth only to have the longed-for child claimed by the indifferent hand of death. She thought perhaps this might have been so, and that the bitterness and resentment that Jane Rudd harboured for the absence of children of her own, children who would have been safe and protected within her care had she only been gifted with them, could not sit in silence or extend any compassion towards a woman who had murdered her own living child.

On these thoughts, the spectre of Jen danced into Michelle's mind. There was no real reason for it. Perhaps it was because Michelle was struck with just how easy it was for one woman to hurt another, when there was a complete absence of justification for it. Angie would have called it a breach of the 'girl code', Michelle thought. Jane Rudd had it within her power to give evidence that confirmed Clara's own, that she had no milk with which to feed her child, and it was the knowledge that he was starving that drove her to take him into the water. Not to murder him, but to end his suffering. Yet she chose to cast doubt on Clara's claim, knowing that this would serve to tighten the noose already sitting limp around her neck. And Jen, to sleep with a man she knew to be married, to choose to get pregnant, knowing full well how Michelle had battled to conceive. Jen must have known that her actions were only going to wound her. Yet she chose that path anyway, as though Michelle's pain was an irrelevance in Jen's world, an inconvenient bit of unpleasantness to be forgotten, provided that Jen got what she wanted.

Michelle teared up. She gave herself a shake. This was not the time to indulge in her own pain and sorrow. She was tired, she was emotional and the morning had required her to take a lot in, and she was desperately trying to avoid the knowledge that Nick was lost to her now. It was like being trapped in the murk of a deep swamp, slowly sinking into the belly of the monster, wishing there was something she could hold on to. But there was nothing. She moved back to the transcript, letting the black and white of the words lead her away from her own grim thoughts. It was the testimony of the final witness of Clara's trial:

> *Kate Harris. I am the nurse at the workhouse. The prisoner was there during her confinement and was delivered of a male child. I cannot remember on what day. It was a fortnight or so before she left. She wanted to go. As far as I saw, her treatment of the child was always kind. She called him Douglas.*

There was no cross-examination. But this time, any further questioning would have been to no purpose. The entire courtroom must have seen Clara's actions for what they were:

the desperate act of a vulnerable girl who clearly loved her son. But none of that mattered.

There were only two lines left. Michelle read them out aloud to Ned:

'Guilty. Aged sixteen. *Strongly recommended to mercy in consequence of her distressed state.* Death recorded.'

Michelle read the sentence again. Ned was looking at her as though he was waiting for an explanation, and Michelle had to confess that she had no idea what the words actually meant. Clara had been strongly recommended to mercy and yet it was noted that death was recorded.

Had Clara been executed? Or had some sort of clemency been extended towards her? There was nothing in the record of the trial to indicate that mercy had been granted. And if it had been, how could Michelle track down what had actually happened? There were a lot of questions that now flowed into Michelle's mind, as though water into a reservoir already close to capacity, and they demanded resolution. How she wished she was less tired, adding to the ever-growing list of reasons why spending the night with Nick had been a bad idea, but the thought of finding her way to the outcome of Clara's fate was energising.

Her mind started weighing up the possible avenues to explore. She could ask Toby to dig further into the archived records of the Old Bailey. She could also check newspaper archives. She wondered if the British Library had some digitised newspapers of the time available. Surely there would be a criminal section in *The Times* that would have noted all the executions taking place? The library was on her 'to visit' list anyway and it would be good to have a compelling reason to go there, otherwise she was pretty sure it would end up becoming one of those places, like Greenwich or the Tate, that you always mean to go to, but never actually get around to because, as Michelle told herself all too often, she actually lived in London now and she had plenty of time.

Ned simply watched Michelle as she made a few notes in her notepad, scribbling down her ideas as they occurred to her. She started making a list of bullet points, and without really thinking, reached towards the fruit bowl and grabbed a banana, which she peeled and then held with her left hand, to leave her right hand free to continue writing. Michelle had almost forgotten that Ned was there until she stood up to put her banana peel in the bin, wondering if she had time for another cup of tea before she went into the office. She was startled to realise he was still in the flat. Ned stood before her, waiting with infinite patience. He did not move. He made no noise. There was no warmth around him. There was nothing. And even if she felt wretched, exhausted and overwrought, everything about Michelle pulsed with life.

She put down her pen and considered the spirit that stood before her, the eerie stillness and vast emptiness that he enshrined within the shadow of the body that had once housed him.

'Ned, what's it like?'

'What do you mean?'

'I mean, what's it like? To be dead. Or, I suppose, not living. Stuck.' Michelle shook her head as she wondered why she was expressing herself so badly when she was usually so articulate. 'No, that is not what I mean. I mean, what does it feel like to have the existence that you have now?'

Ned looked at her as he considered his answer. 'I can't say really. I don't really think about it so much. This is the way that it is for me, I suppose, and as there's no getting round it, I just go on. And on.' He paused for a moment, considered. 'It was hard at first, that is, when I first started to think that I were dead. I don't know if I ever did rightly believe in a heaven or a hell, but I didn't expect it to be like this. I kept expecting something to happen, but nothing ever did. I tried to talk to people, but they didn't see me. They didn't hear me either. I thought there might be others like me, and I went looking for them, but there never were. Or if there were, I never saw them.'

Ned paused, but Michelle said nothing. She waited for him to continue. He took a noiseless breath in. It was still unnerving for Michelle to see his form go through the motions of life, yet the air around him stay utterly still. 'I stayed close to my body, because I didn't know what else to do. I didn't want no Burker taking me, so I had been paying into the club. I thought they would bury me close to my Nelly and that when they buried me with her, I would be with her. But after Nelly died, I didn't have anyone to care for me. No one to check that I were buried right. And the landlord of the rookery let the Burkers take my body. I watched as the butchers cut me open, just like they had my boy, took out all the parts of me they wanted, before they threw what was left of my body into a pit.'

So this explained his hatred of forensic scientists, Michelle thought. She tried to imagine what it must have been like to stand and watch your own body being sliced open and picked apart, as though a carcass set upon by ravenous vultures. She wondered if Ned had been able to feel the blade of the scalpel coursing along his skin, the bones of his ribcage being broken and separated like the Red Sea, so that the doctors could expose his heart. She immediately dampened her far too vivid imagination; the last thing she wanted was to slip inside his mind and find herself immersed in the bloodbath of a Victorian operating theatre.

Once more, she was struck by the innate justice in the symmetry aligning between his death and that of Douglas. Life had a way of restoring balance, she thought. Water had killed them both, Douglas by drowning, and Ned from the contaminated water that had infected him with cholera. Both had been subjected to the desecration of having their bodies ripped apart after death. Michelle wondered what they had done with Douglas's body after the autopsy. She guessed, that like his father, he was in a nameless grave somewhere, the transcript of Clara's murder trial being his only epitaph.

'I guess,' Ned said as he reined his anger in, 'I think about the things I used to feel, and the fact that there is nothing there anymore. My hand goes to scratch at my face, but I reach towards nothing but air. I can't even feel where my body used to be. I look down and I see hands. But I can't feel them. I look at the sun in the sky, and I feel no warmth. When it rains, I see the clouds, I see the water falling from them, but I don't feel the drops falling on me, or trickling down me as I walk through the streets, and I miss the feel of that. I miss feeling things. And people, I see people. People everywhere. And I can't talk to them or make them see me. And I hate them for it. I see people drinking in the pubs, watching them pour the drink down their throats as though they don't really taste it, and I get angry, because they can't see what a wonder it is to be able to taste, to feel. And I get angrier because they can't see the joy in being able to be with other people. I see people. But they never see me. I am nothing. I see buildings come down and buildings go up as if only seconds had passed, the city growing and changing in a way I never thought were possible. But then I remember Nelly, and the room that we shared and the feeling of holding her next to me in our small bed each night, and it feels as if it were so long ago that I can't even hold on to the memory no more.

'I have watched London change and grow. I have watched as all you folk have so much more than we could ever have dreamed were possible, yet everyone is still always rushing about, not seeing how good the world is now. And I watch as all you people walk through the streets, as I did once, and you see nothing. And it makes me angry even more. Especially now, when you are all busy staring at those things you walk around with in your hands.' Ned nodded in the direction of Michelle's phone. It was sitting on the kitchen counter, always within reach, and Michelle confessed quietly to herself that she often focused on the screen in front of her, rather than the fullness and vibrancy of the life that was happening all around her. She wondered how little she saw when she was busy looking in all the wrong places, her vision narrowed as though she was crawling backwards down a tunnel, ignoring the brightness of the light that would embrace you once you emerged.

'And all the while I am waiting and watching, I get angry because I don't want to be here anymore. I haven't wanted to be here for a long time. I'm lonely. Always alone. But I don't know how to go or where it is that I should go if I could. I didn't want to die. I wanted to live. Even without my Nelly. But I don't want to be like this either. I don't know why I'm still here when I'm no longer living.' His voice started to rise as he vented his frustration and his accusation turned on Michelle. 'And I keep waiting for you to tell me what it is that I need to do. But all you do is drag me back to my past. And I hate it. I am full of shame for what I have to see again as I show it to you. What I did to Clara. The death of the boy in the water. I were not a kind man.' He finished on a crescendo before his voice fell away almost to nothing and he whispered, shaking his head, 'I were not a kind man.'

Ned stepped away from her as he condemned himself, and Michelle understood the extent to which Ned was gripped by a crippling shame and guilt. No wonder he was unable to move on from his death. He was paralysed by his own remorse.

In silence, she tried to take in what Ned had just said. She was unable to contemplate his isolation, being trapped in a world that whirled and moved at a dizzying pace while he was entrenched in a pit of silence. She thought of how she had got herself through the nightmare of her fracturing marriage over the last few weeks, how she had withdrawn into herself to help her find some way to navigate through her pain. She had sought solitude. She had wanted to be alone. But part of finding her way through the hurt of Nick's betrayal rested in the knowledge that when she was ready all the people she had left waiting for her to fight her way through it would be there for her when she came out the other side. Angie would be there. Her mum would be there, even all her Sydney work colleagues would be there for her. And she knew that there was the possibility of new friendships. Michelle had so far declined all invitations to socialise from her new colleagues in the London office, but soon she would be ready to show them that there was more to her than the successful and ambitious associate that her reputation had labelled her as. Choosing to detach herself from her friends and family was one thing. But being forced into a solitary confinement that consisted of nothing more than being frozen in a moving wasteland, watching helplessly as the world whirled on without you, was another altogether.

The buzzing of Michelle's phone on the kitchen counter

interrupted her thoughts. She picked it up and glanced at the screen. Toby. She swiped to answer and then listened to an almost breathless commentary from him about a phone call he had just fielded from an irate client. As soon as he paused, Michelle gave him a few brief instructions, assured him that she was on her way into work and ended the call. She turned towards Ned.

'I have to go to work.'

He nodded but looked at her with a question in his eyes. 'You don't actually know how to help me, do you?' Defeat sat heavy in his voice.

Michelle sat down on her bar-stool again. As with her clients, it was always best to be honest, and never make a promise she was unable to fulfil. 'No,' she admitted, 'I haven't actually done this before. In the sense of actually trying to help a trapped soul move on. My grandmother could do it, and I remember watching her talk to ghosts at times when I was a little girl. It seemed to make her really happy... No, happy is the wrong word. It gave her joy.' Michelle paused, remembering Ivy. 'I've been able to see lost spirits like you for as long as I can remember, been able to talk to them, but I used to get scared, especially when I was little and it was harder for me to tell who was living and who was dead, and so I made myself stop seeing souls like you. It turns out if you try hard enough you can stop seeing anything.'

She paused for a moment as she took in the truth of her own words. She had not been in London for very long, but there were so many people who walked about with their eyes wide shut. She thought of those evenings when she walked past Westminster Cathedral, of the poor living souls who had to spend night after night in sleeping bags pressed up against the towering walls of the cathedral or the surrounding shops. Most of those who were lucky enough to have a home to go back to simply did not see the lonely misery of the homeless, with their eyes looking at everything but that as they walked past.

There were also the things Michelle did not see. She thought again of all the little clues that told her Nick was being unfaithful: the hair on the floor of her bathroom, the way her things were not quite where she had left them, her husband's out of character unavailability whenever she had been travelling for work. Looking back now, his infidelity was being signposted for her, but she had refused to acknowledge the reality of what was happening in her world. She hadn't wanted to see, just as she had not wanted to see Ned. True sight compelled action. You could not ignore what you chose to see. Which brought her back to Ned and what she was trying to do for him, even if she had not yet come to understand what it was she had to do to be able to assist him.

'So I don't know how to help you, and I am sorry for that. But Ned, I know that I can help you, even if I don't know how to yet. I do know that much. My grandmother, she was like me too, and she always said we could see people like you, ghosts, for a reason. But I was so busy trying to avoid the shadows that haunted me that I never took the time to think over why I could see what so many others cannot. But I do have faith that I can see you for a reason, and we are going to find the way for you to move on.'

Michelle had moved closer to him as she had been talking. If she could have taken his hands within hers and held them to give him even more reassurance she would have done so. But as ever, her impulse for a physical connection with him was thwarted by the reality of his ethereal existence. Ned drifted towards her, almost as if he wanted to breathe the scent of her in, as though he was moving in to kiss her. As she looked into his eyes, a warmth flooded her body, almost enough to convince her that he was physically present beside her.

He reached his hand towards her cheek. Michelle felt nothing but the merest suggestion of a whisper of the dying wind as his open palm brushed past her face. She closed her eyes but opened her heart. It was almost as if she could feel him touching her.

'Thank you,' he said. Michelle smiled gently at him as he faded in that briefest of moments between the opening and closing of her eyes as they blinked, and once more left her on her own in her flat.

A melee of thoughts still tumbled through her mind. Clara's fate was waiting to be discovered, but she also still had her obligations to her employer and her clients to fulfil. She was edging ever closer towards Ned's atonement, but once more he would have to wait, trapped in the stillness that had claimed him. Michelle still had to live her own life. She went into the bathroom, brushed through her hair and otherwise did her best to make sure she looked presentable, which wasn't the easiest task in the world given the canvas she had to work with. Despite her best efforts she still looked pale and tired, but it would have to do. She gathered her things together, ensuring that she threw the packet of Nurofen in her bag, and reminded herself to buy some Berocca from Boots on the way into the office. It had always been her standard go-to cure for a hangover back in Sydney, but with her prolonged sobriety as she tried to conceive, it had been so long since she had need of it that she had not thought to buy any since her arrival in London.

She threw on her coat and hat, stepped out of her flat, went down in the lift, and out into the mid-morning air of a cold December in London. And while the sky was overcast, pregnant with the promise of rain, at least it wasn't dark, as it usually was when she left for work in the morning. After daylight savings came to an end, and the clocks were turned back an hour, Michelle had been shocked by how late the sun was to make its first appearance, and how early the sky dimmed and darkened in the afternoon. Having come from the beauty and sunshine of a Sydney spring, Michelle had been struggling with the fact it was always dark during her commute each day, and the only time she ever saw the light of day was when she was on her way to a meeting or to court, or was able to pop out for lunch rather than relying on the office canteen. It was as though she lived as a vampire, only coming out in the dark. But the darkness that greeted her each time she left her flat or the office had only played to the sombre mood that had plagued her since she had received Jen's email.

She walked to the Cardinal Place entrance of Victoria station, tapped in, and took a seat on the Underground, a treat given that at the time when she usually travelled into work seats were a rare luxury. She was unable to escape from thoughts of Ned's existence, of what it must be like to sit in a world as though trapped behind film, unable to experience all the tactile delights that life had to offer. And as the train slid through the tunnels that wound their way like entrails through the belly of the city, she thought about the life she did not experience because she had chosen to blind herself to the beauty of her gift. Because she was learning that it was beautiful. It was a miracle, really. She had the ability to see so much more than what she limited herself to. And it took such effort to constrain herself, to hold a part of herself prisoner so that she did not become captive to the random possibilities that her gift could throw in her path. But perhaps random possibilities were what she needed? Wildflowers often had greater beauty than a carefully tended garden. She was beginning to appreciate that in releasing her ability to allow her to communicate with Ned, it had been almost as if she was allowing her own soul its freedom to soar. If Ivy had still been around, Michelle would probably have had to concede to her grandmother that when it came to their gift, she may have had a point. Warmth flooded Michelle's heart at the thought of how Ivy would have been so proud of her for making this discovery for herself.

When the train pulled into Blackfriars, she shook herself out of her reverie and made her way into the office, stopping only to pick up a latte in Pret in her reusable coffee mug. Toby was at the office waiting for her, files stacked up on his desk in anticipation.

He opened his mouth as if he was about to start speaking.

'Wait,' Michelle said, before she collapsed into her chair. She was not ready for the full force of Toby's enthusiasm just yet. She pushed her hair back behind her ears and brought the coffee close to her face, breathing in the nutty scent of it, before she took a sip. She savoured the familiar warmth and taste of it on her tongue, closing her eyes only for a moment to collect her thoughts, to take her mind away from Ned, Clara, Ivy and the challenges of her gift and on to the more practical realities of her clients and their parenting tug-of-wars.

She had once watched an old episode of *Ally McBeal* where Ally had stressed the importance of really being in the moment as you took your first sip of coffee of the day. Michelle had loved that TV show and had seen every episode. It had been one of the reasons she had wanted to become a lawyer, even if being a lawyer in real life was nothing like what she had seen on the screen. But for some reason that one episode with the coffee had been one that had stayed with her. It was something about the potent sensuality of Ally's response to what was really no more than the everyday mundane, just a small mouthful of coffee. But somehow, after hearing Ned describe what it was like to be trapped in his non-life, it seemed more important to her that she enjoy this first coffee right now, even if, in this case, it really wasn't her first coffee of the day given all of the early morning drama she had already had to contend with. She swallowed that divine mouthful and released her breath, allowing the tension she had balled up inside of her its freedom, before turning her attention back to Toby.

Before she could begin to speak, Toby, having seen that Michelle's attention had landed back on him, launched in. 'So, you were up all night too?' he asked, rather too brightly in Michelle's opinion.

'What?' Her immediate concern was, that despite her best efforts, she must look bloody awful if Toby could so easily assume that she had been up most of the night.

But her second and more panicked thought was that there was already gossip drifting around the office that Michelle had spent the night with the husband she had come to Britain to get away from. She had not made any friends at the London office yet. Unless you counted Toby, which, she had to concede, she probably could not. She had not been ready to face the inevitable questioning that would come if she tried to get to know some of her colleagues. She could imagine the conversation: 'So what are you doing in London?' An innocent question she had no wish to field. While she was still consumed by grief for her dying marriage, it was easier to drown herself in her work, and keep her colleagues at a distance. And yet it seemed, even with the protection of her isolation, she had still become a target for gossip.

Michelle glared at Toby, trying to figure out if he knew how she had spent last night, whether he knew that her husband had flown over from Sydney to see her. Nick had managed to get her address somehow, and she was pretty sure someone from the office must have given it to him. They had different surnames. Michelle had been determined to keep her own name when she married, long before she had even met Nick, so she supposed it was unfair to expect that people would know Nick was the husband she was trying to evade, or that her colleagues in

London were even aware that Michelle had a husband. Who was she kidding? She guessed everyone already knew and were keeping a tactful silence on the subject.

Toby looked flustered as he absorbed Michelle's hostility, and started to redden. 'I thought you might have been up all night too. The cricket. It was on overnight. It's just that you look a bit tired, so I thought you might have been up watching the cricket. Like me.'

'The cricket?' Michelle said, looking at Toby as if she had taken a wrong step on the dance floor and had no idea where they were up to. At the same time, as she tried to figure out what the hell Toby was talking about, she did have the comfort of a small measure of relief as she realised that she had managed to keep some of her private life precisely that.

Toby continued on. In some ways it was like watching him trying to cross a minefield while he blew himself up with each step that he took, coming back singed but otherwise unharmed, like Wile E Coyote from the *Road Runner* cartoons. And yet he pressed onwards. 'The Ashes. England is playing Australia. England finally put on a decent show, so it was worth staying up all night for.'

'Toby.' Michelle gave him her best withering stare. 'What are you wittering on about? Cricket? What makes you think I care about the cricket?'

As Toby looked at her, Michelle saw worry flit across his face and she was guessing that he wished he had never started this conversation about the bloody cricket. Nick had liked to watch it, but when he had it on Michelle had never been interested in watching anything other than the idiotic English fans in the stadium who dressed in the most ridiculous costumes, especially in the baking heat of the Australian sunshine. She could not understand how a group of men could play a boring game for five days and still not get a decisive result.

'Sorry,' Toby said. 'It's just that you're an Australian so I just assumed that you'd be supporting them. Australia's already won two of the games in the series. Of course,' he continued, demonstrating once again that he still needed to learn when to stop talking, 'everyone knows that Australians in general, and the Australian cricket team in particular, are nothing but cheats and convicts.'

Michelle wondered if Toby was aiming for a diploma in back-pedalling as he realised he had somehow managed to malign his boss. He was certainly demonstrating the various shades of red he could colour his face with, as he no doubt replayed in his head what he had just said to Michelle. An Australian.

'Wait,' he began, 'I didn't mean you, of course–'

'Toby,' Michelle interrupted before he had a chance to continue digging that gigantic hole of his own making he had just belly-flopped into, 'I am going to do you the favour of ignoring what you have just implied about the integrity and honesty of my country and my fellow Australians. Cheats and convicts, I think you said? Let's just leave that parked, shall we? But, as for you making any sort of assumption about how I spend my time outside of the office, I think it's best if you don't go there at all. I'm pretty sure you and I have already discussed the danger of making assumptions in our professional capacities, but when it comes to making assumptions in relation to my personal life...' Michelle trailed off as a thought struck her with all the force of a meteor. She gasped and took a breath in, wondering why it had not occurred to her earlier. It was so bloody obvious she wondered why she hadn't seen it. Of course, she thought, of course.

'Toby, you're a bloody genius,' Michelle said, grinning at him like some sort of lunatic. She ignored Toby's look of bewilderment as she fired up her PC, grateful that he finally had enough sense to stop talking.

As she waited for the login screen to load up, she scanned through the files Toby had placed on her desk. She was able to quickly identify what she actually needed to deal with, compared to what Toby thought she needed to deal with, and then launched into a lecture on the importance of not letting the client's anxiety or irritation persuade you that a matter needed urgent attention when quite clearly it was not necessary. She warbled on about cost effectiveness and efficiency, which had to be balanced against the importance of client care. Toby nodded frequently but said little; clearly deciding that given the changeable mood Michelle was in, it was best to stay silent. She then made a call to the client who had been the cause of Toby's call to Michelle earlier that morning and put his mind at rest. It was easy enough to do. All she had to do was repeat everything she had told him last time she had spoken to him, and remind him that they had to wait until the court had set a date for the hearing of his application, and there was nothing they could do until then. And to once more tell him that the court system in England was notoriously slow but she would do everything she could to try and accelerate the process. She had put the client on loudspeaker so Toby could hear how she handled the call, and then used it as an opportunity to remind her trainee that part of what they did as lawyers was to reassure their clients. In fact, especially when it came to family law disputes, this is what she did a lot of the time. In this instance, Michelle's client hadn't actually needed her to do anything. All he had needed was to know that Michelle was on his side and was doing everything she could for him.

And once she had done that, and had set Toby some work that would keep him busy until at least lunchtime, she sat back in her chair and smiled.

She had it. Thanks to the oblivious Toby she knew exactly where she would find the answer to the mystery of what had happened to Clara. She was only irritated that it had taken Toby to point out what should have been obvious to her.

She opened up Google and typed: *convict transportations to Australia.*

It proved surprisingly easy. After only ten minutes of navigating from one link to the next, her excitement mounting as though she was a joyful child skipping along stepping stones, she had before her a complete record of what had happened to Clara. On 18 July 1839, the convict transportation ship, the *Mary Anne III*, departed from Woolwich bound for Van Diemen's Land. It carried 142 female convicts. One of those was Clara Waters.

The ship arrived on 10 November of the same year. Michelle tried to imagine how Clara must have felt as the ship sailed into the calm waters of the bay of the colony of Van Diemen's Land after nearly four months of being at sea. She remembered from history lessons at school that the female convicts were generally treated better than the male ones, and were given some freedom to walk the deck during the day. But it must have been a frightening crossing for her, being largely confined to the underbelly of the ship as it was tossed about on the open seas on what must have seemed an interminable voyage, across such a vast expanse of water, especially when London had constituted the whole of Clara's world until her transfer to Woolwich for her embarkation on board the *Mary Anne III*.

And as for Clara's first view of Hobart, it would have been so different from the grey and dirty bleakness of what she had left behind in London. Tasmania was known for its towering trees and the beauty of its rugged landscape. What must Clara have thought? Michelle had never been to Tasmania. It had been on her 'to visit' list for the longest time; but somehow, typical of her, she had never got around to going. And now here she was about as far away from Tasmania as she could possibly be. As she traced Clara's journey in her mind, she imagined that it looked a little like the Blue Mountains, with a rich carpet of green vegetation interspersed with the dusty amber redness of the clay earth. There would have been lots of trees, and king amongst them, the silvery green of the leaves of the eucalyptus trees reaching towards the sun, their branches shivering in the warmth of the breeze, fluttering a welcome as they stepped from the cloying smells of the damp mildew of the ship and into the sweetness of the warm, clean air of her new home. She imagined Clara's wonder as she looked up at the night skies for the first time on dry land, the ground moving underneath her feet as though she was still at sea, the cloudless sky unveiling the wonder of the Southern Cross and its companion constellations that did not grace the skies of the north from where she had travelled.

After she had traced Clara's transportation from England, Michelle then found that each of the convicts on the *Mary Anne III* had a digital record of their official existence in the colony of Van Diemen's Land. Her finger hovered over the hyperlink of Clara's name and she took a breath in. Anticipation was prickling over her skin. Clicking on the link, her eyes glassed over with tears as she read the entry pertaining to Clara.

In 1848, the year that Ned had died, Clara had applied for

permission to marry. She had lived. She had not been executed but had been granted the mercy the judge had recommended and sent from certain misery and death in England to a second chance at a new and better life in Australia. Hope for Clara seeded in Michelle's heart, while at the same time it was flooded with compassion for Ned and his mistaken belief that Clara had been killed because he had walked into her life, and then walked away, leaving her to deal with the consequences of their night together on her own. Ned had died thinking himself responsible for the death of Clara, and now Michelle had discovered that Clara had in fact lived. Surely this knowledge was the key to setting Ned free, releasing his spirit from the purgatory of his existence in that bleak and barren plain between life and death? Michelle was certain that Ned's penance was complete.

She couldn't wait to tell him. The thought of calling out to him, bringing his spectral form to her so she could share with him what she had discovered lightened her soul. It filled her with a happiness that had eluded her for months. And with this joy building inside her, Michelle was almost startled by the realisation that her unhappiness had been part of her for a long time. In fact, as she stared into the reflection of her memories, she had to confess that a knot of unhappiness had been tied into her soul for far longer than the revelation of her husband's infidelity, or her struggles with her infertility. It was almost as if keeping her gift bound and hidden left her unable to open her heart to the full potential of joy that was available in the world for her to experience.

She looked at her life with Nick and could finally admit her happiness had not been complete and in telling herself that she had been fully content, she was nothing but a conspirator in her own deception. She had wanted to believe in her life with him. She had wanted to hold on to her marriage. She had wanted to have a child with him, and have the family that she had always craved, growing up with a distant father who she never saw, and a mother who envied Michelle for her gift that Michelle herself did not want. Michelle had been desperate for the normality of family existence. And she had loved Nick. She loved him still, but with his infidelity he had broken her trust and stripped away everything meaningful that had held them together. And now she could confess to herself that this made it easier for her to walk away. It was probably for the best. She had never let Nick see the true her. She had never told him that she could see ghosts.

Michelle took a deep breath as she thought over what she had to say to Nick later that evening. It was not going to be an easy conversation, and despite the fact he had wounded her with his affair with Jen, she did not wish to hurt him, or cause him any pain. Angie would probably have told her he deserved to get a little pain back, but this was not Michelle's way. Holding on to her anger and releasing it through scorn and hate would not help her move forward. But it was pointless dwelling on all this while she still had work to get through. There would be time enough to think about Nick, her soon-to-be ex-husband, when she met him for dinner, when she would have to send him back on his way to Australia without any hope of reconciliation between them. It was over. She only hoped it would be as easy to say to Nick when she was with him, as it was to say it in her mind in the quiet calmness of her solitude.

Michelle turned to her in-tray and started working her way through the contents with a vengeance. All thoughts of fatigue had vanished. She was energised by the sense of purpose that consumed her. She had built an agenda for the entire day in her mind, and while she did have to deal with Nick, which she was not looking forward to, it would culminate in reaching out to Ned and calling him to her flat, to Emery Hill Street near where she had first encountered him, and telling him what she knew of Clara and her fate.

Given that she had got into work so late, she decided to skip lunch, and pressed ahead with her work. Her buoyant mood seemed to lift Toby as well, and she ensured she took the time to go over some of his draft letters with him, highlighting where he had handled an aspect particularly well, as well as pointing out where he could improve the drafting. Taking a precedent and working with it was a skill that could be taught, and she wanted to give Toby the tools he needed to ensure he got better at it.

By 6pm, Michelle was filling out and checking her timesheet for the day and was encouraging Toby to do the same. She had no time for people who left them undone for weeks on end. It was sloppy; unfair on the client, and not a work practice that Michelle wanted Toby to fall into.

When that was done, Michelle looked up at Toby. 'Go home,' she said. 'Enjoy the cricket.' Toby grinned back at her.

As Toby packed up his things for the evening, and returned his desk to order so he did not have to face chaos first thing the next morning, another one of her habits that she had tried to encourage Toby to adopt, Michelle got her own things together. She went to the bathroom to check her reflection. She didn't look anywhere near as bad as she expected to, given her lack of sleep, but she touched up her mascara and lipstick, and ran a brush through her hair, appreciating the way in which the natural waves of it framed her face.

She tried to tell herself that it didn't really matter what she looked like, given what she wanted to say to Nick, but she also told herself this would probably be the last time she would see him, and she wanted to be looking nothing less than fabulous for his last memory of her. 'No,' she said out loud to the determined woman staring back at her from the mirror. 'Not probably.

Definitely. This will definitely be the last time you will see your husband.'

Nodding as she mentally strapped on her armour to face him, she told herself that if she ever did see him again after tonight, it would only be as a work colleague, not as her husband. And, ready for battle, she walked out of the bathroom, took the lift down to the ground floor and left the office. She headed towards Blackfriars to get the Tube.

The darkness of the night sky surrounded her as she walked up the street towards the Underground, as the year drifted ever closer to the winter solstice. But the darkness did not dampen her mood, and she tapped in and walked through the gates of the station as if she was stepping on to the shores of a new land. Almost as if she was Clara, freed from the ship that had carried her across the vast expanse of the oceans, and feeling the warmth of the southern sun embracing her, kissing her skin, as she stepped off the boat that had transported her, and strode forward into her new life.

CHAPTER TWENTY-ONE

Michelle emerged from the Underground at Victoria and headed towards Wilton Road. It had been warm on the Tube, but she pulled her coat around her as she greeted the cold, damp air of the evening. Her phone told her the temperature had not risen above five degrees all day. She wondered how Nick had coped, especially given his haphazard packing. But actually, she really didn't care. With Christmas fast approaching, the London streets were buzzing with people, some of them heading in the opposite direction to Michelle, towards Victoria station to take them home or to some other part of this great city, some off for after-work drinks, or decked in bright Christmas jumpers and illuminated antler headbands going to office Christmas celebrations. Some were anticipating a night at the theatre with both *Wicked* and *Hamilton* playing close by. The restaurants were already filling up.

Festive joy and the fact that it was Thursday and almost the weekend emanated from the people around her, generating an energy which infused Michelle with even more purpose as she made her way along Wilton Road towards Uno where she would be meeting Nick.

As she walked down the busy street, passing the pubs full of cheery drinkers, off-key carol singers and the smell of mulled wine, she went past the salon where Nathan had cut off her hair, and she was pleased to see him inside, armed with a brush and hairdryer, working away at the woman sitting in front of him. The whole salon was decked with Christmas lights and garlands. It looked very inviting. Nathan's client, her hair already sleek and glossy, looked as though she was in high spirits, with a glass of something bubbly in her hand. Nathan was weaving his magic before she no doubt went to some Christmas party. Remembering that she needed to make an appointment with Nathan for her own office party, she popped inside and spoke to the receptionist, managing to get a booking even though she hadn't given them much notice. The party was being held at the Savoy ballroom and was a black tie do with the theme of 'Elegance from a Bygone Age', and she really wanted to look the part. The Savoy conjured up such wonderful images of opulence and sophistication, and she had bought herself a 1920s vintage dress in a stunning shade of red. The thought of slipping the dress on and setting out for the night was a welcome distraction from her rendezvous for that evening. She caught Nathan's eye as she left the salon and waved to him. He smiled at her and waved back, the familiar geometric black shapes of his tattoos looking somewhat incongruent next to the red and green of his Christmas T-shirt. It had a reindeer on it, and as Nathan started dancing around, its nose flashed red. In spite of the fact that she was about to face Nick again, Michelle laughed.

As Michelle grew closer to Warwick Way, she could see the gas fires outside Uno were already alight, the flames dancing in the distance, and she welcomed the thought of the warmth that accompanied them. Hopefully the restaurant served mulled wine, because she fancied a warming glass of it. As she approached, she could see Nick was sitting inside at a window table, a bottle of wine already ordered and decanted. There was a small amount of red wine in his glass, and she guessed that he had tasted it, then waited for her arrival. He had also ordered bread and olives, both of which were sitting untouched, also waiting for her. Nick hated olives. Michelle should have been pleased that he had ordered them for her, but it was hard to be grateful for the small things, when the bigger picture was so monumentally fucked up.

Michelle handed the waiter her coat as she entered. She went to join Nick. He jumped up as she approached the table, and held her chair out for her, a level of courtesy she had not seen from him since they had first started dating.

Nick waved the waiter away and poured the wine himself, filling Michelle's glass first. His hand reached across the table towards hers, as if he wanted to take hold of it. She picked up her napkin and placed it on her lap, moving both hands under the table at the same time, a barrier between them, like those that existed in prison visiting areas, the clear Perspex window preventing any suggestion of physical connection.

'You're still wearing your rings,' Nick said, as Michelle twisted them round her finger under the table.

'Yes,' she said, 'I keep meaning to take them off.'

Nick sighed and asked how her day had been.

'Tiring,' she replied, wondering how on earth she could possibly even begin to explain her day to Nick. It would mean talking him through Ned, her ability to communicate with people like him, and everything she had discovered about a transported convict who had lived and died close to two centuries ago. She wondered if he would ever believe her if she were to tell him. As she thought this, she realised she didn't actually want to talk to Nick about any of that. And it occurred to her that she had already started to let him go. So instead, she stayed with subjects he would understand, and briefly talked about the legal issues she had dealt with that day and about what the office in London was like compared to the one in Sydney.

And then Michelle asked Nick what he had been doing, and if he had managed to get out of the hotel to see any of London. It seemed he had not, choosing to spend most of the day watching the highlights of the cricket and sleeping to help him get over both his jet lag and the lack of sleep he had suffered after his night with Michelle. Indeed, he did seem to be fully rested and full of energy while she was battling her fatigue. It seemed to have come back to embrace and subdue her the moment she walked into the restaurant and set eyes on Nick. A wave of negativity had fallen on her, and like a swimmer battling to free herself from a rip tide, the very thought of having to deal with him sapped her of all her strength.

They discussed what they were going to order, and Nick talked about the Italian restaurant in Neutral Bay they had once loved to visit. Her sadness intensified as it dawned on her that she would never go there with Nick again. She knew it was going to hurt her to have to say goodbye to him once the evening had come to a close, but she was already feeling utterly bereft from his absence even though he was still sitting across the table from her. It didn't matter what they had once meant to each other, or how close they had once been. What he had done had put a bigger distance between them than even the combined volume of the waters of the Indian and Atlantic oceans.

Nick moved on to talk about the gourmet pizza place where he had taken her on their first date. She could see he was trying to evoke their happy, shared memories, and by this tactic hoped to impress upon her what they stood to lose if they were to part. But it didn't really matter what they talked about as they sat there filling in the time between when the waiter came to take their orders and the arrival of their first course. It was as if, by silent accord between them, whatever they said at that point was only small talk, as they avoided getting to the heart of the issue that had brought them together that evening. It was all obfuscation and delay. Neither one of them wanted to say goodbye to the other. But Michelle knew she had to give voice to the imperative that had brought her to confront her husband that night.

Their starters arrived. Michelle took a mouthful, chewed and swallowed, not really tasting the food. 'Nick, you do know you have to go back to Sydney?' she said, placing her fork down.

'I know,' he replied, 'but I don't want to go. Not without you.'

She wished she wasn't having this conversation. She wished he had never come to London. But most of all, she wished there had never been a Jen in Nick's life.

'I'm not going with you, Nick. I'm not going anywhere with you ever again. You know that. You had an affair. You broke my trust and you broke my heart, and every time I think of you and Jen together...' Michelle trailed off, shaking her head, as her emotions threatened to take control of her. She took a breath in. Having banished the threat of tears, she said, 'I can't come back to you. I can't even bear the thought of being in the same country as you. Go back to Sydney. There is nothing for you here.'

She had said the words she needed to say, and the echo of them sat there between them, silencing them both. She picked up her fork and started eating again, but although she had not had lunch, nor a proper breakfast to speak of, she was not hungry. Food could never fill the void that now sat in the core of her.

'Is there nothing I can do?' Nick asked after the silence had seemed to swallow them both.

'No,' she said softly, looking at him with gentle kindness as she delivered the fatal cut that would sever the tie between them. 'Go home. Go back to Sydney. Go back to Jen. Go back to your baby.'

She didn't want him to see how close to tears he had brought her, so she turned her eyes towards the window, and let them settle on the gas-fired heaters flaming outside. She watched the rush of fiery heat travel upwards towards the heavens. As her vision blurred and the hazy orange-red of the flames kaleidoscoped across her vision, the shadowy image of Ned shimmered in and out of focus behind it. He was holding his blue cloth cap in his hands, wringing it with his impatience. Michelle sensed him calling her.

'Nick,' Michelle said, placing her fork on her plate and abandoning her starter, 'there is nothing more that we need to say to each other. I'll send you details of my solicitor and we can let the lawyers take it from there.' She pushed back her chair and stood up abruptly. 'I have to go,' she said.

She did not wait to say goodbye. She did not wait for him to say anything at all. She picked up her bag and she walked to the door of the restaurant. The waiter, who had been listening to their conversation with rapt and dedicated inattention, hurried to retrieve her coat for her, not waiting for her to hand over the coat ticket. Michelle took it and walked out of the door.

'Michelle!' she heard Nick call as she started the walk towards Vauxhall Bridge Road to get back to her flat. 'Michelle, wait.'

She did not stop. She kept walking but turned her head to catch one last glance of him. The last thing she saw was Nick standing up from the table, knocking over the decanter that was still full of wine, and the glass shattering all over the floor, the red wine pooling like blood over diamonds.

CHAPTER TWENTY-TWO

Michelle reached her flat and walked through the door, feeling like a prisoner released from death row. She hung up her coat and carried her bag into the kitchen, then poured herself a cup of red wine, musing that she really must order some new wine glasses. Who knows when the rest of her stuff would get to London. As she took a sip, she thought about the wine that had been spilled all over the floor at Uno. She rather regretted the waste of it. But she thought it a fitting epitaph for the end of her marriage, and the end of her life with Nick. There was nothing left to do except mop up the waste and open another bottle.

'Cheers,' Michelle said, lifting the cup up to herself, taking a sip and savouring the rich, deep taste of it. Closing her eyes, she reached out and thought of Ned, of that shadowy figure fading in and out of her life. 'Okay, Ned,' she said, 'where are you?'

When she opened her eyes, Ned was in the flat standing before her. He was waiting. Always waiting.

'You know, don't you?' he asked.

'Yes,' she replied, smiling, and deciding there was no point trying to create some sort of dramatic tension she launched straight in. 'Clara's trial was in 1838. You know that already, because you were there. But you never saw what happened at the end. Clara was found guilty.'

'I already knew that,' Ned said. 'And the judge sentenced her to death.'

'Wait. She was found guilty. And the judge did sentence her to death. But he also recommended that Clara be shown mercy. And she was shown mercy. Clara did not hang.'

'What?'

Disbelief coloured his face. Shock, even.

'She didn't die. Her sentence was commuted. She was transported to Australia about eleven months after her trial. I don't why it took so long, and I don't know where she was held while she waited for transportation, and I'm pretty certain she would have had a fairly unpleasant time of it in prison while she waited, but she lived, Ned. Clara lived.'

Ned stood as though frozen. But Michelle could see that his mind was furiously trying to make sense of what she had just told him. She waited for him to process the information. As she waited, she noticed that her flat seemed suddenly lighter, as though someone had turned the dimmer switch up. Something about Ned brightened too, as though he had swallowed a handful of stars, and the light of the heavens filtered through his skin.

'She were a Transport?'

'Yes,' Michelle replied.

'Where did they send her?' he asked.

'Australia, Van Diemen's Land, as it was known in your time, although we call it Tasmania now. It's an island off the south-east coast of Australia. It's a beautiful country. Australia, it's where I'm from.'

She wondered what he was thinking as he searched his past,

his thoughts turned inwards to his memories, all of them based on false assumption.

'Did she make it?' he asked. 'Did she make it to this Van Diemen's Land?'

Michelle nodded. She wished she could take his hands and assure him with more than just her words. 'Yes, I've seen the records. She landed in Australia towards the end of 1839. She made it to Van Diemen's Land. The records don't actually tell you a lot about what happened after her arrival, but I know from my history lessons at school that she would most likely have been sent to a female factory, which is where they processed all the female arrivals into the colony, and then she would probably have been given a job in service, especially since she had experience in domestic work. There were good opportunities for young women who had just arrived. Most of them went on to marry.'

'Do you know if Clara... if she were wed?' he asked. Michelle suspected that there was a part of Ned that did not want to hear her answer. But she gave it anyway.

She nodded again, her eyes filling with warmth, grateful that Clara had found at least a chance to put the horror of her past behind her. 'She applied for permission to marry in 1848. All convicts who had not reached the end of their sentence required permission to marry. And it was nearly always granted, especially for women. So I'm pretty certain that Clara would have married shortly after she applied. I'm sorry, Ned, but I don't have any of the details. I don't know who she married, or when. I suppose I could try to find out but I would have to find some way of searching through the historical archives back in Australia and it would take a bit of time, and I–' Michelle broke off as she saw Ned shaking his head.

'It don't matter,' he said. 'None of that matters. All that

matters is that she lived. That she didn't hang. She lived?' he asked again.

'Yes.'

'I didn't kill her?'

'You did not kill her.'

Ned staggered backwards and seemed to collapse into himself, as if the knowledge of Clara's fate had freed something captive within his soul. When he looked up at Michelle, tears ran down his face.

'I killed my boy,' he said. 'And I thought I had killed her. And I thought that was why my Nelly and our bairn were taken from me. Because I didn't deserve them after what I'd done to Clara.'

'It doesn't work like that, Ned,' Michelle said, wondering why she was saying something that she did not know, but feeling the truth of her words as they embraced him. 'Nelly didn't die because of what happened between you and Clara. She died like lots of women did in your time. She died in childbirth. If she had been giving birth today, Nelly would have lived. What happened to Nelly had nothing to do with you.'

'I blamed myself for all of it,' Ned told her. 'For all the time I lived after poor Nelly had died, I blamed myself. For Nelly and our little one dying, for Clara being hung, and for the drowning of Clara's baby. My boy. Douglas. I blamed myself for it all.'

It had not just been those mortal years that Ned had lived where he carried his guilt with him as though it had been sewn into the fabric of his flesh. In death he had imported it with him, carried it across the threshold, and it weighed him down as though he had been chained to a boulder.

And as Ned talked, took in the truth of Michelle's words as if they were a serum, he seemed to lighten even more, and Michelle saw the pale-blue mist forming around him, shimmering like beams from the sun across the still waters of the harbour, obliterating the shadows of guilt that had haunted his soul.

'I wish I could have telt her that I were sorry,' Ned said. Michelle knew that he was talking about Clara; not Nelly.

'I think she knew,' Michelle said, again wondering where her words were coming from. Yet her words were once more clothed in truth. It was almost as if she was giving voice to Clara herself, her forgiveness stretching across the oceans, through the years, reaching out to him, undoing the links in the chain of his guilt.

Ned's eyes were still brimming with silent tears, conduits for releasing his self-loathing and blame that he had held pent up inside of him, inside his heart, as though it had been wrapped in the barbed wire of his remorse. The pale-blue aura intensified around him, deepening in colour as though shrouding him in a meteor shower of sapphires. Michelle could feel the warmth of it caressing her skin. She remembered Ivy. She remembered her joy.

Ned's eyes lifted towards the light as the endless expanse of shimmering blue opened up to him, and then he looked at Michelle as though he didn't know what to do.

Her gaze was drawn to where the ceiling of her flat should have been, but saw only that celestial great vastness of vivid, crystal light shining down upon them. It seemed to her a miracle that she should see it. It was breathtaking, unreachable, like sailing in the sunset towards that point where the ocean met the sky. She breathed in the serenity it offered. She let the joy of it unfold over her. Joy. Pure joy.

'It's okay,' Michelle whispered to Ned. 'You can go.'

Ned seemed almost afraid to move towards it, as if he still could not believe it was time for him to move towards the promise inherent in the shattering splendour that had opened up before him.

Silenced by the unearthly beauty that surrounded her, Michelle nodded at Ned. He looked as if he were going to dive into the fathomless depths of the opalescent blue that was still unlocked before them, but he came towards Michelle instead. He reached his hand towards her, and Michelle lifted her face as if she could meet his hand, and opened herself to his touch, feeling his thumb trace across her cheek as though it were the tiniest feather from a hummingbird.

'There is something coming to you,' he said. 'Something from across the sea. There is something from Ivy.' Ned paused. 'Who's Ivy?' he asked.

'My grandmother,' Michelle whispered.

'There is something of hers that you must see,' he said, with a certainty that Michelle thought he did not understand, and then he looked into the distance of the shining blue, as if he was seeing something that Michelle was unable to focus on, because her mortal eyes could not accommodate the light. Ned, his deep-brown eyes bright with joy and hope, turned to look at her and recited, as though saying his prayers:

'Creeping where grim death has been,

'A rare old plant is the Ivy green.'

Michelle's heart lurched with the familiar singsong call of it. It was something Ivy used to say to her, in a calming voice, as though she was singing a lullaby, on those evenings when she had looked after her when she was a little girl, as she was tucking her into bed. Michelle remembered her grandma telling her that her own mother, Michelle's great-grandmother, had named Ivy for this poem because she too had shared the gift that had been bestowed on the women of her family. She could almost feel Grandma Ivy standing beside her, as if her spirit danced in the shining blue light that surrounded her. She remembered the warmth of her voice, the comfort of her words, and how she had been the only one who could calm the terrified fears of a little girl who could see the dead.

Ned shook his head and looked confused. But he repeated, 'There is something of hers that you must see.' Michelle nodded her understanding, although she had no idea if there was anything of Ivy's that she had not already seen. Michelle and her mother had been through all of Ivy's things after her death, and had set aside anything that might have been of importance to them.

The light called to him. Michelle could hear the faint strains of a multitude of voices, in harmony, but Ned was still waiting for her. There was nothing more to be said. Michelle was overwhelmed by both joy and sorrow. It was almost harder for her to say goodbye to Ned than it had been to say goodbye to Nick. Her eyes pointed Ned towards the golden heart of the light that bathed them both, and he turned towards it. He turned back once more and nodded at her. He said nothing, but as he drifted into the depths of the light, Michelle was flooded with his gratitude. It soaked into her soul and her whole body responded as she was infused with his joy. She smiled at him, and silently willed him forward. Ned turned his back on her and leapt into the very heart of the light, and disappeared into its fathomless brightness.

It was as though he had stepped through a trapdoor. Ned vanished and her flat was plunged back into the darkness of the electric light, and she was once more left in solitude.

Her skin tingled as she looked at the empty space where Ned had been standing. He was gone. She would never see him again.

'Goodbye, Ned,' Michelle whispered into the eerie silence. 'I will miss you.'

CHAPTER TWENTY-THREE

Michelle's alarm sounded at 6am. She was still tired after the marathon that the day before had turned out to be, but she wanted to get into work early as she would be leaving earlier than normal. It was the day of the office Christmas party and her appointment with Nathan was for that afternoon. Michelle reached for her phone to turn off the alarm. She saw there was a message from Nick. As she read it, she was filled with a curious concoction of both sadness and relief:

> Mich, by the time you get this I'll be on my way
> to Heathrow. There is no point in staying in
> London any longer. I know I have said it
> already, but I probably can never say it enough.
> I'm sorry for hurting you. I hope London is
> good to you. You deserve to be happy. I love
> you. Nick x

Her finger hovered over the screen as she considered her reply, then she placed her phone back on the side table and got out of bed. She had nothing to say to him. That part of her life was over.

Michelle got ready and went into work. There was an

undercurrent of excitement in the office, with people already looking forward to the party. She found the energy contagious, as if there was a collective hum that she could not help but be a part of. She couldn't wait for the party. Toby was already in the office when she arrived and was his usual exuberant self, although Michelle noticed with a small degree of amusement that he let her have her first sip of coffee in peace before he launched into conversation. As a steady stream of words poured from his mouth Michelle noticed that her trainee, rather sensibly, made no further reference to the cricket that was still going on back in Australia. He was a fast learner.

She felt strangely at a loose end. On the surface nothing had really changed, she was still, as she had been the day before, a single professional woman living in London. She thought of the loss of both Nick and Ned as though it had been a type of double amputation, cutting off the parasitic twins that feasted on her heart. It had been right to let them go, and she had no regrets over sending them both on their way on a path that she could not take with either of them. But she found herself thinking of them both.

She was therefore grateful when she opened up her emails and realised she was in for quite a busy day. She usually was this time of year. It didn't matter what had been previously arranged between parents after carefully negotiated agreements or hard fought for court orders, you could almost guarantee that as soon as the holiday season rolled around there would be arguments between them about where their children should be spending Christmas, whose turn it was to make sure the children were with the appropriate parent at the right time, or who was to be responsible for looking after the family dog. And within about five minutes of whatever the issue was between them being raised, tempers were lost, threats delivered, angry phone calls made, and emails sent to lawyers. As Michelle scanned through the emails that had come in that morning, she was almost grateful she had never had children. The hatred and spite bubbled to the surface. So much for the season of goodwill to all men and all that:

> I do not want my daughter meeting his new girlfriend. They have only been together a few months, and he will probably be bored of her soon enough. Besides, this new girlfriend is only ten years older than our daughter. Can you write to him and tell him it is inappropriate…

> She wants to take the twins to her parents in Finland for the holiday season. I know she is allowed to have them for a week over Christmas, but I can stop her from taking them overseas, right?

> She has been letting them get filmed for her trashy reality TV show. I do not want them exposed to her quest for further fame…

Michelle sighed and got on with dealing with the queries, hoping to sort them before they escalated into yet more battles between warring parents that would cost them a lot of money, with no discernible benefit to the children they were supposed to be fighting for. She forwarded a few of the emails to Toby and asked him to draft replies. She wanted to see how he would approach these types of requests from clients. If she had been doing her job of teaching him properly, she should be able to use some of his drafts. It would be a test of both what he had learned and how effectively she had taught him. And so the day continued.

As the afternoon was coming to an end, and the time that Michelle was planning to leave was approaching, she considered her day. She wasn't quite sure how she had got through it. She kept thinking about Ned, a part of her still wondering if she would see him when she went home that evening, while at the same time knowing she would never meet him again, at least in this life. There was no coming back from the place where he had gone. And the day was also difficult for her knowing Nick would have been taking off from Heathrow, flying across the globe back to Sydney, and returning to a life that she was no longer a part of. A life where he would become a parent, while she faced a single life alone. Their house would be sold, and their lives ripped apart like a corpse upon a Burker's table.

But there was no point dwelling on what was gone. She had to move forward with her own life, and she decided she was not going to think about Nick, or Ned, or about the babies that had been lost. At least not today. Today she was going to see Nathan and let him do something fabulous with her hair, slip on that vintage scarlet dress, and go and drink champagne at the Savoy. She was going to spend some time socialising with her colleagues rather than avoiding them. She was going to get to know them, but more importantly, let them get to know her. She was going to embrace her new life as a single woman in London. Really, it was about bloody time.

She tidied her desk, putting everything back in its place. Toby looked startled to see her getting ready to leave for the day. In the couple of months they had been working together, she had not once left the office before him.

'See you at the party tonight,' she told Toby, as she walked out of the door, enjoying the look of surprise on his face. She was guessing Toby had assumed she would not be going, given she had not yet been to a single social occasion organised by work.

Michelle headed to Blackfriars and jumped on the Tube, taking her familiar journey home from work, and got off at St James's Park. She started walking back to Emery Hill Street. She had left herself enough time to get back to the flat and have a shower before her appointment with Nathan. But she had only taken a few steps outside of the station when her phone buzzed in her coat pocket.

'Hello, Michelle Sikes,' she said into the phone, and then stopped walking as the caller announced who she was speaking to. It was a representative from the packing company. The one Harpers had hired to wrap her possessions in bubble wrap, pack them into a box and transport them from Sydney to England. She apologised for calling so late on a Friday afternoon, but they had just arranged to be in the Westminster area on Monday for another delivery so they would be able to deliver her crate as well, if she was available to receive it.

Michelle's blood stilled for a moment, and her skin prickled over, as her mind returned to Ned's message that there was something coming across the ocean that had belonged to Ivy that she had to see. She had assumed that whatever it was, it must have been packed into her crate. But she couldn't think what it might be. She had asked the packing company to liaise with Nick when it came to her possessions, requesting that all of her clothes, her personal items, and some of her more expensive homeware be shipped over to her. At the time when she had left, her only thoughts had been those of flight, not the practicalities associated with an international move. She had not given much thought to the furniture and paintings they had bought together. She had figured she and Nick could sort the rest of their stuff later, even as she knew she was avoiding dealing with it at the time because she was still hoping that somehow, they would be able to move past his betrayal. But as she thought through what Nick would have picked out for the company to pack for her, her mind could not settle upon anything that had belonged to Ivy that Nick would have thought to include in the items sent out to her. This item of Ivy's was an enigma.

Deciding she had to let it go, and stop turning over the possibilities in her mind, at least until the crate arrived at her flat, she arranged with the packing company for them to bring it to her on Monday. She would have to take the day off work, but given she had no court appearances or client meetings scheduled, and that she was way ahead of budget in terms of billable hours, and also that she had started work earlier than what had been agreed, she was sure there would be no issues. She ended the call, looking down at her phone to drop the diary entry into her calendar.

Once the calendar entry had been made, Michelle looked up. She was standing still, in a city that moved all around her. It never stopped moving. She observed the people scurrying around Victoria Street, half of them with their heads down looking at their phones. She recalled what Ned had said, how people of today had so much, and yet saw so little. She slipped her phone into her pocket, and continued walking home, absorbing the delights of the street illuminated with festive lights, taking in the backdrop of the magnificent cathedral next to the enormous Christmas tree. It was almost Christmas card picture-perfect. As she walked along, she thought of Ned.

Even though it was only 4.30pm it was getting quite dark, and as she turned on to Emery Hill Street, Michelle's eyes searched for Ned leaning against one of the black street lamps. But the glow from the electric bulbs threw its light down on nothing but an empty pavement, illuminating only his absence.

Michelle went home, had a shower, and threw on some running clothes, before walking across to the salon where Nathan was waiting, a glass of champagne in his hand in readiness for her. Christmas carols were being piped through the sound system, and Michelle walked in to the strains of 'God Rest Ye Merry Gentlemen'.

'Merry Christmas, beautiful,' Nathan said, pressing the glass into her hand.

Michelle smiled at Nathan's T-shirt as she sat down in the chair. He seemed to have an extensive collection of gaudy seasonal T-shirts. This one depicted emoji Brussels sprouts in Christmas hats. She sipped at her champagne, enjoying the sensation of the bubbles fizzing and popping inside of her mouth, and let Nathan get to work on her. He chatted away as he washed and styled her hair, until just over an hour later, he was getting ready to add the finishing touch. Michelle had found a silver diamante vintage-inspired headband, which Nathan placed along her forehead, and fixed in place. She smiled as she looked in the mirror. She thought that with the headband and the hairstyle, she and Nathan had nailed the 1920s look. The headband had three crystal stars across the centre of it, so it looked as though she was adorned by Orion's Belt. She watched the way they glittered in the light.

Promising Nathan she would take a selfie and send it to him once she was in her dress, Michelle returned home, put on her make-up, and then studied the dress, which she had left hanging on the door of her bedroom. Taking it off the hanger, a shiver of anticipation coursed down her spine. Surprised by the intensity of her emotional response, she traced her fingers over the elaborate beading that followed the neckline, trailing down in a symmetrical pattern along the centre of the front. The fluted hem was similarly beaded. She slipped the dress on, and then put on the black Mary Jane shoes she had bought, bringing the straps across her ankle and buckling them up. Completing her outfit, she pulled on a pair of elbow-length black gloves.

She looked at herself in the mirror and then smiled, which was starting to come more readily now, after she had spent weeks forcing it on to her face. She thought she looked beautiful, but as she had no one to tell her, and trying not to let her mind drift on to thoughts of her husband, she found her phone and took a photo in the mirror, sending it to Nathan. She was pretty rubbish at taking selfies but even she thought that she looked good in the picture. Nathan immediately messaged back:

> Wow. You are simply stunning. Totally beautiful. Have fun at the party, and don't forget to tell me about all the gorgeous men who flirt with you. Nathan xxx

Smiling again after reading the message, she turned her attention back to the mirror to take one last look at herself. But as she gazed into the reflection, she saw something. Her smile vanished. She was sure she had seen something. A shadow flitting behind her, like a moth at dusk. A presence. Ned? The flat was empty. Trying to calm her racing heart, she reminded herself that Ned was gone. But she saw something. She was sure of it. Or had she just imagined it? She looked around again, her eyes searching the corners of the room, looking into the shadows. There was nobody but her in the flat.

Unsettled, Michelle went to her wardrobe and pulled out the black velvet coat she had bought to go with the dress, and slipped it on, loving the way it felt on her skin, as if a silken cat was caressing her. She took enough money out of her purse to pay for a cab later that evening, and placed it, together with her lipstick and her phone inside a black beaded clutch bag. She had already decided she was going to walk to the Savoy. While she was not wearing the most practical clothing for walking across the city, she figured that with the usual Friday afternoon traffic and the additional Christmas congestion, it would be quicker to walk than get a taxi or take the Tube. And since that first morning in London when she had gone running around St James's Park, Michelle had come to associate it with a feeling of calmness. It was a place where she felt she could be herself, with no one's expectations to carry with her. To get to the party, she planned on walking around the perimeter of the park, before cutting across to Horse Guards Road, walking through the arch to Trafalgar Square, and then up the Strand. She estimated it should take her just over thirty minutes.

As she left her flat, and entered the crisp cold air of the evening, a few reluctant flakes of snow were starting to fall from the stars. Michelle smiled. She would so love a white Christmas. A bitterly cold winter was already being forecast, but all the Londoners, including Toby, scoffed at the suggestion. They all told her it rarely snowed in London, and it never got that cold, especially in December.

But as she made her way to St James's Park, the snow was starting to come down in earnest. She pulled her coat more tightly around her, praying that the snow wouldn't ruin her hair or cause her mascara to run. It was a novelty for an Antipodean like her, and might have been pretty, but it was also wet. She was thankful that her Mary Janes did not have particularly high heels. She worried the ground would turn icy and cause her to slip. She made her way to the east of the park, and walked along the path by the lake, slowing to admire a large white swan, sleeping with its head curled into its wing, sitting by the side of the lake, the backdrop of Buckingham Palace visible in the distance. It was like looking at London through a shaken snow globe, the glittering flakes falling onto a magical frozen scene, entrancing her.

As her step slowed, Michelle's heart began racing, colliding with the sense of unease she had not been able to shake since she thought she had seen a presence in the reflection of her mirror. She looked across the edge of the lake, with the dark waters moving gently with the breeze. Michelle could see a shadow taking shape in the distance. And that shadow was looking at her.

She closed her eyes. Not again. Not now. But, remembering Ned, remembering the joy of his departure into the serenity of the ephemeral opalescent blue, how could she continue to pretend that she could not see? She opened her eyes, and she opened them fully. The shadow had materialised and was standing close to the edge of St James's Park lake. She was a young woman, Michelle would have guessed no more than twenty years old, with fair hair cut into a bob. She had pale-blue eyes that appeared to reflect the ice and cold of the winter evening. And those icy speculative eyes seemed to pierce Michelle as the woman considered her. Michelle's skin prickled over with goosebumps as she saw what the woman was wearing: a mirror image of Michelle's scarlet dress. Michelle closed her eyes again, sighing, as she realised that the beautiful vintage dress she was wearing, the one that she had thought so elegant when she had seen it hanging on the rail of the vintage clothing store on Upper Tachbrook Street, must have once belonged to the spirit she now saw, looking at Michelle, contemplating her. Michelle realised that her own anticipation at wearing the dress had been infused with and magnified by the lingering memories of this woman's when she had first worn it. Once more Michelle had been drawn, unwittingly, to something that connected her with the dead.

Before Ned, she would have closed her eyes to the girl, refused to see her. But Ned had given her something. She could never choose blindness again. She looked into the eyes of the woman, hoping to see them thaw, took a step closer to her, and held her hand up, beckoning to her, bidding her welcome. But the woman shook her head and stepped towards the waters of the lake as if she was wading in for a swim, and disappeared into the darkness of the evening, just as the snowflakes gently falling from the sky vanished into nothingness as they settled on the surface of the cold water.

The lake was disturbed only by the slightest suggestion of a ripple circling outwards, but the swan lifted its head, stood, startled, and stretched out its wings as if it were readying itself to take flight. Michelle observed the creature in the disconcerting stillness of the evening. As the swan's wings curled back to its sides and it settled into the thin layer of snow and tucked its head back into its wing, a feather of the purest white floated from the stars and fell at Michelle's feet.

She bent down to pick it up, contemplating what she had seen. Whoever this young woman was, Michelle supposed that she was not yet ready to move on and chose to remain earthbound. Michelle could only hope that if she needed her help, she would find her when she was ready.

The park was quiet and serene. The swan slept; its rest only briefly disturbed by the supernatural wanderings of humanity lost. Michelle looked up to the sky and let the snow fall on to her face, feeling the icy cold of it tease her senses, enjoying this one rare moment of life that she would never experience again. Then picking up her step, she continued on her way to the party.

CHAPTER TWENTY-FOUR

Michelle woke late the next morning. How could it already be so close to 10am! It was as though she had slept for a week. She must have really needed it. She was grateful that it was now the weekend and she had three whole days to herself before she had to go back to work.

The anticipation of her delivery on Monday caused a surge of excitement through her body, and she started feeling more awake than she had done for days. She got out of bed, put on her dressing gown over her beloved Peter Alexander pyjamas, and made herself a cup of tea, glancing briefly at the red dress she had hung back up on the door of her bedroom. Each time she glanced at it the sequins along the front of it seemed to glimmer in the light, teasing Michelle with the suggestion that the spirit she had encountered in the park the night before had returned to her. The mystery of who the woman in her red dress had been tantalised her, but she pushed it out of her mind. You could not look for answers when you had not yet formulated the questions. Besides, she wanted to focus on herself. She wanted to email Angie.

She went into the kitchen and sat at her kitchen counter,

unable to avoid thinking of all those conversations she had with Ned while sitting at that very spot.

She began typing:

Hi Angie

Michelle thought about all the things she wanted to tell her friend: about Nick coming over to see her, about the end of her marriage, the end of her hopes and dreams of having a baby with him, about how much it hurt to know she was never going to see him again. And she wondered if she would ever be able to talk to Angie about Ned. She supposed that if she wasn't able to talk to Angie about him, she wouldn't be able to talk to anyone, except maybe her mother, and that would bring with it its own set of difficulties that she had no wish to bring into their already fraught relationship. Her mind drifted to her mum, wondering if she would have any idea what it was of Ivy's that she was supposed to see. But her mum had always hated it when she brought up anything to do with her grandma, especially after Ivy had died.

But right now, Michelle didn't want to think about any of that, and instead, typed:

Hope everything is going well in Sydney and you're all not missing me too much! You will never guess what has happened. Well, actually, you probably will. Nick did show up in London, just as I suspected he might. But I don't want to talk about that over email. I think we should talk about it together. And I am not thinking Skype or FaceTime either. Christmas. I am guessing you are still in between boyfriends, and I am definitely single for the first time in a long time. We always talk about how much fun we had when we backpacked around Europe. I know we can't go back and do it all again, and I think neither one of us wants to stay in youth hostels or budget hotels ever again. And, as we are now sensible grown-ups committed to adulting, I suppose it would be irresponsible to take huge amounts of time off work. But Christmas is coming up, and we both have some holiday time accrued. So how do you feel about Christmas in New York?

Michelle smiled to herself as she typed the words. Knowing Angie, she would jump at the suggestion. It would give her the perfect excuse to avoid a family Christmas, with her Italian mother forever asking when she was going to settle down like her brothers and sister. Michelle was not ready to return to Sydney and it felt unfair to ask Angie to come all the way to London just to see her. It was such a long flight. New York seemed like a good compromise, and they had talked on and off for years about going there together. It was another one of those places that Michelle had always wanted to go to, but never did. But last night at the party, when Toby had asked her about how she was spending Christmas, she found herself telling him she was going to New York. And although it was random, it was impromptu, and a little mad, once she said it, it seemed like a good idea.

We can get a really fancy hotel, eat bagels for breakfast, go to that ice-skating rink you always see in the movies, and fall over a lot, and Angie, think of the shopping we could do.

And then in the evening, we can find some posh wine bar and I can tell you all about Nick.

So, what do you say? New Year's Eve in Times Square would be pretty amazing as well. It would make a change from Sydney Harbour.

I miss you, crazy girl.

Talk soon,
Mich xx

Michelle pressed *send* on the email. Given that it was already Saturday evening in Australia, and that Angie would no doubt be on a date in her latest quest to find herself a boyfriend, Michelle suspected it might be hours before she heard back from her best friend.

But by the time Michelle had showered, and thrown on a pair of jeans and a warm woolly jumper, she was pleased to see a reply from Angie already sitting in her inbox. She had changed the title of the email to NEW YORK CITY HERE WE COME!

Michelle read over the email, saw Angie's proposed dates, and before she had time to change her mind, had booked a return flight to New York, leaving the day before Christmas Eve, and flying back on New Year's Day, and had managed to find a nice hotel that had a room available for them to share. She smiled, imagining the week she was going to have with her best friend, what fun they would have together, like they were having a week-long slumber party. She then filled out the online holiday request form for work, confident it would be approved. It was hard not to get excited as she made the arrangements, and she emailed the confirmation to Angie, who was booking her own flights to co-ordinate with Michelle's, trying to pick an arrival time as close as possible to the one Michelle had booked.

Next, Facebook. It was the first time she had been on social media since she had discovered Nick had been cheating on her with Jen. But she didn't dwell on her newsfeed, worried that what she could see would hurt her. Instead, she brought up her list of friends, and then unfriended both Nick and Jen. Not that Jen had ever been a friend in the first place, really. Now that she thought of it, Michelle wondered if Jen had used Facebook as a way of keeping track of what Nick was doing. He tended to post photos of the TV and beer whenever Michelle had been travelling for work. It would have been a sure signal for Jen that she could turn up and deliver some 'important papers' in the full knowledge that Michelle was not going to be at home. Michelle forced her mind to turn away from Nick and Jen. Unfriending them on social media was just another way of putting up a barrier. She didn't see the need to torture herself with what they were doing now, and the thought of seeing scan pictures, photos of the 'bump' or of their baby when it was born was just too painful to contemplate. It would only remind her of what she had lost, and the babies she would never have.

Finally, she sent a private message to an old friend of hers from uni, Meena Singh, who had recently set up her own practice as a family and divorce lawyer. Michelle was smart enough to realise that despite the fact she was an expert in family law custody dispute cases, she would be a poor advocate for herself. She would not be able to detach emotionally from the legal process. But, at the same time, she needed to get the divorce proceedings underway. There was no point holding on to something that had fractured and spoiled, to let it fester and spread its tentacles of infection through the rest of her life. It was time to start the process of dissolving the bonds of matrimony that tied her to Nick.

She looked at the time. It was getting on towards 11.30am, and she had nothing else to do except wait until Monday, when her crate would be delivered, and the mystery of what item of Ivy's it contained would be revealed to her. Her restlessness started jarring at her. What should she do to fill in the time?

She looked at her PC and thought about getting on with some of the less urgent work she had not yet dealt with. But she closed her laptop.

It was too easy to bury herself in work. It was time to start seeing some of the things Michelle had told herself she would get around to seeing one day. It was time to start living her own life, on her own terms, and following her own dreams. She pulled on her boots, grabbed her bag, and set off. She would go to the Tate.

But as she walked out of the door to her flat and waited for the lift to take her down to the ground floor, she hesitated, and as she left the building, instead of walking south towards the river, she started walking in the direction of Victoria station. It was as though a compulsion had taken hold of her. She took a Tube to King's Cross, and then, following the blue dot on the Google Maps app on her phone, she walked with steady determination.

Twenty minutes later she looked up at the doors to the entrance of the Foundling Museum. Ned was gone, so there was no real reason for her to have made this pilgrimage, but Michelle's heart was still full of unanswered questions. Michelle wanted to see where Clara had lived, where her childhood had been spent. She wanted to understand. She wanted to see the place that had failed Douglas, and failed Clara.

As she walked through the doors of the museum, pulling out her purse in readiness to pay the entrance fee, Michelle could almost hear the wails of an orchestra of babies plucked from the breasts of their mothers, and the maternal choral symphony of sorrow that accompanied their tragic requiem of loss.

CHAPTER TWENTY-FIVE

fter paying the entry fee to the museum, Michelle wandered in, not really knowing what to expect. She had, of course, done a quick Google search of the Foundling Hospital shortly after she had waded into Ned's memory of Clara returning to him with Douglas in her arms, telling him that she would take the baby to the Foundling. She had confirmed what it was, and that it now operated as a museum. But as she made her way towards the first room, she was starting to realise it was more than that. It was also a standing archive of children loved and lost, babies separated from their mothers because this had been the best that the charitable impetus of a few kind-hearted souls could do for a woman who was unfortunate enough to find herself pregnant and alone.

She walked slowly through the first room of the exhibition, coming to a standstill before a display of billets, as they were called. They were random everyday objects, ranging from torn playing cards, paper, scraps of fabric, tokens and metal. Some of the items had been ripped in half. She stood before the display with sadness anchoring her to the ground as though her feet were sinking into mud. She remembered Clara pressing into

Ned's hand the scrap of torn fabric from the fraying shawl she had swaddled Douglas in, telling him he could use it to reclaim his child.

She read the information that the museum had put up for its visitors, learning that the intake of the hospital had not been restricted to the babies of unwed mothers, but also the children of wives and widows. Those women whose husbands had died in the workplace, or vanished at sea, or simply abandoned their wives, leaving them to live by their own wits. In fact, as she discovered, it was the wives and widows who were most likely to find themselves 'relieved', to borrow the language of the trial transcript, of their babies, because women who had married before their child was born were considered worthy. Girls like Clara, who allowed themselves to be taken into bed before a marriage had taken place, well, what had they done so that their babies deserved the charity of the hospital, when there were so many demands for the few places it could offer?

Michelle looked through the coldness of the glass display, at the book of billets, each page setting out a description of the child, giving the child a number, giving the child a new identity with a new name, and affixing the item that the mother had chosen to leave with them. The name that had been given to the infant by their mother was not recorded. The institution stripped everything from each child that was taken into the care of the hospital. It was a sobering thought. That piece of fabric that had been so important to Clara was the only thing that would have connected Douglas to his parents, if the Foundling Hospital had agreed to take him. She thought of Douglas, his lifeless body floating on the waters of the Thames.

The billets swam in front of her eyes. Every single one of them was soaked with the many tears of loss and despair of the mothers whose babies had been stolen from them. That loss ran through the whole building as though a river, with its tributaries reaching into every last hidden corner of what had once been the Foundling Hospital. Michelle thought of Jen, and Nick's suggestion that she should take Jen's baby from her. What had Nick been thinking? She thought about what that would do to Jen. A mother separated from her baby. She thought of Clara, her desperation to save her son. A wave of anguish crashed over her. Too many babies parted from their mothers. Too many babies lost. She had to get out of there. She hurried towards the exit, crashing out the door, taking deep breaths of the cold air, tears turning to ice on her face.

She remembered that Clara had been a Foundling child. That Clara had grown up in that place of loss, a child ripped away from her mother, growing up to be a mother who had her child torn away from her. Michelle remembered Clara in the dock at her trial. How broken and defeated she looked, grey with grief, sodden with sadness. Michelle's heart wept for her. She wondered what her life in Australia would have been. If Clara had gone on to find happiness and peace in her new home. Maybe one day, she thought, she would try and find out.

CHAPTER TWENTY-SIX

Michelle was dressed in jeans and an old jumper that had once been Nick's before she had shrunk it in the wash, ready to take delivery of her crate. She made herself a coffee and was idling on her PC not really able to settle to anything. She peered down at her fluffy lilac slipper boots as she sipped her coffee, enjoying the wriggling nugget of excitement that was building inside of her. It was as though Christmas had come early this year, and she was as restless as she had been when she was a young girl waiting, wide awake in bed, until the clock reached the magic time of 5.30am, which was the earliest her mum would allow her to get up. She couldn't work so she wasted time scrolling through Twitter before logging on to Facebook. She was grateful there were no pictures of Nick or Jen to greet her in her newsfeed, despite the fact they did have a number of mutual friends.

She typed into her status update:

Up bright and early on a dark winter morning, waiting for my crate to be delivered to me in London at last. Looking forward to being reunited with my things, especially some wine glasses!

She pressed *post* and sat back and considered what she had written. It was her first status update on Facebook since she had left Sydney and she was aiming for a casual and breezy message. She guessed she was hoping her friends back home would see it and know she was doing okay. Because, all things considered, she was starting to believe that she was going to be fine. Nick had wounded her, and it would take a long time for that wound to heal completely, but she was making progress and she was going to be in control of her own life once more.

She heard the sound of a truck on the street outside, jumped to her feet, and ran over to the window to see if it was a delivery van. It was the first of many such moments as the minutes ticked over through the course of the morning. Every time she heard the sound of a large vehicle, her heart leapt into her throat, and she would race over to the balcony to see if it was her crate arriving. As she waited impatiently, Michelle's mind kept drifting back to her visit to the Foundling Museum on Saturday.

The ringing of the entryphone interrupted Michelle's dark thoughts. A flutter of anticipation travelled through her veins as she answered and gave access to the delivery men. She could hear them discussing how they were going to get everything up to her, before one of them asked through the intercom system if it would be okay with her if they broke into the crate and brought up the boxes one at a time. Michelle agreed and waited for the first box to come up to her door. She had a strange feeling in her stomach, almost as if she was eight years old and waiting for Grandma Ivy to hand her the Rainbow Paddle Pop she had bought from an ice-cream van on a hot summer afternoon.

It was difficult for Michelle to wait, but she managed to restrain herself from wrenching open the first box as soon as it was brought up. She waited until all eight boxes had been deposited in her flat, ignoring the less than subtle hints for cups of tea and mince pies. She then signed the paperwork in triplicate, and the delivery chaps took their leave, Michelle ushering them out of the door with an almost ungrateful haste. She looked at the boxes, stacked together in the living room of her flat, each pile the height of up to her shoulder, taking up nearly the entire floor space.

Somewhere, hidden inside one of the boxes, there was something of Ivy's waiting to be discovered.

She walked around them, tracing her hands along the outside of each one, her fingers gently gliding over the rough wood, listening for the hum that would tell her this was the box she was looking for. As she circled around them she was quietly repeating over and over to herself the words of her grandmother:

'Creeping where grim death has been,
'A rare old plant is the Ivy green.'

The words were as a talisman to her, an enchantment. She stopped before one of the boxes, her hand caressing the side of it as though it were human skin. It felt warm to the touch.

This was the box she wanted.

Reaching for the hammer she had bought from the hardware store on Warwick Way, she used the claw end to prise it open. As the side of the box fell away, Michelle was pleased to see how carefully everything had been packed, most items in individual cardboard boxes, with everything wrapped in layers of protective paper and bubble wrap. She set to work, opening each of the boxes in turn, taking items out one by one, and peeling back the packaging as if she were a bioarchaeologist unwrapping an ancient mummy, looking for the treasures concealed within the layers.

It was a slow process. Grandma Ivy had been an avid collector of what Michelle liked to term knick-knacks and as much as Michelle had a horror of clutter, she had held on to a number of ornaments and decorative items that Ivy had been particularly fond of. She found a decorative hand fan that Ivy had bought in Venice, opened it by spreading the blades apart and traced her fingers over the delicate pale-blue fabric and lace. It still carried faint traces of Ivy, and as Michelle held the fan close to her face, the faded scent of lavender and jasmine was almost enough to persuade her that her grandma was in the room with her. But it was not what she was looking for. She closed the fan and carried it over to the kitchen counter and placed it on the top. She did not want it damaged while she continued her search.

She continued hunting through her possessions, reflecting on how far they had travelled. It was as though the detonated remnants of the flotsam of her life had been gathered together and returned to her, another step that would help her move on from Nick. She opened up a cardboard box and smiled as she saw what it contained. It was Ivy's antique globe. Michelle had always been fascinated by it. She spun it around, as she had done countless times as a child, almost hypnotised by the moving countries and oceans. Her fingers rested for a moment over the outline of Australia, allowing herself to feel the pull of her home country on her soul, before tracing her finger along her own path from Sydney to London. She glanced over the names of countries that had long since ceased to exist. The world had been a different place back then, she thought, as she rotated the globe around again. Each revolution seemed to bring some sort of change. Countries lost, countries changing names, countries being swallowed by the greed and ambition of others. Michelle took the globe and placed it on the counter alongside the fan.

She then discovered some of Ivy's books. She had taken as many of her grandma's books as her mum had allowed her to at the time. Her mind drifted back to when she and her mum had gone through Ivy's possessions one by one, shortly after her grandmother had died, her mother wanting to throw most of it into the skip that she had hired, getting rid. But there were some things, Michelle had known, even at only eight years old, that Ivy had wanted her to keep, and when she looked at her mother, and told her Ivy had wanted her to have something, her mother had looked around her, as though she was trying to see what Michelle could see, and she had not argued. Michelle drew her fingers over the spine of the first edition copy of *The Turn of the Screw* and smiled. Ivy had been a wise woman. Opening up the cover, she saw Ivy's handwritten name in distinctive cursive inside: *Ivy Lane.* Michelle's finger rested on the name as though she was reaching out to touch Grandma's hand.

More of Ivy's items followed, and they were placed reverently on the kitchen counter, as if Michelle was making some kind of shrine to the memory of her. But, with Ned's message still echoing around the chambers of her heart, Michelle had not found anything that she thought Ivy needed her to see. Not yet. And as she delved deeper into the box, her frustration was rising in a symbiotic fusion with her disappointment.

'Dammit, Grandma,' Michelle said, looking at the discarded packaging strewn all over the floor, and the mounting pile of her own possessions that she would need to find a home for. 'What the hell is it I am supposed to be looking for?'

She stooped and stepped inside the near-empty box, as if she were a tomb raider entering a sarcophagus. As her eyes quickly adjusted to the near imperceptible change of light, she bent down into a crawling position on her hands and knees and moved towards the bottom right-hand corner. There was a small package resting there.

She crawled backwards out of the box on one arm and two

legs, cradling the parcel in her other arm. When she emerged, she kneeled, and sliced through the wrapping. There was something different about this package. It was as though she were a cardiologist slicing open the chest of a patient, ready to expose the beating heart that lay beneath the protective casing of skin, muscle and bone. She was precise and careful, ensuring she would not damage whatever was inside.

The packaging fell apart in her hands, and she turned over a small wooden and mother-of-pearl box, fastened with an intricate silver butterfly clasp. It reflected the light of the room, like moonlight on a lake. Was it her jewellery box? No. It was Ivy's jewellery box. Michelle remembered that her mum had taken out all of Ivy's jewellery, thinking she had removed everything of value, and handed the empty box to Michelle. The shell adorning the box glinted shades of turquoise, silver, blue and green. The colours were still vivid, and the casing shimmered in the light, reminding her of the celestial portal that she had seen Nelly and her baby, and later Ned, drift through. She remembered the fluttering of crystal luminosity that she had seen leaving the body of Nelly's baby, in the oasis of serene light, like a butterfly in the morning sky. She gently touched the silver butterfly clasp of the box and smiled.

She opened the jewellery box, a real-life Pandora. But she was not afraid of the mysteries she would find inside. She pulled out a silver chain with a star pendant that Nick had bought her and let it slide through her fingers, before spiralling it down in a pile next to her on the floor.

She next pulled out a shell necklace that had belonged to Ivy's younger daughter Dora. Michelle had loved that necklace when she was a little girl. Ivy had told her that Dora had been given the necklace by her boyfriend when he had returned from serving with the navy. Michelle could not remember her Aunt Dora. She had only seen pictures of her. She had always thought Dora looked like one of those beautiful women from a Rossetti painting, with long flowing auburn hair, and skin as pale as porcelain. Ivy had not liked to talk about her, telling Michelle only that Dora had died young. That was all she knew of her.

Michelle emptied out the remainder of the jewellery box and examined every piece one by one. But there was nothing in it that had been Ivy's. She examined the box. It was empty but it had that hum, and she knew she was missing something vital. Listening to the faint traces of the melody that seemed to emanate from somewhere inside it, she traced the index finger of her right hand along the red velvet lining of the interior of the box, as if she was a man seeking the heat inside of a woman, waiting for that moment when all inhibition was liberated.

And she found it. Michelle realised there was a certain give in the lining of the bottom of the box, and she used her fingernail to slide underneath it, and lift it open. She extracted the red velvet bottom and peered into the hidden base of the box.

It was a faded piece of paper. She lifted it out, and opened it up, carefully unfolding the yellowed page that Ivy had left. At first glance it seemed to be a rough sketch of her family tree. But it only had the names of the women. She saw a series of female names, coupled with the years of birth and death:

> *Michelle Sikes 1986*
> *Diane Chesterton 1955*
> *Dora Chesterton 1967 – 1986*
> *Ivy Lane 1928*
> *Claire Unwin 1900 – 1967*

Michelle recognised her grandma's writing. It was the same cursive that she had used to sign her name on the inside cover of all of her books, and she realised that no one had updated it to record Ivy's death. She saw not only her own name, but the names of her mother, aunt, grandmother, and great-grandmother. Four of those names were shaded in blue. The only name that remained unvarnished was that of her mother, Diane. She tried to scan upwards to read the other names that were written there, but as she looked at the piece of paper in her hand, the names blurred as her eyes were drawn to what had been left in the bottom of the box, hidden underneath the piece of paper that Michelle had just pulled out.

She was sure she had seen it before.

Her fingers reached in and she lifted out a thin, frayed piece of fabric. It was as light as gossamer silk, yet it felt heavy in her hand. The colour was so faded it was almost grey, but Michelle could still see the faint traces of warmth in the fibres. It was delicate, like the wings of a butterfly, so fragile that Michelle thought it might fall apart in her fingers, crumble into ash and disappear, almost as if it had never existed.

She held it with infinite tenderness, in between her first finger and her thumb, holding it up to the light. Her heart leapt into her throat, pounding as though someone was playing timpani.

She tried to stand, but she could not get to her feet.

She continued to stare at the fabric. She had seen it before. She had seen it nearly two hundred years ago. The shawl that Douglas had been wrapped in. She had seen Clara handing a piece of it to Ned. But no matter how long she stared at the fabric, willing it to yield the answers to her, she did not understand how Ivy had come to have in her possession Clara's one connection to her lost child. Everything tilted and whirled around her, and Michelle watched as the bleached colours of the scrap of material in her hand seemed to brighten and shades of copper and red flowed through the fibres of the fabric as though blood through the veins of a reanimated corpse.

She tried to hold on to the present but found herself dragged into a vortex, a spiralling mass that hauled her backwards through the years. She was unable to resist the power of the storm that she had been caught in.

When the storm stilled she looked down at the fabric, still in the fingers of her right hand. She was sitting in muddy sludge, with waters creeping up around the middle of her thighs. A part of her panicked as she realised she had slipped into Clara's memories. It was too real. The water was cold, wet, urgent, yet as she saw the world through Clara's mind, she was serene even as the tide continued to swell the river, threatening to swallow her whole.

She was holding a baby in the crook of her left arm, resting the bulk of his slight weight on her knees. Her baby. No, Michelle told herself, not her baby. Clara's baby. All her babies were dead before they had even been born. Doomed before her husband's seed sought fusion with her egg. Clara's baby, she told herself, as she gazed down at the infant in her arms. He was sleeping. He was at peace. Michelle kissed his forehead, and she found words coming out of her mouth, a haunting song that she did not know the name of.

The water was creeping higher. It wasn't cold. It was as though she had settled in a bath with the water still running. As she sat there, waiting for the waters to rise, Michelle tracked backwards through Clara's memories as though she was pressing reverse on a remote control.

She was sitting. Michelle recognised the nearby building. She had been there just two days previously. She was waiting by the gates of the Foundling Hospital, her son in her arms, a piece of fabric in her fingers ready to give to them. She was not alone. There were other women there. Other mothers cradling babies close to their breasts. And the only thing Michelle was aware of was a growing desperation. She had to save her son.

The babies mewled as the light darkened and the night grew cold. Mothers whispered comforting words to their infants, placed an engorged teat within an open mouth. And they settled into the darkness, praying to whatever god they believed in to guard their children, to keep them safe, to let them find refuge within the walls of the hospital they had come to as supplicants. Michelle tried to get the child in her arms to attach to her empty breast, but there was nothing for the child to take hold of. She had nothing. She was empty. The only thing inside of her was a gaping void.

She looked up to a sky filled with smoke and smog so that all the stars, like hope, were invisible to her, and prayed that her son would be spared. But she feared for her son because she was unhallowed. She could feel the seed of a man that she had not wanted, that she had taken for the coin that he could pass to her, seeking succour in her womb, like a tapeworm bedding down in her intestinal tract. It settled in the lining of her uterus just as a layer of filth settled on the top of the River Thames, a dirty, slimy mess that crusted over the surface of the river, the heart of the city, contaminating it so that it could never be clean.

Michelle was overwhelmed by Clara's shame and sorrow; complicit in her own violation, and she wanted to give in to weeping. But she was strong. Such strength from this mere slip of a girl. The only thing that mattered was her son. She shook her head, trying to free it, to remember that these were not her memories. He was not her son. He was Clara's son. Douglas. And Michelle could only despair as she remembered there would be no hope for this sweet baby that she held so close to her, giving him the only comfort she could.

Clara waited all night, holding her child close to her breast, and the torn fabric as though it was an amulet that would protect her boy. She waited her turn. And when the morning came, she pleaded her cause.

They turned her away. They would not take her son. They took the child of the mother whose husband had been killed while he worked on the railway line near Euston. She had been married. They took the baby from the parlour maid who had been raped by her employer. But when Clara told them of her drunken seduction by a man who bought her drinks they would not take her son. She was turned away with the other women who had brought their disgrace upon themselves.

And she had nowhere left to go. Nobody to turn to. But she knew what she had to do.

Michelle found herself back in the rising tidal waters of the Thames. She looked down. She brought the sleeping child closer to her breast, felt the gentle rhythm of his breathing, and let it calm her. It would not be long now. The waters were coming up to her waist, ready to take them both. She could hear the noise of people calling to her from the distant bank of the river, but it was as nothing to her. She was going to help her baby. She was going to make sure no one could hurt him, that he would never feel a leather strap biting into his skin because someone thought him a bad boy, to ensure that he would never again feel the crippling pangs of hunger, or the cruel pains of a bitter winter's evening spent seeking warmth in a hostile city.

She unwrapped the ripped shawl that swaddled her child, her heart swelling as she took his tiny feet into her hands, marvelling at their perfection. She kissed him lightly on his forehead, and then the tip of his nose, the feathery touch of an angel, taking in the sweet scent of him.

Something inside Michelle was screaming. But Clara was numb. Nothing could reach her. Michelle found herself watching with horror as she lowered her arms and Douglas drifted away from her, straight into the welcoming waters of the river. There was no displacement of the water, no cries. He simply disappeared into the dark depths as though he had never been. And Clara was empty. There was nothing in her but a bleak hollow that stretched between deserts. Michelle scrunched the fabric into her fist as Clara waited for the river to take her. She felt nothing. The darkness of the sky deepened into a cobalt blue. The waters started lapping at her breasts.

It would be over soon.

CHAPTER TWENTY-SEVEN

Nothing. It was as though she existed within a void of blackness, where no light could penetrate. Nothing surrounded her, engulfed her, and consumed her. Clara waited with utter disinterest as the waters rose up to her shoulders, and Michelle, trapped inside the darkness of Clara's mind, could only watch in frustrated, impotent horror. She could not see her baby, but she could feel him calling to her. The first rays of the moonlight reflected on the river, and the light danced over its surface, as if someone had strung a myriad of slowly flashing fairy lights beneath. Michelle closed her eyes searching for her baby.

Behind the curtain of Clara's closed eyes, Michelle could see her son floating in the purest of shimmering crystal-blue waters, waiting for her to come to him. He was still sleeping. She reached her arms towards him, submerging them into the waters that surrounded him, exposing her heart, rendering herself vulnerable. The vivid blueness intensified as if struck by a multitude of lightning strikes, and Michelle submitted to the calm and serenity the depths promised.

But at that moment when she was moving closer to join her child in the soothing light, the sudden jerk of hands grasping hold of her arms, pulling her away from her baby brought her back to her desolate reality. There were people in the river with her, and they were trying to pull her into the shallows. They would not let her die.

They were trying to pull her away from her son. But her skirts had been weighted, and their fight to free her from the clutches of death was frustrated. They didn't understand, she thought. Death was not to be feared. It was to be welcomed. It was life that was unbearable. It was trying to survive that broke you. She struggled to free herself, to return to the bosom of her own demise, and as she broke free and plunged into the depths of the river, she found herself sinking into an abyss as the water covered her mouth, and her nose, preventing her from drawing breath.

She was under the water and she was serene. She opened her eyes, and could see the moonlight penetrating through the surface, as if lighting the path to her afterlife. And as she looked ahead of her, it was as if she had dived into an underwater cave with a celestial light that illuminated the entrance, offering a path into the fiery heart of a priceless opal. The blues, greens and reds beguiled and bewitched. They called to her. They had already received her son. Now they waited for her.

The cold breath of the evening air hit Clara's face like a slap on her cheek, and tore asunder her path towards that unspeakably beautiful light. She was coughing and spluttering. Multiple hands had hold of her, dragging her further away from the alluring brightness that called to her. They called her a lunatic.

Clara's resistance flooded Michelle's body, and fighting against the arms that restrained her, she heard cries of 'My baby, my little boy. I have lost my baby,' coming from her mouth.

The light was dimming and the grey reality of life was pressing down on her. Something powerful was awakening from the darkness that had taken her into the river. It was as though she had given birth to a monster that wanted to tear open her chest and pluck out her heart. She wanted her baby, and she fought to free herself so she could continue her search for her son. Where had he gone? She had been holding him. They had been so close to the shining brilliance. Clara's body tensed with resistance as she tried to fight the hands that held her and pulled her away from her child. She heard an unearthly wail, the keening of a banshee. It took her a moment to realise the sound emanated from her own soul. She screamed her grief for her lost baby, a child taken by the tide. They pulled her out of the rising waters, and they collapsed with her into the tidal mud that formed the boundary between the river and its bank. They said they would make her go to the police station.

Michelle watched through the bleak lens of Clara's vision. She sensed her submission as Clara let them take her. She told them she had killed her child. She had murdered her son. All that was left of him were her memories and the piece of sodden fabric still clutched tightly in her hand. They marched her from the river, her saturated skirts falling heavily around her legs. As they impelled her forwards, she opened her fist, staring at the fabric. Michelle focused on it as the ground underneath her feet shifted and whirled. She watched the fabric age in her hand, the years taking their toll on the fibres, the last of the colours bleaching out of it, the dye fading, like the memory of Douglas, lost somewhere in the vast attic of time.

She looked around her as the familiar safety of her flat swam back into her vision.

Immobilised by the shock of her return from Clara's last moments with her son, she choked back tears, gasping for breath, trying to understand what it was she had just seen.

Clara had killed her child. But Michelle could not condemn her. She had run out of options. There were no choices left to her. She was only a child herself, and yet she had a baby that she could not hope to provide for. She could not feed him. And she could not bear to watch him suffer. The dark waters of the Thames sang their siren song, beckoning her with the only comfort she could offer him. Michelle had seen Clara's heart. She had felt it. It had been a heart swollen with love.

Michelle placed the small scrap of material back inside Ivy's jewellery box, her eyes full of tears. But she still did not understand how Ivy had come to have Clara's fragment of her baby's shawl. Michelle picked up the piece of paper that had been on top of the fabric. Ivy would have placed it there for a reason.

She looked at the names and years once more. All of them except two were shaded in blue.

> *Michelle Sikes 1986*
> *Diane Chesterton 1955*
> *Dora Chesterton 1967 – 1986*
> *Ivy Lane 1928*
> *Claire Unwin 1900 – 1967*
> *Jane Taylor 1874 – 1900*
> *Elizabeth Morley 1850 – 1914*
> *Clara Waters 1822 – 1900*

Clara. Clara Waters. Michelle read the name again.

Her heart stilled as though a silent teardrop was falling into still waters, the echo of the fall resonating through her soul.

She understood at last. It was as though someone had stripped the veil off a mirror and she could see her true self. The strength of her connection with Ned and with Clara had not been random. Michelle's gift had not just come from Ivy. It had come from a chain of women stretching back through the years to that one moment when Clara had taken her son into the dark waters of the Thames to die. Michelle took her mind back through Clara's memories, of her seeking her death in the womb of the river. When she was under the water, waiting to drown, courting death, Clara had seen her child floating, but, Michelle realised, she had not seen his body. She had seen him because he was dead. Because she could see the dead. Clara could see ghosts, just like Ivy, and just like Michelle.

Still on her knees, her head bowed, Michelle examined the paper in front of her like she was a penitent reading a prayer book. But reality was creeping back into her body, and her calves were cramping due to being confined in a kneeling position for what seemed like hours. Her shoulders ached, and it was as if she could feel bruises appearing on her arms from where desperate hands had grabbed her and tried to haul her free from the expectant mouth of the river.

She got to her feet, unsteady at first, shaking out her legs to try and restore some blood flow into them. She still had the piece of paper in her hand, and it seemed to get heavier the longer she thought about it. The list of women seemed like a legacy to her, but also a responsibility and she was starting to feel as though she was betraying it by her inability to have a child of her own, a daughter of her own, to carry forward the gift that had been bestowed on her.

Moving to the kitchen counter, she stared at Ivy's possessions. What had been the point of keeping them, if it all ended with her? She lost herself in dark and morbid reflections. Ivy's lace fan meant something to her, but when she died, who would value it? It would just be thrown in a skip, designated as nothing more than tat by whoever was unfortunate enough to be given the task of going through her things after her death.

She placed the fan back down on the counter and picked up

Dora's necklace, running the little shells between her fingers and thumb as though it were a rosary.

A small breath of air shifted behind her as though someone was standing there, out of sight, and she could have sworn that a finger pressed against the back of her neck. But when she turned around, there was no one there. She turned her eyes downwards again, to consider the shell necklace that she was running through her fingers.

There was a gentle pull, a warm gentle wind fluttering across her face, and when she looked up, she could see a young woman walking along a beach towards the rising sun at dawn. The sky was streaked with pink and gold. The woman was a long way in the distance, and Michelle had to squint to try and make the vision clear, but it was still a long way from her. As her eyes strained to make out the detail of what she could see, a picture started to take shape in her mind. The woman had long loose-flowing auburn hair, which was flying about her pale face in the soft sea breeze. She was laughing and pointing out towards the never-ending waves as they came in and broke over the shore.

Michelle recognised the woman.

'Dora,' she whispered.

Dora was not alone. She was holding a small hand within her own, the little girl looking up at Dora with love and an unworldly patience for one so young. The child stopped to pick something up and stood to show Dora the string of shells she had plucked from the sand. It was identical to the one Michelle was holding in her own fingers. The child then turned her curious gaze back towards Michelle, her bright and shining eyes the same green as her own, and even through the haze and mist that blighted her view of Dora and the child, her heart was flooded with an intensity of fierce love that she had only encountered once before.

It was the same love that Clara had held for Douglas. It was visceral, primitive, violent and urgent. It was maternal.

Dora and the child turned away and disappeared into the mist, leaving Michelle sitting at her kitchen counter alone in her flat, trailing the shells through her fingers.

She looked down at the paper with the names of generations of the women of her family. She thought of Clara, of Ivy, of Dora and the promise of the child who had not yet come into the world. Her daughter. And she opened her overcharged heart to the future, and let it fill her with joy. With hope.

'Hope,' she whispered into the silence of her flat, 'I can wait for you.' She folded up the yellowed paper and returned it to the box, covering it over with the red velvet lining, tracing her fingers along the silky richness of the fabric. She closed the lid, fastening the butterfly clasp, before getting to her feet.

She walked over to her balcony, still carrying Ivy's jewellery box in her hand, and pulled back the curtain, looking out on to Emery Hill Street. She was a woman who would always be haunted. She would always be able to see the dead and she could no longer pretend this was not a part of who she was. Ghosts would come to her, and she would see them, hear them. But it didn't scare her anymore. How could it? She remembered the words of her dear Grandma Ivy, telling her that it wasn't the dead that could hurt her. She thought of her elation as Ned moved into the eternal completeness and purity of the jewelled light. She thought of her vision of Dora, and the child she had seen walking hand in hand with her.

Michelle opened her heart to the fullness of her sight and the promise of her gift, to the joy that it could flood her with, and although she stood alone in her flat in a city that swarmed with life, she was not lonely.

The night was gathering in on her, as London crept ever closer towards winter. She looked out into the gloom and darkness of the evening, out towards the black lamp post where she had seen the ghost of Ned and, bringing the box close to her heart, she smiled.

THE END

AUTHOR'S NOTES

The poem 'The Ivy Green' was written by Charles Dickens and can be found in *The Pickwick Papers*.

The quote 'If there were no bad people, there would be no good lawyers' is from *The Old Curiosity Shop*, again by Charles Dickens.

The end of the novel draws on another of Dickens's characters, David Copperfield, who reflects that he is 'haunted by the ghosts of many hopes.'

The transcript of the trial of Clara draws heavily from Old Bailey reports of infanticide or murder from the period of 1837 – 1841. These can be found at https://www. oldbaileyonline.org/. I chose this time period because of the number of legal and social imperatives that made it virtually impossible for a working class unmarried mother to provide for her child. In 1834, the Poor Law Amendment Act came into force with the philosophy of making the workhouse as 'repulsive as consistent with humanity', as one clergyman of the time said. Fathers were not financially responsible for their illegitimate children. In 1837, an amendment to the Ellenborough Act made all abortions illegal. Prior to this Act, abortions had only been illegal if they took place after the 'quickening', or when the mother had felt the baby moving within her womb. The penalty for a breach of this law was death. I also needed to work within a time period where transportation to Australia was still ongoing. While officially, transportation ended in 1840, ships continued to be sent to Australia until 1868.

In researching these cases, I came across the transcript of the trial of a woman named Harriett Longley on 5 April 1841 and I knew that I had found the case that is the most comparable to that of what I had already imagined for Clara. Harriet threw her three-week-old infant daughter into the Thames. The case is interesting in that, somewhat unusually, two surgeons were called as witnesses. The first one had not performed an autopsy, assuming that the child's death had been from drowning. The second performed an autopsy. I suspect the defence requested it because it was hoped to prove that the child was dead or dying before Harriett cast her into the water. Unfortunately, the autopsy proved that the child was alive when she entered the water, and the guilty verdict was inevitable. It is easy to condemn women such as Harriett, but from the comfort of our twenty-first century life it is even easier to forget that nineteenth century England was not welcoming of unmarried impoverished mothers. There was no birth control. Abortion was punishable by death. Harriett was homeless, starving and unable to breastfeed her daughter, and had been released from prison for vagrancy with only 18d (worth about £6.38 in today's terms). Her daughter's name was Eliza.

Like Clara, Harriett Longley was sentenced to death for killing her child. Also like Clara, Harriett was spared the gallows, and was transported to Van Diemen's Land (now the state of Tasmania in Australia) aboard the *Garland Grove* on 23 June 1841, arriving on 10 October 1841. It seems Harriett was also able to start her life over. She applied for permission to marry on 5 May 1843.

In January 1866, Queen Victoria met with the Lord Chancellor and they discussed proposed reforms to capital punishment. Queen Victoria was anxious that unfortunate women should not be hanged for infanticide, as she believed they were often driven to it by despair. However, when the Capital Punishment Amendment Act came into force in 1868, it only stipulated that executions were no longer to be public and must take place inside prison walls. It was not until 1922, with the passing of the Infanticide Act, that the death penalty for a woman who killed her newborn baby was effectively abolished.

ACKNOWLEDGEMENTS

I would like to acknowledge the support of my sister, friend, and fellow author Sharon Ibbotson, who read over this book while it was in the early stages and had the courage to tell me what was wrong with it. Her advice helped me to make it the best version of the story that I wanted it to be. I am also grateful to Louise Walters for her editorial review and her comments on one of my earlier drafts. I want to recognise the outstanding editorial work of Abbie Rutherford to get my book ready for publication, as well as the entire Bloodhound Books team for helping me through every stage of getting my book ready for the world to see. I am very grateful for all the support I have been given.

Finally, this book would not have been written without the encouragement and support of my family, for whom I want to acknowledge my appreciation and love, especially to my children, Euan, Rowan and Kate. I hope you take with you the message that there is always hope, even in the darkest of times. I love you.

ABOUT THE AUTHOR

Deborah Siddoway was born in the North East of England and grew up in Sydney, Australia. She is currently a PhD candidate and tutor at Durham University, where her research interest is in nineteenth-century literature and the law, with a focus on matrimonial and divorce law. She has a particular love of the works of Charles Dickens and is an active member of the Dickens Society. She lives in Northumberland with her children and her dog Brontë.